QUESTIONS OF LOVE

How could an unfashionable young lady like Lady Frances shine in the eyes of Lord Julian Mainwaring amid the glittering whirl of the London Seasons?

How could a proper young lady like Lady Frances compete with the improper but indisputably attractive Vanessa Welford, Mainwaring's notorious mistress?

How could a brilliant young lady like Lady Frances convince Mainwaring that a woman's intellect was to be as highly prized as her other, more evident attributes?

Frances needed not only her head but her heart to find the answers. . . .

After studying eighteenth-century literature in college, *EVELYN RICHARDSON* decided that she would have preferred to have lived between 1775 and 1830. She wrote this, her first novel, at her home in a seacoast village south of Boston where she lives with her husband and her cat, Sam. She is currently working on a sequel.

The Education of Lady Frances

by

Evelyn Richardson

A SIGNET BOOK

NEW AMERICAN LIBRARY

A DIVISION OF PENGUIN BOOKS USA INC.

To My Parents
Hugh and Madeleine Johnson

NAL BOOKS ARE AVAILABLE AT QUANITY DISCOUNTS
WHEN USED TO PROMOTE PRODUCTS OR SERVICES. FOR
INFORMATION PLEASE WRITE TO PREMIUM MARKETING
DIVISION, NEW AMERICAN LIBRARY, 1633 BROADWAY, NEW
YORK, NEW YORK 10019.

SIGNET, SIGNET CLASSIC, MENTOR, ONYX, PLUME,
MERIDIAN and NAL BOOKS are published by New American
Library, a division of Penguin Books USA Inc.,
1633 Broadway, New York, New York 10019

First Printing, November, 1989

1 2 3 4 5 6 7 8 9

PRINTED IN THE UNITED STATES OF AMERICA

1

L ady Frances frowned in concentration as she searched once again for the error that was keeping the accounts from balancing. She sighed and looked out the window hoping to clear her mind. That was a mistake. A second glance proved the figures no more comprehensible than they had been before. The sight of fields beginning to sprout after the last few warm wet days, and the fringe of green buds on the tree by the mellowed brick of the garden wall, made her long to be out-of-doors, smelling the newly washed hedgerows and feeling the warm sun on her face. "Botheration!" she exclaimed, and shut the ledger with a decisive snap. This interrupted the sound sleep of the terrier at her feet. He woke with a start and looked up expectantly, as did his more lethargic companion, a large, battered tabby cat who opened an inquiring eye. "Come on, Wellington," she called. "I've had enough for one day. Let's get some fresh air." Unfortunately, as they headed for the door, they were stopped in mid-escape by the sound of hooves on the gravel drive. Wellington sat down with a snort of disgust as a very agitated young lady burst into the entrance, brushing aside Higgins, the butler, in her haste to pour out her problems to Frances.

"Oh, Frances," she wailed, "my uncle has returned from Vienna and positively orders me and Cousin Honoria up to London. He insists that I come out this Season! You know Ned would be miserable there, and we can't possibly leave him here. Besides, I don't want to be a lady of fashion, simper all day long, and think of nothing but shopping and changing clothes. I want to be like you, free to enjoy the country and my books and not have to pretend to care about doughty dowagers and their eager, eligible prospects." Here she paused for breath while Higgins took her hat and gloves.

Kitty Mainwaring was a diminutive girl with large brown eyes, tumbled brown curls, and a pert nose. The impish features were overcast with worry, but otherwise it was a face that should have made its owner look forward to being the toast of the Season rather than an unwilling participant.

"Do come in, Kitty. Higgins will bring some tea directly and we can consider this further. In the meantime, come into the library. There's a fire to take off the chill, but the windows afford us a view of spring." Kitty allowed herself to be ensconced in a chair with a cup of tea and then waited patiently as Lady Frances settled herself. "Now, then, I quite agree with you that balls, flirting, and endless shopping make an empty life, but hundreds of people seem to enjoy that sort of life above any other, and it can be amusing for a while." Lady Frances tactfully refrained from mentioning the misery of standing alone at Almack's for lack of partners who would discuss something beyond the set of their coats and their hopes for favorite race-horses. Nor did she speak of her grateful return to her own books and country pursuits when the death of her father and his unusual will placed her at twenty in charge of the entire estate as well as the nine-year-old twins, Cassandra and Frederick. "Besides, my dear, you're far too lively and pretty to live alone the rest of your days. And you certainly have no prospects around here to share your life."

Kitty frowned. "But you aren't alone. You ride whenever you wish, wherever you wish. You read and write your children's books." She lowered her voice in alluding to this activity, which was a carefully guarded secret. "And you're constantly avoiding Lady Featherstone and her daughters because they're always discussing the latest fashionable *on-dits*."

"Yes, but I am older and more serious than you are. I don't necessarily avoid marriage, but I have found that anyone serious enough to talk of something other than fashion usually wishes to prose on about himself and his estate. I wouldn't mind sharing my life with someone interesting, but I have never met such a person. I am sure that with your looks and address you'll attract a swarm of young eligibles, and surely one among the crowd would suit." Lady Frances spoke as though she were an antidote, when in fact it had been a combination of intelligence and natural reserve rather than lack of countenance that had kept her in the less-crowded ends of London ballrooms. Eager partners initially attracted by her classical features and elegant figure were rendered uneasy by the glint of humor they saw creep into her expressive hazel eyes if they spent more than one dance describing the difficulties developing a cravat style that was intricate enough to be distinctive without being so elaborate as to be laughable. This humorous look was instantly interpreted as criticism by uneasy young aspirants to fashion, and it was not appreciated in the least. Lady Frances had not been successful with the members of her own sex either. Though brunettes were all the rage, her straight nose, tawny hair, delicate complexion, and generous inheritance made her enough of a threat to her marriage-mad companions that they were only too delighted to label her as "blue" because she actually listened to the plays and concerts she attended and refused to ridicule Lady Lucinda D'Arcourt, who, in spite of being an earl's daughter, and a wealthy one at that, was a shocking quiz and insisted on wearing the most outmoded frocks and huge bonnets. Nor would she discuss the latest escapades of Lady Caro Lamb, maintaining that she was sorry for the creature despite her shocking behavior and dampened muslins. But as the Season wore on and novelty wore off, Lady Frances had found herself left more and more to her own devices. It was with a queer sort of relief that she learned of her father's death and his unusual wish that she look after the estate and her family. His loss was severe in a family as close and loving as the Cresswells, but all of the children knew that Lord Cresswell had never been happy after their mother's death ten years before.

Lord and Lady Cresswell had been unusual in their devotion to each other. Both scholars of considerable standing, they had spent the early years of their marriage traveling around Greece and the classical world, working on their own translations of the more obscure Greek poets, and even venturing into Egypt until driven home by Napoleon and his designs on the world. It was their example of close friendship, love, and shared intellectual passion that provided Frances with a model of marriage that was both inspiring and, given her limited choice, discouraging. Having explored the temples of Greece and Rome as a child, and having received an education as good as if not better than that of most of her male counterparts, she soon found herself bored and slightly disgusted with the local gentry.

Kitty broke in on these unfortunate recollections. "Perhaps you are right. It would be fun to see the Tower and all the other London sights. And how delightful it would be simply to go to Hatchard's to procure the latest books! I suppose I am mostly put off by the suddenness of it and the peremptory tone of his letter. You know how I still miss Mama and Papa and the good times Ned and I had with them. They were always so affectionate and gay that the idea of having anyone as a guardian in their place, especially Lord Mainwaring, is daunting. I am sure he is haughty and cold. Why, he never visited us when they were alive, and he barely even acknowledged our existence until they were killed. I have heard that he's terribly fashionable. And, you must admit, the idea of leaving dear old Camberly to lead a terribly stiff and *à la mode* life in some imposing town house is more frightening than exciting." With this, Kitty produced a heavy sheet of crested stationery and handed it to Frances for her perusal. "My dear niece, Lady Streatham has agreed to chaperone your come-out. I shall send my groom and the post chaise for you in three week's time. Mainwaring."

"It does not sound as welcoming as it might, but remember that Lord Mainwaring is a busy man and probably considers his providing you with a Season generous rather than threatening. You mustn't attribute his previous disinterest to coldness. After all, he has spent the last year attached to Castlereagh in Vienna, and several before that attending to the business interests in the colonies left him by his uncle. So you see, my dear, even were he devoted to you and Ned, he would not have been much at Camberly.'' Examining the bold black script and the forcefulness of the scrawled "Mainwaring," Frances privately agreed that its writer was probably as arrogant as Kitty feared.

All further reflection and conversation were halted by the eruption of a whirlwind as the large and battered tomcat dashed across the room and leapt into the safety of a nearby chair. He was closely followed by Wellington and two rather disheveled eleven-year-olds. Wellington came to a screeching halt in front of the chair, while the cat, surveying him from the safety of his perch, switched his tail tantalizingly and made a swipe with a chubby paw. ''Arf, arf!'' was the encouraging reply as the dog, followed by his feline companion, raced to the other side of the room, narrowly missing the tea table. ''Cassie, do grab Nelson before he overturns the cake stand. It's all very well for them to chase each other, but must they always do it at teatime? Freddie, pick up Wellington and put him by the fire. However did all of you get so muddy and wet? And say hello to Kitty, both of you.'' The twins, with mops of curly blond hair and rosy cheeks now lightly smeared with mud, were barely distinguishable except for dress. Both grinned and did as they were bidden.

''Well, you see, we heard Wellington barking, so we followed and discovered that Nelson was stuck in a tree. You know that with only one eye he can see well enough to climb up but not well enough to get back down, silly thing. Freddie tried to climb up to get him, but he wasn't tall enough to reach the first branch so I had to stand on his shoulders. I slipped the first time,'' added Cassie matter-of-factly, pointing to a grass stain on the front of her frock and her muddy footprints on the shoulders of her brother's jacket.

''Oh.'' Frances accepted the explanation with aplomb, wondering aloud to no one in particular, ''When will Nelson learn to extricate himself from his scrapes on his own? If Wellington hadn't pulled him out of the pond when those nasty village boys threw him in, we never would have had him in the first place. It's not as though he were a fine specimen of the feline species, are you, Nelson?'' Nelson smiled apologetically as he rubbed against the hand that rubbed just the right spots.

Freddie spoke in their pet's defense. ''But he's such fun for Wellington because he knows just how to chase him and play hide-and-seek.''

''Arf, arf,'' agreed Wellington wholeheartedly.

Frances rang for Higgins to bring more tea and cakes, the earlier supply having completely disappeared the minute the twins entered the room. London and Lord Mainwaring were forgotten as the children related the latest tale of the hole in Farmer Stubbs's fence, which had allowed the sow and her piglets into the lane and nearly caused the wreck of the squire's gig. ''You should have seen it, Frances,'' said Freddie through a mouthful of cake. ''The squire came round the corner into the lane at a slapping pace and almost ran over the runt. Wellington saved the day, though, because he herded them all to one side. What a Trojan!''

''Arf, arf!''

''And then Cassie nipped in and grabbed the runt just as the wheel came by.''

''So I see,'' Frances remarked, surveying the splashes on Cassie's pinafore.

Unable to refrain from adding her bit to the tale, Cassie burst in, ''Squire Tilden was so angry. You should have seen him! His face was all red and he was shouting and calling Farmer Stubbs a good-for-nothing. And he is too, because he said it would have been better for the runt to be killed. Can you credit such meanness? The runt couldn't help it that it was the smallest of the litter. So I took the dear little thing because it was squeaking so and I gave it to John Coachman because I didn't think you would want it in the house in spite of its being quite clean and pink with the sweetest ears and curly tail you've ever seen. Can we keep him, dearest Fanny, please?''

Fully aware of her younger sister's passion for animals of any type, Frances recognized that she was in for a long battle. She grimaced, but nodded, adding, ''Off with you now. You must run get cleaned up and then we'll review your history lesson from this morning.''

"What a good sister you are! No wonder they love you," Kitty observed.

"Well, you know, having such a pet is the best way to teach any number of valuable lessons in responsibility, estate management, even natural history, if you will. And you know how much I value my own excellent education, which was all the work of both Father and Mother. I feel, if nothing else, that I owe it to them to share it with the twins." The touch of sadness which had crept into her voice was quickly banished as she gave herself a mental shake, ringing for Higgins and adding briskly, "But you mustn't be leaving your own brother to a lonely tea. Here's Higgins with your hat and gloves. Off with you now. I shall ride over tomorrow after I've thought it over, and see if I can devise some way to help you turn Mainwaring's orders to your best advantage."

"Oh, thank you ever so much, Frances. I do hate to burden you when you have so much to attend to, but Cousin Honoria, though she lends propriety, is too flighty to contribute much else, and I have had no one to advise me how to go on since dear Papa and Mama . . ." Here Kitty's voice was suspended by tears.

"It's no trouble at all, and I am happy to help," Frances assured her, but refrained from commenting that advice from her was probably far more sensible than any Kitty would have gotten from two such hopelessly romantic and indulgent parents as the late Lord and Lady Mainwaring had been.

2

A t that moment the perpetrator of Kitty's dilemma sat staring into the library fire at a forbidding mansion in Grosvenor Square. A man of action who ordinarily avoided the social demands of life in the *ton*, the new Marquess of Camberly would have preferred to remain in his smaller, less-imposing establishment in Mount Street, but on succeeding to the title he had recognized the foolishness of maintaining two London residences. Reluctantly he and Kilson, his valet, butler, and general factotum, had left the freedom of their former abode for the formality of Mainwaring House.

Lord Mainwaring frowned down at the letter just delivered to him. "Blast, there's nothing for it but to go down to Hampshire and straighten this out! Thank you, Kilson." The flickering firelight revealed a dark, rather harsh-featured countenance rendered even more harsh by its owner's present expression. At thirty-five, Lord Julian Mainwaring, the new Marquess of Camberly, was a man more accustomed to the excitement of politics and the administration of business interests inherited from his uncle, a nabob of immense wealth and influence in the empire's financial circles, than he was to the more pedestrian concerns of estate management. These he had happily left to his brother, never dreaming that he would suddenly become responsible for the lands as well as the children of one who was only a few years older than he. Because of his far-flung financial concerns, constant attention to international politics had been a necessity and Mainwaring had rapidly become a man whose advice was often sought on the economic consequences of certain aspects of British foreign policy. It was for this expertise that he had been asked to join Castlereagh in Vienna. To a man of action, Castlereagh's policies had seemed hopelessly timid and tentative. Julian Mainwaring was more inclined to favor the economic sentiments of Castlereagh's opponent Canning, though when closely questioned by his intimates, he was known to criticize the insular nature of Canning's foreign-statesmanship. To an independent thinker such as Mainwaring, political loyalties and party theory were less important than the practical economic questions posed by the issues raised at the Congress. For this reason he had consented to go to Vienna. There he had found his element in the dealing and intriguing, where the incredible collection of heads of state, ministers, and hangers-on of every description made it easy to communicate with a variety of states, principalities, and nations, all of whom were committed to the creation of a new Europe. He had found this sense of making history an exciting and heady atmosphere, and it was with extreme reluctance that he had returned to England at the notice of his brother and sister-in-law's deaths in a tragic coaching accident. The scenes of glittering soirees and heated conferences faded as he turned back to the humdrum problems of country estates: tenants' complaints, cottages to be repaired, fences to be mended, fields to be drained.

It was Kilson's second "Ahem," preceded by a conspicuous opening of the library door, that broke his train of thought. "Lord Charlton to see you, sir . . . beg your pardon, milord." Kilson was having difficulty adjusting to the new formalities of his situation. He had preferred the free-and-easy life traveling in the colonies and on the Continent, but realizing that the new responsibilities and settled existence were even more onerous to his master, he did his best to see they both remained aware of and accustomed themselves to the changes.

"Send him in and bring a bottle of port. I've a feeling I'll need it."

"Julian, my boy, good to see you home!" The elderly statesman greeted him heartily as he came to warm his hands in front of the fire.

"Thank you. I wish I could share your sentiments, but I find it damnably dull to be here." There was a distinctly sardonic note in Mainwaring's voice.

"Well, yes," Lord Charlton agreed. "I expect anything would be sadly flat after rubbing shoulders with potentates and intriguers from every corner of Europe, but you know as well as I do that foreign policy begins at home. And at the moment we need you rather desperately right here, old boy."

"Oh?" Mainwaring tried unsuccessfully to keep the interest out of his voice.

"Rather. You know that sentimental idealist Alexander has dreamed up this romantic twaddle of the Holy Alliance—the most ridiculous piece of tripe you can imagine! It will simply mean that he will be even more free to meddle in European affairs and pontificate to his heart's content. We must keep Prinny from agreeing to such a thing. You are as familiar as anyone with his theatrical bent, and sometimes Alexander's playacting as 'Savior of Europe' can be rather more attractive to him than is good for England. Prinny is inclined to dismiss all of us as a bunch of power-hungry politicians, but perhaps he'll listen to you, since your friendship has more to do with aesthetics than politics."

"I'll try, George," the marquess sighed. "But just because Prinny consults my knowledge of Oriental architecture and admires some of the pieces I've collected here and there doesn't mean he'll pay the slightest attention to anything else I might say. He may have revolutionized artistic vision in this country, but politically the man is a complete fool. I only put up with him because he at least can offer an amusing conversation on something more stimulating than crop rotation. I'll put it to the touch, though."

"Thank you, my boy. We'll be very grateful for anything you can do. Now I must go. I promised I'd attend this affair at Sally Jersey's with my wife. Can't think why women like these things. Can't stand them myself, but we're puffing off Caroline this Season and Maria wants to be sure that Sally gives her a voucher for Almack's—ridiculous place.''

''My sentiments exactly,'' the marquess said sympathetically. ''At least there will be two sane people there. You'll be someone I can look for. I must get rid of my niece as well this Season. Got my cousin, Lady Streatham, you know, to do the real work dragging her around, but no doubt I shall be dragooned into appearing at some of the most important of these functions.''

It was in a much cheerier frame of mind that Mainwaring returned to the fire. In fact, he felt invigorated enough later to look in at his club, where he was welcomed both for his own attributes as a talented pugilist and noted judge of horseflesh and for the news he brought from the Continent. This reception further inspired him to stroll to a certain house in Mount Street.

There he was certain of his welcome. ''Julian, my dear, how charming to see you,'' exclaimed the opulent brunette rising seductively from an exceedingly becoming pink couch. ''It's been so long,'' she complained with a pout of full red lips and a sigh that called attention to beautifully rounded shoulders and bosom.

''I know it has been a tediously long time.'' He bent his dark head to kiss a perfumed hand, continuing the caress up to a dimpled wrist and elbow. ''But must we now waste our time dwelling on how long it's been?''

The beauty smiled a slow, confident smile. ''Ah, you think to make me forget how you've neglected me.'' She sighed voluptuously, leaning back against the satin pillows.

His gaze dwelt on her appreciatively. ''No, I came here to make *me* forget.''

''Trifler! I must demand some forfeit for such shabby treatment.''

''Naturally, your generous nature will keep you from such rash behavior,'' he murmured, kissing the nape of her neck, forcing her to abandon any further attempts at reprimanding him.

Unlike many of his cronies, Julian Mainwaring considered it a waste of time and money to pursue the numerous opera dancers and barks of frailty who constantly sought to attract his attention. The petty jealousies and competition for favor that were a necessary part of such a scene held no allure. He preferred the more mature charms of a sensible woman of his world. Lady Vanessa Welford was the perfect partner. Married at a very early age to a doddering peer who combined the advantages of immense wealth and an early demise, she had no intention of ending the freedom of her widowhood in another confining marriage. She juggled her many liaisons with such discretion that it was only the highest sticklers of the *ton* who could find the least objection of her. She had enjoyed her freedom immensely until she had met Julian at the Duchess of Marlborough's ball some months ago. Accustomed to manipulating her many and varied lovers without becoming emotionally involved in the least, she recognized, after being guided masterfully around the dance floor, that the new Marquess of Camberly was accustomed to dominating every situation—financial, political, or amorous. Gazing seductively into his dark blue eyes framed by fierce black brows and high cheekbones, she read a great deal of appreciation for her charming appearance but nothing of the blind adoration she was accustomed to inspiring. Intrigued, she had invited him to call the next day, and again found him completely charming and completely disinclined to become involved. Having thus set out in a spirit of pique to capture his attentions, Vanessa found that she rather than he was becoming captivated. An experienced woman of the world, she knew better than to make demands of him. She found his lovemaking, detached and infrequent though it was, more and more necessary to her existence. In fact, he was becoming an obsession with her—so much so that she had of late decided, against all her principles, to become Lady Mainwaring and had embarked on a discreet but intensive campaign to accomplish this.

For his part, Julian enjoyed the attentions of a clever, beautiful woman who exhibited an insatiable appetite and a thorough knowledge of the art of dalliance, but never having felt the need for female companionship or a family, he had not the least intention of going beyond a purely physical relationship. In fact, it was with rather a sense of relief that he left her house in the early-morning hours. After the cloying intimacy of her perfumed satin boudoir he found the prospect of a drive to Hampshire and a few days in the country a refreshing and welcome change.

3

U naware of the impending arrival of her "villainous guardian," as Kitty with her love of the romantic was wont to call him, Kitty and Lady Frances were strolling together in the conservatory at Cresswell, hatching a scheme to render the former's visit to London as unintimidating as possible. Lady Frances had conceived the notion that some of the worry might be taken out of the approaching ordeal if Kitty had a friend such as Lady Frances there with her. "But you loathe London and the Season and all that entails," Kitty protested.

"That was many years ago, when I was young and had entirely different expectations and aspirations. I might just enjoy it. For, you know, it would be a very good thing if I were to visit my publisher right now. I have done something slightly different in this latest book and I would wish to consult with him before I go further. Besides, Cassie and Frederick have never been to London. I am sure they would find it extremely diverting, as well as full of new opportunities for further mischief. I also confess to a great desire to see the marbles Lord Elgin brought back from Greece. He was a great friend of Father's and Mother's, you know. We met him in Athens, and such a wonderful time we all had," she said with a slight catch in her voice.

"Oh, that would be wonderful above all things," her companion said with enthusiasm. "Ned could come too, and we could have a fine time. With Lady Streatham to take me about, we shan't need Cousin Honoria, who is the greatest bore imaginable. And she will be happy because she can go visit that insipid niece in Bath whose perfections she is forever throwing up in my face when she considers I've been the least bit gay or impertinent."

"That's settled, then. I shall direct Higgins to have the staff open the house in Brook Street. It will be terrific work, I am sure, as no one has used it this age. But it should be ready within the month and it will certainly take me that long to convince Aunt Harriet to leave the country. We shall probably have to take all those orchids with us," sighed Frances, looking with dismay at the large and varied collection around her.

Ordinarily she loved the conservatory, which was her aunt's chief interest in life. She often came there to sit in its peaceful tropical atmosphere to think or to soothe her nerves after a long day poring over accounts or dealing with tenants. But at the moment she could only view the exotic blooms as an encumbrance. She dearly loved her aunt, whose acerbic wit and down-to-earth attitude had bucked her up after her unhappy time in London, but her eccentricities did complicate the Cresswells' existence. It was Aunt Harriet who had convinced Frances that there were many other ways for a woman to enjoy herself and feel successful beyond making a brilliant marriage or winning a name for herself as a diamond of the first water. Lady Frances had certainly had her own mother as an example of a happy, successful woman, but then Lady Cresswell had been married to someone who encouraged her interest in scholarly pursuits. Such companionship in marriage was unusual, if not highly unlikely, judging from the scandalous *on-dits* Lady Frances had heard in London. Harriet Cresswell had been born with the same scholarly inclinations as her brother, except that her passion was horticulture rather than history. While Lord Frederick Cresswell and his family were traipsing around the classical world, she had remained at Cresswell Manor enjoying free rein with its gardens and constructing an elaborate conservatory to house her growing collection of orchids. Ever since she had encountered Captain James Cook at a friend's dinner party forty years ago, she had become passionately interested in tropical plants, especially orchids. She had managed, via a mysterious network of naval and seafaring connections, to convince captains of various vessels to seek out and bring back any samples of exotic flora they could find. Undoubtedly her generous remuneration of the least of these efforts encouraged the captains' loyalty and ensured the regularity of these botanical delivery services. By now the household and surrounding countryside had become accustomed to the sight of some swarthy seaman uncomfortably astride a horse riding up the drive carefully clutching an oddly shaped package from which emerged some strange-looking greenery covered with brilliant blossoms.

When Lord and Lady Cresswell had returned from their travels, Aunt Harriet had made some halfhearted offers to remove to a house in Bath, but having put so much into the gardens and conservatory, she was quite relieved when no one paid the slightest attention to her. So she remained a fixture at Cresswell, largely ignoring the children and the world in general. She did take an interest in her eldest niece, especially after Frances returned from the Season disappointed in what the *ton* had to offer and as little interested in becoming a society matron as Aunt Harriet had been.

It was Aunt Harriet who, listening to the imaginative way in which Frances taught Cassie and Frederick their history lessons, had convinced Frances to write down these lessons and send them off to her father's publisher in London. And it was Aunt Harriet who shared in Frances' surprise and delight when Mr. Murray had written back that he was honored to print "these extremely edifying histories for young readers" and had requested more. By degrees, Aunt Harriet had proved to Frances that a lack of success in London by no means presaged an equal lack of success in the country. She encouraged her niece to read anything and everything, from politics and agriculture to literary and artistic reviews. Slowly the sound opinions and good judgment Lady Frances developed were appreciated and made her sought-after by local gentry and tenants alike. She still retained her natural reserve. Only her family and the Mainwarings were aware of her fun-loving side, her wonderful sense of humor and extravagant imagination that invented mythical beasts and hair-rising adventures for hours on end. This same sense of humor allowed her to be amused rather than discommoded by her aunt's eccentric ways, her habit of putting any visitor out of countenance either by cutting him dead or, if the slightest interest were evinced, by subjecting him immediately to an extended horticultural tour of Cresswell. Frances knew how much the prospect of cramped quarters, poor air, uneven sunlight, London society, and the parting with the Cresswell rose beds would upset her aunt. But she also knew that the *ton*, which was not only censorious but remarkably well-informed, would soon discover and comment on her behavior if she were to set up an establishment with only Freddie and Cassie as companions. She may have considered herself well on her way to being a respectable spinster at the advanced age of twenty-two, but the scandalmongers would be more than happy to gossip unless she had a more respectable chaperone than a pair of mischievous eleven-year-olds. There was no help for it but to drag Aunt Harriet along with them to Brook Street. Though, she mused, the constant attention required to check the insatiable curiosity and incessant antics of the twins makes them far more effective chaperones than an aunt who would continue to putter with her plants while thieves carried off the silver and ravishers abducted her niece.

Pushing these thoughts aside, she resolved to tackle her aunt by offering her the baggage coach and the services of James, the footman, for the plants a week before the rest of them were to travel, in addition to the enticement of having the front bedroom and dressing room as well as the morning room—all very sunny—at her complete disposal. Having settled that to her satisfaction, she bade Kitty good-bye and rewarded herself with the prospect of a long ride in the soft afternoon sunshine.

Half an hour later, having donned a new riding habit just arrived from the dressmaker and having ascertained from a quick glance in the mirror that the severe cut and jaunty hat were as becoming as she remembered, she strolled out to the stables to be greeted by her favorite mount. Ajax was eager to be released and could barely wait for her to be tossed into the saddle and be off. A handsome Arab, he seemed too strong a mount for a lady, but Frances was a skilled horsewoman and took great delight in the challenge of handling such an animal. The wind whipped the cobwebs from her mind, while the sight of the countryside with its delicate touches of green and the smell of fresh earth made her begin to regret her decision to exchange it for the crowds and the pavements of London. For some time she galloped along, letting Ajax choose the way across the fields, jumping hedgerows and slowing down to canter through the woods, both of them relishing the exhilaration of freedom. But soon thoughts of a myriad of tasks she had left undone intruded and she knew she should return to them. Regretfully she took one last jump and headed home to finish the accounts waiting for her on her desk.

Her good intentions were not to be fulfilled, however, for upon her return she was forestalled by Higgins, who informed her that a gentleman awaited her in the library. Alerted by the somewhat anxious expression on his normally wooden countenance, Frances questioned him further. "It's the new Marquess of Camberly, milady." Then adding in a confidential tone, "And he looks to be in not the best of tempers." Thus forewarned, Lady Frances removed her hat, smoothed a few unruly wisps of hair, and shook out the skirts of her riding habit. Then, fortifying herself with a deep breath and assuming as much dignity as possible after such an invigorating ride, she entered the library.

If he had not been a great deal too angry to care, Lord Julian Mainwaring would have described his first impression of Lady Frances Cresswell as charming rather than beautiful or dignified—an excellent figure, hazel eyes sparkling, and cheeks flushed after a ride. Her graceful entrance and melodious, "Good afternoon, my lord," added to the impression and further exacerbated Mainwaring's temper.

He had been intensely annoyed several days prior to this encounter to receive notice of an action led by the local magistrate against the agent at Camberly, which had forced him to abandon several interesting political projects in London and post down to Hampshire. He had been even further annoyed to discover that the action had been precipitated by the complaint of a Lady Frances Cresswell. If there were anything Julian Mainwaring loathed more than interference in his affairs, it was interference from an officious busybody spinster who had nothing better to occupy her time than causing trouble for everyone else. Years of dealings with a host of aunts and cousins bent on running his life had perfected his technique of discouraging such meddling. An aloof, coldly polite demeanor dampened the curiosity and helpful suggestions of even the most inveterate of busybodies. He had been perfectly confident that the use of this weapon, an icily polite setdown, would solve his problems with Lady Frances as effectively as it had with the others. The shock of encountering someone who was not only a mere slip of a girl instead of a withered-up spinster, but also a girl who did not conceal an annoyingly understanding humorous twinkle in her fine eyes and revealed a charming smile completely deprived him of his usual resources. Accustomed to dominating every situation, he felt himself at a loss in dealing with this one. Frustration merely added fuel to his anger with the situation and with his hostess.

Frances, waiting for his reply, had ample time to study her opponent. The fierce set on an arrogant jaw, the tightening of well-shaped lips, and the lowering of black brows over intensely blue eyes did nothing to dispel her original reading of his character from his letter. He was a man accustomed to command, arrogant and impatient of other people. The gracious manner and smile that good breeding forced her to adopt disappeared immediately and she faced him warily, determined not to be dominated.

"It has come to my ears, madam, that you have had the effrontery to complain to the magistrate about the conduct of my agent." If she had been bent on resisting him before, she needn't have worried. Her determination, which had sprung from her natural resistance to anyone overbearing, was now fueled by anger. An excellent estate manager herself, she had long been annoyed by the irresponsible behavior of Camberly's shiftless Synthe. Fair-mindedly she had to admit to herself that it was none of her business that the estate was poorly managed, but waste and disrepair upset her whenever and wherever she saw them. In some ways she had been affected. Common fences that had fallen down allowed Camberly livestock into the well-

ordered fields of Cresswell's tenants. After all her complaints
had been totally ignored, she had repaired the fences herself,
but her annoyance had remained. She had been almost glad when
her youngest housemaid's tale of woe had revealed Snythe to
be a villain as well as negligent. Frances had surprised Sally
in tears one morning, and after much cajoling had discovered
that he had been forcing most unwelcome attentions on her.
When she had rejected him he had threatened to turn her father,
one of Camberly's oldest tenants, off the land. Her father's
tenancy had been guaranteed by the late Lord Mainwaring's will,
but Snythe had enlisted the aid of a disreputable solicitor from
the nearest town and had managed to convince Mr. Clemson
that it was in his power to remove him from the farm. Sally
had been at her wits' end. Much as she loathed the slimy Snythe,
she loved her family and knew the miseries of the certain poverty
that threatened them should they be turned off. Having heard
the entire story, Frances had bidden her dry her eyes and had
ridden straight to Sir Lucius Taylor, the local magistrate. Bluff
and honest, Sir Lucius had been Frances' adviser in all estate
matters since her father's death. He had been glad of the
opportunity to bring Snythe to account, something he had been
longing to do even longer than Frances.

Thus it was with some asperity that Frances replied, "Yes,
my lord, and you may be sure it should have been done long
before this, for that man has been running the estate into the
ground this age."

His expression became truly alarming. "How dare you interfere in my affairs, madam!"

"I assure you, I restrained myself with difficulty from
entering your affairs long before this. It always grieves me to
see an estate mismanaged, but I refrained from any action,
feeling confident that surely someone would recognize Snythe
for the scoundrel he is. Obviously I was guilty of misplaced
optimism. It was only after his neglect destroyed some of our
seedlings and he threatened my housemaid and her family with
ruin that I took any steps at all."

If Lord Mainwaring had been annoyed before, he was furious
now—furious because he had not had the time to follow up on

his original suspicions of Snythe and come down to investigate, and furious because he had been put in the wrong by a girl little more than half his age. "And I suppose, my girl, that it never occurred to you that the most honorable and expedient way to handle this matter would have been to complain to me," he retorted contemptuously.

Lady Frances flushed. Though privately she acknowledged the justice of his remark and its good sense, she was not about to give in to such high-handed behavior. "I had no reason, sir, given your total disregard for Camberly and its people, to believe that you would pay any attention to a communication from a . . . a 'girl,' " she replied, her eyes kindling at his slighting form of address. "And now, seeing how arrogant you really are, I am surprised you should have paid the least attention to my complaints."

"I had to attend to my own and my brother's affairs in London before I could consider Camberly," he answered, further exasperated at having to defend himself to her. He continued, "As to the rest of the people at Camberly, who are also no concern of yours, I have arranged to bring out my niece this Season under my cousin's aegis, and I will thank you to stop interfering there."

"Interfering? I?" gasped Frances, angry beyond all decorum at this unexpected attack.

"Whom else must I thank for putting such prudish and blue-stocking notions into her head that she writes to me that she does not want to be 'sold to the highest bidder on the Marriage Mart,' as she phrases it? Where else must I look to find the example that makes living in the country, following 'simple, educational pursuits,' seem so attractive? Living in the country and managing an estate may be very well for one such as you, but you know that someone such as Kitty, who has the most naive outlook on life and possesses such romantic propensities, is not the type to enjoy it for long. Better by far that she come to London and learn the untaxing role of a young woman in society so that someone stronger and more sensible than she can take care of her."

Privately Lady Frances was in total agreement, but it would

never do to let this overbearing person know that. "Yes, and suppose no such paragon appears—then what will she fall back on?" was her swift rejoinder.

A cynical smile touched the corners of his lips. "Never fear. What young buck could resist the trusting simplicity of those big brown eyes?"

Before she could stop herself, Frances commented tartly, "Well, obviously men such as you could." Heretofore she had maintained her dignity in spite of being in such a rage, but as these words escaped her lips she realized how rapidly she had descended from a rational condemnation of Lord Mainwaring's business to peurile comments on his personal affairs. Guiltily conscious of this, she put a hand to her mouth and in a remorseful tone added, "Oh, I *do* beg your pardon."

This rapid change from the furious, contemptuous mistress of Cresswell to someone who suddenly looked like a school-room miss caught in an illegal escapade completely threw Mainwaring. Unwilling amusement crept into his eyes as he agreed, "Yes, but I am not the marrying kind anyway, you know."

That left Frances without a thing to say, but rescue was at hand as Higgins entered bearing a decanter of port, which he offered to his lordship. This interruption brought Mainwaring to his senses, and though he thanked Higgins, he declined, saying that he must be off to Camberly, where he was expected for tea. With that and a curt "Good day, ma'am," he strode off, leaving Lady Frances to smile gratefully at her butler.

"That was excellently done, Higgins. I do thank you."

"I thought perhaps his lordship was in need of some restorative," he replied, his impassive countenance belied by twinkling eyes.

It wasn't until he was halfway back to Camberly that Julian realized that though he'd received an explanation, he had certainly not received anything that remotely resembled the apology he had ridden over to demand. "In fact, it was *she* who seemed to think *I* was in the wrong," he muttered bitterly to himself. "Any man would have apologized openly, honestly, shaken hands, and been done with it." His eyes kindled. "In fact, no man would have interfered in such a damned officious manner without coming to me in the first place.'' Thoroughly irritated by the thought that a mere girl had dared to tell him how to go on, he refused to admit that he had been in complete agreement with her over the original problem. He urged his horse to a gallop. ''Damned foolishness! Imagine leaving the management of an estate to a woman—and a girl at that!''

4

During Lord Mainwaring's short tour of inspection at Camberly, it was rapidly borne in upon him that young and female though she might be, Lady Frances Cresswell commanded the respect of the surrounding countryside. He could see for himself her well-drained, well-tilled fields, her neatly maintained cottages, and the excellent quality of her livestock. Sir Lucius confirmed this as they enjoyed their port together following an elaborate repast at his comfortable manor. "At first I couldn't believe that Cresswell would do such a damn-fool thing. Even if he did spend most of his time with his moldly old books, he was a mighty clever fellow. But Frances not only has a good head on her shoulders, she seems to know how to handle her people. Of course, she's got an excellent man in Dawson, her steward, but he tells me she knows all the accounts inside and out and can hold her own in any conversation with a farmer. I hear that she's always having the latest agricultural tracts sent from London. She has a quiet way with her that seems to reassure people and inspire trust. And it isn't easy having care of those twins, either. A rarer bunch of scapegraces I've never been privileged to see. Fine rider too." He waxed eloquent: "Never seen a better seat or lighter hands.'' From such a purely old-fashioned country gentleman as Sir Lucius Taylor, this was high praise indeed. Mainwaring departed in a thoughtful mood. He respected the older man's judgment but not to the point of describing Lady Frances Cresswell as someone with a "quiet way" about her.

Of course, in his niece Kitty's eyes she could do no wrong. At any other time he would have been amused at her naively enthusiastic description of such a paragon, but it did not suit him to be forever hearing the praises of someone who had had the impertinence to interfere in his vastly complicated affairs. And then to imply that he wasn't succeeding very well at them was outside of enough. In fact Lord Mainwaring was beginning to find the companionship of Kitty, charming though she was, slightly tedious. Even in his salad days he had never had much use for the awkward enthusiasms or, worse, the false sophistication of young misses, and had done his best to avoid them at all costs, choosing instead the more amusing company of older women whose married status did not threaten his bachelor existence. Liaisons with them gave him freedom to choose charming flirtations or relations of a more intimate nature. In both cases each party was perfectly aware of the rules. In fact, young people of any age bored him. He could not understand his cousin Lady Streatham's extraordinary interest in her own offspring, let alone those of her friends. Having led a solitary life himself, abandoned largely to the care of nurses and tutors, he could see no earthly reason for parents to spend any more time and thought than was absolutely necessary on creatures who had no intelligent conversation to recommend them and who were more likely than not to make a mess of the drawing room. All in all, he was quite ready to leave the restrictions of marriage and families to his friends, while he retained the freedom to choose his own amusements.

It was not long before Lord Mainwaring was eager to leave Camberly and return to the more scintillating companionship offered in the metropolis. He had had his fill of dinner conversations that seemed to consist chiefly of a discussion of the varied and mysterious ailments that threatened Cousin Honoria and the manifold accomplishments of Kitty's idol, Lady Frances. Since these consisted of the decidedly dull ability to tutor her brother and sister, manage an estate, and write books, he was less than charmed. If there were a class of women who bored Lord Mainwaring even more than simpering misses, it was the bluestockings, whom he stigmatized as women forced to affect eccentricities because they were too tedious or unattractive to command attention in any other manner. It was fairly easy to avoid the languishing eyes of hopeful young ladies and the blandishments of their matchmaking mamas. A man as wealthy and distinguished as Lord Mainwaring learned this skill from the moment he entered the *ton*. Far more annoying, because less obvious, were the tactics of these women whose only aim in life seemed to be to meddle in others' affairs and to advise them on how to conduct themselves with more propriety, more social conscience, more virtue, more serious-ness of purpose, and always—as in the case of his bevy of aunts—to marry and produce heirs.

It was thus with relief that at the end of the week he bid good-bye to his niece, gave final instructions for her journey to London, climbed into his curricle, and set his powerful grays on the road to London.

Lord Mainwaring was not the only one relieved that his visit had come to an end. Kitty, having endured his rather critical company for several days, felt her confidence at handling the rigors of a Season fast slipping away. It was not that her uncle had actually voiced any actual disapproval of her dress or behavior, but his entire bearing and conversation betrayed such exacting standards that she despaired of ever living up to them.

She could see that at the very least her conversation was uninteresting to Lord Mainwaring, and at the worst, it annoyed him. Several awkward dinners had left her desperately wishing that her parents' rather liberal interpretation of Monsieur Rousseau's maxims had not encouraged them in a blithe neglect of formal education. Rather, they had allowed their children to educate themselves, following natural inclination at the expense of a discipline which would have forced them to attend to the newspapers and books likely to cultivate not only their minds but also, more important, their conversation. Instead of following such a program, as she knew Lady Frances had, Kitty had familiarized herself with every dramatic episode, every improbable plot in the latest novels from the circulating library. However, her natural optimism, one thing that had been fostered in the indulgent atmosphere of Camberly, soon reasserted itself. The arrival of a letter from Lady Streatham, cautioning her not to purchase any of her wardrobe until they could consult the modistes in London, assuaged any lingering doubts she had about the forthcoming Season. So it was that before she had seriously begun it, Kitty abandoned the rigorous reading program she had devised for herself in favor of poring over the latest *Belle Assemblée*.

Lady Frances, lacking a guardian who ruthlessly ordered her affairs, had spent the better part of her week cajoling and effecting compromises among various members of her household. Cassie and Frederick had raised a loud wail of protest at the prospect of removing to town. "We won't have any places to explore, and we'll have to be clean all the time, with nothing to do but listen to a lot of dull conversations," complained Freddie.

"And there won't be any trees to climb at all," Cassie chimed in with disgust, only to break out again as a new, more terrible thought struck her. "We won't have our ponies to ride, or Wellington or Nelson to play with."

"Of course I would never leave our friends behind," Frances defended herself indignantly. "Do you think for one moment that I want to give up riding Ajax? John Coachman and some of the stableboys will take all the horses to London before we go, and then will return to drive all of us to London, including Wellington and Nelson. You don't seriously think I'd leave those two mischief-makers here, do you? They would have the place all to pieces in no time, I daresay." She continued wistfully, "It won't be as exciting to ride in the park for any of us, but we shall certainly ride. Who knows, you may make some new friends there. Of course we shall be sure to visit the Tower and Astley's Amphitheater. And no one visits London without tasting the ices at Gunter's. Perhaps, if we're lucky, there will be a balloon ascension." By the time she had finished describing some of the delights to be enjoyed in the metropolis, the twins were reconciled.

"And," Frederick assured his twin, "if we're *that* busy, we can't have time for too many lessons!"

Aunt Harriet was rather more difficult to convince. "Never heard of such a stupid notion! Leave Cresswell when the gardens will be coming to their peak? You are all about in the head, my dear. And you know that the aphids on the roses were so terrible last year that I must be particularly vigilant this spring." A cunning look came into her eyes. "You know that once people hear you are in town you'll be invited to balls, routs, and every type of frivolous amusement those fashionable fools can devise. Surely Kitty will insist that you accompany her to Almack's, at least the first time."

"Yes, but I shan't mind this time, now that I won't be disappointing the family if I don't snare some unfortunate for a husband. Having discovered I am not the romantic or marrying sort, I won't be the least bit upset if no one pays much attention to me. In fact, the less attention I attract, the better time I shall have. I don't believe a man I would enjoy marrying exists, so I shan't be hoping to meet him as I once might have done. Besides, I shall amuse myself observing the idiocy from the safety of the chaperones' corner. You see, you can't worry about me on that score. I thought we could have a few select dinner parties and invite Sir John Perth, now that he has returned from India. Perhaps he will have discovered some new horticultural wonder you know nothing about. Besides, he's a great friend of Sir Humphrey Repton and would perhaps agree to bring him along. Papa knew Sir Humphrey, but not well enough that I could invite him to dinner."

If Frances had counted on sparking some interest with the name of the botanist and noted landscaper, she was only partially successful.

"That's as may be." Aunt Harriet eyed her suspiciously. "But what about my orchids, miss? You know I can't leave them with Swithin. He thinks they're too outlandish." Her aunt dismissed the head gardener, her chief crony at Cresswell, with scorn.

"No, I had thought to take them with us. James will take them to the baggage coach when John takes the horses. You may have the front bedroom, which, in addition to being very sunny, has a dressing rom. If that's not sufficient, there is the breakfast parlor for the rest of your horticultural darlings." A wicked little smile accompanied this generous offer. "And surely you would like to visit Kew again?" her niece quizzed her.

"Very well, miss. I only hope you are not sorry you went to all this trouble for a silly chit like Kitty." She continued, nodding sagely at Frances' raised brows, "You're going about things in your usual style, putting yourself to a great deal of trouble on someone else's behalf without the least thought for the inconvenience to yourself. Kitty's a very sweet girl, but even you will allow that she's rather flighty. Any number of eligible young men will do for her, and she won't need your help or support in finding them. I had certainly better come to London to protect you from your own generous impulses." With that Parthian shot she swept out, leaving Frances in her wake, prey to conflicting feelings of amusement, exasperation, and gratitude.

It only remained for Frances to organize the twins and herself and leave instructions with the rest of the staff for the closing of Cresswell and preparation of the London house for their occupancy. This monumental task was far easier for her than convincing the people she loved to leave a place to which they all were so strongly attached. She truly did need to meet with her publisher, and though it was unconscious on her part, she did long for the mental stimulation of the metropolis with its plays, operas, exhibitions, and bookstores. It would never have occurred to her to think her life dull. Between the duties of the estate and the education and rearing of her younger brother and sister, she never had a quiet moment, but she did miss the interesting discussions she had enjoyed so much with her father. There was no one in the immediate area who understood her intellectual interests, much less shared them with her. Sir Lucius and his wife, though jovial and as kind as could be, didn't seem to feel the need to know or think about anything beyond the immediate concerns of farming and family, and looked with some suspicion at anyone who did. They had both adored her father, but whenever they had been with him, there had been something in their attitude that suggested apprehension that might at any minute burst into wild philosophical speech rather like a madman.

The following week found Kitty and a protesting Ned ensconced in Mainwaring's impressive mansion in Grosvenor Square, while Cassie, Frederick, Frances, Aunt Harriet, Wellington, Nelson, and the orchids were beginning to settle in close by in an elegant but less-imposing house in Brook Street. Within a few hours of arrival the household had reverted to normal. Cassie, summoned by Wellington to rescue Nelson from a precarious position in a tree, had torn her new pinafore. Freddie had discovered that the mews of London had far more horses and stableboys to befriend than the combined stables of Camberly and Cresswell. Higgins had taken the cook to task for selecting a scullery maid who was obviously in an interesting condition, turned the wench off, and procured a neat and willing young person much more suited to a genteel household. And Aunt Harriet, having bullied James, the youngest footman, was tenderly placing her orchids in the most advantageous positions, commiserating with them all the while on the miseries of a coach trip to London. Seeing that everyone and everything was in order, Frances, mindful of her most pressing reason for visiting the metropolis, dashed off a note to Kitty informing her of their safe arrival.

5

The note was delivered as that young damsel was trying on a bewitching confection just arrived from a very expensive milliner. Its high crown and broad brim trimmed with delicate plumes set her delicate features off to perfection and contrived to make her look both innocent and enticing. The bright red—*ponceau*, the modiste had called it—ribbons matched the trim and ruching on her striped walking dress, complimenting her large brown eyes, delicately rounded chin, rosebud mouth, dimples, and dusky curls. All in all, it was a very satisfying transformation from her serviceable brown merino. London would be thoroughly delightful, she thought, if she had a properly appreciative audience. The Cresswells were not the ideal audience for an attractive young girl, but they were an audience. And at present, they were the only ones she knew in town, so she decided to afford them the first taste of her newly fashionable appearance by taking a cup of tea with them and sharing news of the *ton* gleaned from her few previous days in the metropolis.

Just as she had ordered that odiously superior Kilson to procure a chair—she was too much in awe of her uncle to dare to ask for the use of his many conveyances—the knocker sounded and Lady Streatham was ushered in. Elizabeth, Lady

Streatham, cousin to Lord Mainwaring and the only relative he had not labeled a "dead bore," had been a reigning belle in her day. A merry rather than beautiful face, vivacious nature, and abundant energy had won the hearts of scores of eligible young men. To everyone's surprise, given her fun-loving nature, she had chosen the quietest and shyest of them all, Lord Streatham, and retired happily to his country seat to raise a promising young family. In answer to her friends' protests against such a seemingly unequal match, she had maintained that for her to marry someone as lively as she was would be to court disaster. For sanity's sake she had chosen someone she could dominate. Her closest friends, seeing the warmth in her eyes whenever she was with her husband, recognized that, unlike most of her contemporaries, she had married for love to someone who could give her a constant supply of admiration, support, and emotional security. These same friends, while they missed her gaiety and humor, realized that these lovable traits now found an outlet with her four equally fun-loving and energetic boys. In fact, the joy she derived from being mother to a lively family far outweighed the gaiety of London. It had been years since she had spared a thought for all that she was missing, buried in the country until her youngest had begun to spend more time with his tutor than he did with her. Just as she realized with a slight shock that she was middle-aged and had not attended for years anything more formal than a country assembly, she had received Mainwaring's missive begging her to chaperone his niece. With some trepidation she had broached the subject to her husband. "I do think I ought to help him out, as I am the only female in the family with whom he is on speaking terms. Don't you agree, John?"

Her husband looked at her fondly, marveling that in spite of her years and children she didn't look much older than she did when he married her. "Of course, my dear, it's time we used the London house ourselves. We all could do with a little town bronze. I have some affairs to attend to in the city." He continued, with an understanding twinkle, "Elegant as you always are, I am sure you are years behind the London fashions. My riding boots are in tatters. Come to think of it, we could all stand to replenish our wardrobes as well."

Lady Streatham, knowing how much her husband loved the country and how difficult the social whirl was for someone of his shy nature, fully appreciated his sacrifice and the generous spirit which prompted it. Tears stung her eyes as she flung her arms around his neck. "Oh, John!"

"There, there, my dear, no need to get in a pother about it," said her husband, returning her embrace and smiling down into misty eyes. "I've selfishly kept you to the boys and myself all these years. It's time your friends enjoyed your company again."

"You're so good, my dear friend," she replied. "But won't you dislike it excessively?" she questioned anxiously.

"Not when I've got the gaiest member of the *ton* to watch out for me." Her husband smiled. "Now, no more. It's settled," he added, silencing her with a kiss that was unexpectedly passionate in such a reserved man. So it was that the entire Streatham household was removed without a great deal of fuss to their house in Bruton Street, not too far away from Mainwaring House. And Lady Streatham lost no time in becoming acquainted with her charge for the Season.

She had already met Kilson, who allowed the faintest of smiles to cross his countenance as he opened the door to her. Pulling off delicately shaded lavender gloves, she greeted her protégée. "I see you're on your way out, and looking vastly charming too, if I may say so."

"Yes," responded Kitty, highly gratified by such notice, "I've just received word that Lady Frances has arrived in town, and I do so want to see her. Won't you come too? I need your support because I know she means to avoid most of the social functions and I think it would do her good to attend them. She says she refuses to burden any hostess with someone for whom partners must be pressed into service, but I hardly see how that could be. I think she's very elegant and certainly easy to talk to. But she says people don't want elegance and conversation. She keeps telling me that she is not at all the type that is admired, but I think that her opinion is a result of her one and only Season, when she was taken about by Lady Bingley, who is excessively silly herself and moves in such fashionably empty-headed circles that Frances was bound to feel awkward and out-of-place. Do

come and help me convince her at least to start off the Season
by accompanying us to Lady Richardson's ball.''

Lady Streatham had not spent a week escorting Kitty to every
fashionable establishment in London without having heard about
Kitty's unusual neighbor, and her curiosity was aroused. Her
own lively family and a devoted elder brother had given her
enough confidence to enjoy her come-out and to view making
the acquaintance of hordes of unfamiliar people as an exciting
opportunity for discovery, but she knew she had been unusually
lucky in her family and friends. Too well she could imagine
the loneliness of a girl whose parents' tastes had kept them apart
from the fashionable world and deprived her of the security of
recognizing familiar faces among the *ton* crushes. The fact that
the distant relative who had chaperoned her scarcely shared a
single thought with Frances would merely have added to her
sense of being completely out-of-place. ''I agree. We must see
what we can do to change her mind. Come along. My carriage
is just outside,'' offered Lady Streatham, drawing on her
recently discarded gloves.

''We must be back by three o'clock, because Lord Mainwaring is taking me to tea at his grandmother's,'' warned Kitty
in a tone tinged with misgiving at this prospect.

By the time they arrived at Brook Street Frances had
succeeded in persuading Cassie into a fresh pinafore and lured
Freddie away from the stables with promises that he could take
a large lump of sugar to his pony after lessons. She intensely
disliked playing the martinet, but knew the children would feel
more comfortable and the household would run more smoothly
if a routine were immediately established. Consequently it was
a well-behaved, well-scrubbed schoolroom scene that welcomed
Kitty and Lady Streatham as they entered the drawing room.
This model of decorum instantly disintegrated as Cassie jumped
up to greet Kitty, upsetting the globe in the process. Lady
Streatham, whose maternal reflexes were never far from the
surface, caught and righted it dexterously while extending her
other hand to Frances, saying with her infectious smile, ''I am
so glad to meet you. I apologize for coming uninvited, but Kitty
persuaded me that it would not bother you. She was desperate
that I should meet all the Cresswells. Besides, having rusticated

for so long, I feel in need of support from another sensible woman if I'm to help Kitty sort out admirers. From what I hear, you're just the ally I need.''

She couldn't have chosen a more advantageous method of attack. What Frances would not do for herself, she would do for someone else most willingly. Appealed to in this way, she could only laugh as she rose to greet her visitors, removing the somnolent Nelson from her lap as she did so. Having deposited him in an equally comfortable spot, she extended a welcoming hand to her visitor. ''I shall do my best to help you, ma'am. But with my experience, or lack of it, I am more likely to scare off suitors than to introduce Kitty to them.''

Looking into the frank hazel eyes fringed with thick lashes, the delicate features lighted now by a warm, generous smile, Lady Streatham agreed with her charge that Frances' one and only Season must have been badly mismanaged. Surveying the scene further as Frances directed Cassie and Frederick to make their bows to their guests and pushed Wellington from a perch on the sofa—illegally snatched in all the confusion—she reflected on what a great pity it was that someone who commanded love and respect as naturally as Frances did should so quickly resign herself to spinsterhood. No sooner had she decided this than she began to plan a strategy to avert such a tragedy. I shall force Mainwaring to help me, she resolved. To lend Kitty countenance, he will just have to overcome his dislike of the place and escort us to Almack's and to several balls as well. He detests partnering the young girls and their rapacious mamas so much that he should be only too glad to dance with someone as sensible as Frances. He'll get intelligent conversation and protection from matchmaking females at the same time. At this point she remembered hearing Kitty repeat Frances' account of the rather disastrous first encounter between the two. Never daunted, she set out to remedy this immediately by asking if one of the Cresswells' footmen could deliver a note to Lord Mainwaring requesting that his lordship call for Kitty at the Cresswells' on his way to his grandmother's. ''For it's much more convenient and will give us more time together. How did we not think of it before?'' she wondered aloud. Once Mainwaring was at Brook Street, she felt fully confident of her

powers to cajole him into meeting Frances and renewing their
acquaintance on a better footing.

Her schemes were interrupted by a distinct tug at her skirts.
She looked down to discover Wellington and Frederick looking
at her hopefully. "Excuse me, Lady Streatham," broke in
Freddie, "but Kitty says you have a boy about my age. Is he
here in London with you? I should like ever so much to meet
him if he is." He lowered his voice confidentially. "The thing
is that I want someone to play with my soldiers with me. I have
the dandiest collection! Cassie's a great gun. She can run and
climb trees as well as I can, but she hasn't the knack for playing
at soldiers. Frances knows ever so much about battles and
history and such, but I don't really think she likes the thought
of bloodshed. So if your son were here . . ." He trailed off
rather wistfully.

Lady Streatham's infinite experience with small boys
prompted her to respond with just the right note. "How
delightful! I should think Nigel would like to above all things.
He has a set of his own, so you two could have a whole campaign
instead of one paltry battle. I'll discuss it with him when I return
home this evening." Her eyes twinkled in a conspiratorial way
that had won the hearts of countless children through the
years.

"Oh, famous!" breathed Freddie, hardly daring to hope for
such luck.

"Woof!" agreed Wellington with enthusiasm. The two dashed
over to Frances, breaking into Kitty's excited recital of all the
advantages to be found in London.

"You must come to Hatchard's with me straightaway," she
was saying when Freddie burst in.

"Fanny, I say, Fanny. Lady Streatham has a son who is about
my age and he has his own soldiers and she thinks he might
like to visit and play with me and she's going to speak to him
about it directly!"

"That sounds like great good fun," approved his sister.
Catching sight of Cassie's forlorn face out of the corner of her
eye, she added, "While you and Nigel are together it would
be an excellent time for Kitty and me to take Cassie and Ned
with us for ices at Gunter's."

The woebegone look vanished instantly from Cassie's, to descend on her twin's. "But, Fanny . . ." he wailed.

"Now, Freddie, you can't do two things at once, you know, so you must choose." With only the briefest of hesitation he selected the more bellicose amusement, as she had known he would.

"Besides," she teased him, "I couldn't bear the strain of taking both you and Cassie there at the same time, when either one of you alone is a walking disaster. Together, I shudder to think!" The twins grinned good-naturedly, but neither one could let such a remark pass without a spirited defense. These rather vociferous protests were cut short by the entrance of one of the footmen bringing tea and cakes. Neither Lady Streatham nor Kitty, looking forward to the forthcoming tea at the dowager Marchioness of Camberly's, was able to do more than nibble daintily, for which Cassie and Freddie, not to mention their furry friends, were abundantly grateful.

"Kitty tells me that you brought not only your entire household and stables, but your conservatory as well," Lady Streatham commented with some awe. Looking at the twins, she felt that she would be unequal to anything greater than shepherding those two lively charges. Her esteem for Frances rose mightily when she saw how surprised she was that anyone should consider it an effort.

"Oh, yes." Frances laughed. "We have brought all the comforts of a country home, and then some."

Here, Freddie, who had barely finished his cake in time to enter the conversation, burst in eagerly, "Lady Streatham, does your son ride and does he have his own pony?" Assured on both counts, and having arranged to meet Nigel in the park very soon, he was satisfied, and the ladies were left to compare notes on the various unpleasantnesses encountered in removing to town for the season.

This agreeable conversation was interrupted by the entrance of Higgins. "My Lord Mainwaring," he announced, wondering as he did so whether milady and milord would wind up having another set-to. Certainly milord had looked rather forbidding as he strode up the steps, the wind whipping the folds of his many-caped driving coat.

He had, however, underestimated Lady Elizabeth, who, deftly stepping over Nelson and Wellington's teatime tussle, extended both hands to Lord Mainwaring. "Thank you for coming to collect Kitty here. It has saved me taking her back to Mainwaring House, and I'm late for Nigel's tea as it is." Then, plunging on with her irresistible smile, she added, "I know you've met Lady Frances before, but you two haven't been properly introduced. I daresay if you had, each one of you would have been much more civil to the other and wouldn't be looking daggers at each other right now." At this direct attack the two principals, who were both ramrod-stiff and eyeing each other warily, looked slightly sheepish.

Appreciating the humor in the situation, and recognizing a master stroke when she saw one, Lady Frances extended her hand, saying in her frank way, "How do you do, my lord?" No proof against the lurking amusement in her eyes, Lord Mainwaring thawed slightly to extend his own.

"There," Lady Streatham chined in gaily. "Now, if we're all to survive this Season and bring Kitty out in proper style, perhaps we'd best put country matters out of our minds." She looked meaningfully from Kitty to the two who had established an uneasy truce.

Frederick, who had been gazing with rapture out of the window at something in the street below, could bear it no longer. Pointing at Mainwaring's elegant equipage, he asked, "I say, sir, are those grays yours? What an absolutely bang-up pair! They look to be very sweet goers. You must drive to an inch if you can hold them. Do you, sir? How are their mouths? They look as though they'd respond to the lightest of hands. They must go like the very wind when you spring 'em!"

The forthright speech and blatant admiration of a scrubby schoolboy were something totally beyond Lord Mainwaring's vast experience. He discovered, too late, that he was no proof against them. "Yes, they are mine. Would you care to have a look at them?"

Frances noted with surprise that he spoke as casually as though her brother were one of his driving cronies. She had not thought to discover such sensitivity in one who had previously shown himself to be unpleasantly blunt—to put it mildly. Mainwaring had certainly won her brother's undying loyalty.

"Shouldn't I just!" exclaimed Freddie as he dashed downstairs, leaving Mainwaring and the others to collect themselves. "We mustn't keep Grandmother or the horses waiting. Good to see you in town at last, Elizabeth. Since you've commandeered me for Lady Richardson's ball, I hope you'll drag Streatham along with you so there will be at least two men of sense there to support each other." With that and a "Good day" to Lady Frances, he followed Freddie's tumultuous descent in a more leisurely manner and handed his niece up into the curricle. His lips twitched slightly at the sight of Frederick earnestly debating the grays' good points with his tiger, who, seeing his master, bade a speedy good-bye to the boy and leapt up behind.

Lady Elizabeth stayed long enough to invite Frances to dinner with them before the ball, thus ensuring her presence. She forestalled the protest she knew was coming. "My dear, you simply cannot forgo all social intercourse while you are here, you know. You must come because I shall be very busy with Kitty, and someone must keep an eye on Streatham and Mainwaring. Both of them loathe these things so, and they are being so good in attending them for Kitty's sake. But if you aren't there, Streatham is bound to fall asleep in a corner and Julian will be besieged by matchmaking mamas or, worse, their daughters. Such chivalry should not be so poorly repaid. I know you found these scenes a dead bore before, but how could it have been otherwise with Lady Bingley and her set? Why, they have more feathers on top of their heads than they do inside them."

Lady Frances laughed outright at this, but Lady Streatham could see that she had been struck by the truth of the remark and its interpretation of the cause of her previous disenchantment with the fashionable life of the *ton*.

6

Though ill health had forced the dowager Marchioness of Camberly to relinquish her former role as one of society's leading patronesses, it had not deprived her of an active interest in or reliable information on all of its comings and goings. Julian Mainwaring, who possessed a spirit and intelligence to match her own, had always been her favorite among her children and grandchildren. It had always seemed unfair that he and not the soft and sentimental John was the second son, when Julian had all the natural attributes befitting the master of Camberly. She had been delighted when his uncle, recognizing these abilities, had made him heir to his vast interests at home and abroad, though it had saddened her that fulfillment of these responsibilities made it impossible for him to visit her very often. However, whenever he was in England, he made it a point to come see her before seeing anyone else. She enjoyed his rather caustic wit, which recognized and ridiculed pretension as quickly as she did, and she greatly relied on his interpretations of social and political events for knowledge of the true state of affairs in the world, where she was no longer able to observe and judge for herself. The one point on which the two of them were not in complete agreement was matrimony.

Lord Mainwaring categorically refused to see any value in an institution that forced people of dissimilar interests and propensities to endure each other's presence under the same roof. To his grandmother's acid suggestion that there was such a thing as love, he had replied that she might be right, but as that usually didn't last very long anyway, surely it was unwise to hasten its demise by marrying, when it could be enjoyed perfectly well and perhaps longer outside of marriage. She knew she would sound uncharacteristically sentimental to him if she were to suggest that the passion to which he referred and true love—a combination of that passion and mutual respect—were two very different phenomena. So she had held her tongue, hoping against hope that he would discover his error and find someone to share his life and interests just as she had. So far he had closed his eyes to the type of female who might be expected to be both companion and lover, concentrating instead on the entangling and purely passionate liaisons with expensive and experienced matrons of the *ton*. She hoped his succession to the title and the obvious necessity of introducing his niece to society would force him to abandon these and look around for a suitable partner. Though he might not choose matrimony, Julian had enough respect for history and his family name to recognize his duty in providing an heir. In order to discover his sentiments on that subject, and to give herself the chance to exert at the outset what little influence she had, the dowager Marchioness had invited him and Kitty to tea immediately upon their arrival in town.

They entered the ornately decorated drawing room to find her well-wrapped in a variety of richly embroidered shawls, ensconced on a sofa before a roaring blaze. "So, Julian," she barked as she extended her hand for him to kiss. "It's about time you took a position in society instead of skulking on the sidelines with the excuse you were too busy or gallivanting all over the world. And this is Kitty. Come here, child, and let me have a look at you. Very pretty. Not quite so lovely as your mother, but you'll do. And very well-behaved too," she observed as Kitty shyly curtsied to her. "You should have no trouble at all firing her off, Mainwaring. I congratulate you on having charge of a charming ward." Then, turning to Kitty,

who was trying to keep her awe of this alarming old woman
from showing, she continued, "How do you like town life?"
Kitty responded shyly that she liked it very well but had not
been about a great deal yet. "You will do, my dear, you will
do. And soon you'll be in such a whirl you'll not have a moment
to yourself."

Further observations were cut off by the entrance of her aged
butler staggering under an enormous tea tray, which, in addition
to a hugely ornate tea service, contained incredible quantities
of sweetmeats. It was fortunate for Kitty, who possessed a
healthy appetite, that there was an abundant supply, as she was
totally ignored while the dowager pumped her grandson for the
most recent political news as well as the most scandalous *on-
dits*. These he recounted with such skill that she was soon
laughing merrily and contributing her own share of satiric
comments. Never being one to wrap things up in clean linen,
she soon broached her main reason for inviting them, demanding
in her abrupt fashion, "Have you given Lady Welford her congé
yet?" The amusement vanished from Lord Mainwaring's eyes.
"Don't poker up at me, my boy. Do you take me for a flat?
We both know it's all very well to live the gay bachelor
existence, but as head of the family you now have responsibilities that go beyond managing the estate. You need a
marchioness and an heir. Dancing attendance on someone like
Vanessa Welford, who is no better than she should be and greedy
to boot, won't do." Correctly interpreting Julian's raised eyebrows and quick glance at a round-eyed Kitty, she snorted,
"Don't worry about Kitty. It's time she learned a thing or two.
I have no patience with these niminy-piminy modern gels and
their overnice scruples. Far better that she go into the world
with her eyes open than to cry them out later when she discovers
her husband has 'another interest.' "

Seeing that the old lady was becoming agitated, Julian took
a beringed hand in his firm clasp, remarking, "Just so, ma'am,
but we'll discuss this some other time. You must save your
strength to rake me over the coals another day."

The dowager gave him a sharp suspicious look but the genuine
concern she read in his eyes demonstrated that his remark had

truly resulted from solicitude rather than evasion of a sore point.
Sighing, she agreed that she was just the slightest bit tired, but
only the slightest, and rang for Biddle to show them out, murmuring, "Do please come often, Kitty, to share your latest
adventures and conquests with me."

Mainwaring laughed. "As to that, Grandmother, you will
know all about her conquests even before Kitty does, probably."

"Off with you, you wicked boy!" The dowager was inor-
dinately pleased with his assessment of her incredible network
of social reporters.

Kitty was unusually silent on the ride home, digesting this
latest piece of information about her guardian. Less in awe of
him than she had been at first, she no longer annoyed him with
numerous nervous attempts to engage him in conversation, but
behaved more naturally—to the relief of both of them. They
rubbed along as well as might be expected of a worldly thirty-
five-year-old man and a sheltered schoolgirl of seventeen. Try
as she would, she could not picture her reserved and haughty
Uncle Julian in the passionate embraces of some ripe beauty.
The vision of him as a lover just did not coincide with all that
she had heretofore seen of him conferring in his library with
distinguished-looking peers, discussing voyages and the status
of his colonial enterprises with captains recently returned, or
pursuing the purely gentlemanly pursuits at Brooks's, Gentleman
Jackson's, Manton's, and Tattersall's. Kitty resolved to pay
more attention in the future, hoping to elicit some interesting
details from her new abigail, Alice.

This recent addition to the household was only too happy to
regale her country-bred mistress with interesting tidbits about
the ornaments of London society. It was to this lively damsel,
more than to Lady Streatham, that Kitty owed her growing
knowledge of what was "done" and what was "not done" in
the *ton*. Those belowstairs had an even more rigid code of
conduct for those they served than did their masters. For it was
better to be a mere housemaid in a house of the first stare of
respectability than to be abigail to someone of more dubious
reputation, such as Lady Welford. Alice hoped to ensure her
own position by keeping her mistress on the most narrowly

virtuous path. The best way to do that was to keep her informed of the pitfalls along the way and to warn her of the disastrous mistakes that less-well-informed maidens had made.

When Kitty approached her, she was more than willing to talk about her employer's formidable reputation as successful wooer of some of society's most dazzling women. Kitty listened openmouthed as Alice, not a little proud that her master was so dashing, added one name after another to the list of his conquests. "But, Alice," she gasped, "those ladies are all married!"

Her preceptress nodded. "Aye, so they are, my lady. Them's the sort that gets married as quick as possible to some bloke who is as dull as he is rich so they can live like they really wants to and choose their own lovers."

The description of the standard marriage of convenience was all news to Kitty, whose parents had been unfashionably and madly infatuated with each other, and she remained a little confused. Still unable to envision her forbidding guardian in the role of ardent lover, she asked incredulously, "But is he in love with all these ladies at once, then, or one after the other?"

Alice snorted. "Good Lord, no! He's just—ahem—'attracted' by their beauty, if you understand my meanin', miss. He's a reg'lar conoosewer and won't be seen with nothin' but the best, most fashionable ladies. You won't catch his lordship with anyone who isn't what you call a reg'lar diamond. But, Lord, he ain't even that good friends with them. They don't understand all the complicated political things he's into and they don't want to bother their pretty little heads trying. They're happy just so long's he keeps givin' them jewels and takin' them to the opera and suchlike, for they be right proud to have caught him and they want all their friends to see them with him."

Kitty admitted to herself that she had seriously underestimated the variety and magnitude of her uncle's abilities. She knew that to succeed with women in these days of social refinement, any man must possess a good deal of address. She could not picture the Uncle Julian who corrected her conversation, and who was more likely to point out what was wrong with her appearance than compliment her on it, whispering gallant nothings into some lady of fashion's ear. Alice assured her that, contrary to appearance, her seemingly taciturn uncle was famed for his expertise in the art of dalliance when he wished to put forth the effort. Kitty could hardly wait to share her discovery with Lady Frances and to discover whether she were any more conversant with the *à la mode* way of marriage. If she were, it would certainly go a long way toward explaining her distaste for the London season with its universally acccepted goal of the advantageous match. Mulling all this over, she gave herself up to Alice's deft ministrations in preparation for dinner.

7

T he marquess, feeling that he had done his duty and endured enough female company for at least a week—certainly for the day—strolled to Brooks's after dinner in search of convivial company. Luck was his. He encountered the Honorable Bertie Montgomery, exquisitely garbed in delicately shaded pantaloons and a coat that had taken the best of his own and his valet's efforts, as well as an inordinate amount of skill, to smooth onto his slender form without a wrinkle. The Honorable Bertie had been a close friend of Julian's since their days together at Eton and then Oxford. It was a friendship that continued to puzzle many who failed to see that the constantly cheerful Bertie provided a relaxing companionship for his more serious friend, while Julian's intelligence and adventurous nature flattered the sociable Bertie and provided him with a glimpse of exciting worlds without involving him in them.

"Hallo, Julian," he greeted him, his amiable face lighting with pleasure. "Hear you've become an ape leader this Season. Don't do it, my boy. M'mother was in a rare tweak all last year trying to pop off Susan."

Julian tried vainly to conjure up a vision of this damsel, but having been abroad much of the time, gave up.

Sensing his difficulty, Bertie came immediately to his friend's rescue. "A nice little thing, Susan, but a bit on the mousy side. You wouldn't remember her."

Looking at his friend's open but undistinguished countenance, Julian could readily believe this.

"Get your niece betrothed quickly," continued Bertie. "Mother found someone for Susan directly, and we were much more comfortable after that."

Julian smiled, "I shall keep your advice in mind, but I shall have very little to do with it. Lady Streatham is taking Kitty under her wing." The marquess handed his cape to the servant at the door and ordered a bottle of port from another who rushed up to attend to their wishes. "I shall leave everything in her capable hands and lend my presence only when absolutely necessary. I would be exceedingly grateful to you, Bertie, if you would come support me tomorrow at the first fulfillment of my guardian duties at Lady Richardson's ball." Lord Mainwaring rarely asked anything of anybody, but this time the look he directed toward his friend was definitely beseeching.

"Certainly, Julian, but Lady Richardson's ball is the opening event of the Season. Everyone will be there. It should not be so onerous a duty as all that."

The sardonic curl of the marquess's lips and the arrogant lifting of heavy dark brows were eloquent testimony to this gentleman's expectations of such an evening.

"Oh, don't be so damned high in the instep, Julian! Such an evening can be quite entertaining. And not everyone there will be on the catch for you. I tell you what, my boy, it would do you a great deal of good to encounter some woman, any woman, who is not after you for herself or her daughter."

A distinctly cynical look settled on his friend's handsome features. "It may surprise you, Bertie, to hear that I have met such a female, but I don't find prudes any more attractive than I do the most rapacious mama or her daughter."

"Whoever was it?" Bertie questioned, agog to discover the identity of one female who had not fallen victim to Mainwaring's fortune, social position, attractive harsh-featured countenance, or reputation as a perpetual bachelor.

"It was Lady Frances Cresswell," was the unwilling reply.

"Fanny, a prude?" Bertie gasped. "Upon my word, she must have been more shattered by her father's death than I thought."

"You know Lady Cresswell?" Julian asked, wondering at the same time if he had been entirely fair in labeling the lady in question a prude. After all, it was only on the basis of Kitty's description of her learning and his own single experience of estate matters that he had decided she must be a bluestocking. In his experience, most bluestockings were shocking prudes, among many other equally unattractive things. But the more he thought about it, the more he realized that he had been rather hasty in assigning her this trait. No prude would have spent a minute unchaperoned in the company of any man, let alone a man of his reputation, in the library or any other room. Lady Frances had spent fully half an hour alone with him trying to put him in his place, without showing the least sign of discomfort. It was true that she objected to Snythe on moral grounds, but her opinion of the slimy agent was no more censorious than his own. A true prude would have dropped her eyes, blushed, and meekly given in to any of his wishes instead of standing her ground, cheeks flushed, and eyes looking directly and angrily into his own. Not only had she not been meek, she had gotten the better of their encounter. No, he admitted ruefully to himself, whatever Lady Frances was, she was not a prude.

Bertie had been watching the variety of expressions flitting across his friend's face with interest. He would have given a great deal to be able to read them accurately, but, being the good friend he was, contained his curiosity, merely volunteering, "I knew her father."

Julian's patent disbelief in the friendship between one of London's most dedicated dandies and a scholarly recluse forced Bertie to defend himself. "Dash it all, Julian, you needn't look at me as though I'm a half-wit. If you knew the least bit about these things, you'd know that it takes more than a tailor to make someone an arbiter of fashion. It takes exquisite taste, my boy, and exquisite taste demands long and careful cultivation. I first met Cresswell in Greece when I was on the Grand Tour and he and Elgin were convincing the Greeks to sell them bits of the Parthenon. He knew a devilish lot about Grecian art and had some very interesting aesthetic ideas of his own besides. He took me home to see some of the objets he'd collected on his travels. We became quite friendly and I visited him and his family fairly often while I was there. Frances was only a child at the time, but mature beyond her years, and she used to join us and listen to our discussions.''

Harking back to his visit to Cresswell Manor, Mainwaring couldn't remember anything distinctly, but cudgeling his brains, he did dimly recall an impression of lightness and elegance which had given a clue to the artistic interests and eclectic tastes of Lord Creswell.

Bertie continued, ''When they returned, I visited them down at Cresswell. Not long after, Lady Cresswell died and Frances took over the care of the twins. At times she seemed little older than they were, ready to engage in any romp from tree-climbing to punting on the lake. Well, at any rate, she certainly didn't seem as though she were eleven years older. Lord, I remember one night when she dressed up as the headless horseman reputed to haunt the district. She had us all quaking in our boots, what with her bloodcurdling yell.'' He chuckled heartily at the memory. ''No, Frances never cared two pins about what anyone else would think.''

Julian, who had found it difficult to picture Lady Frances Cresswell as anything but self-possessed, certainly had no difficulty agreeing with his friend on this last point, but confined himself to remarking, ''Well, you'll have a chance to judge for yourself. She's to be one of my cousin's party at the Richardsons' ball. It is one thing to partner Kitty, simpering miss that she may be. After all, she is my niece, but I draw the line at Frances Cresswell. She and I have nothing to say to each other, and if I know Elizabeth, she'll consider me at least as responsible for amusing Kitty's friend as I am for squiring Kitty herself. Be a good fellow, Bertie, and do the pretty for me with Lady Frances.'' Lord Julian Mainwaring rarely felt the need to ask a favor of his fellowmen, but there was a distinctly cajoling note in his voice.

''Always happy to oblige a friend, Julian, always happy to oblige,'' Bertie agreed good-naturedly, relieving his friend of the unpleasant task, which had intruded on his thoughts at the most inauspicious moments. That settled, they could turn their minds to the contemplation of an excellent bottle of port and several games of whist before going in search of more enlivening entertainment onstage and off at the opera.

8

L ord Mainwaring was not the only person looking forward with some misgiving to the Richardsons' gala. Kitty, though highly excited at the thought of her first ball, was beset by all the ordinary fears of a young lady making her first entrance into the adult world of fashion. Would she know how to go on? She had been able to dance delightfully with Ned and her dancing master, but performing complicated steps with one's brother in one's own empty drawing room was a good deal different from executing them with a total stranger in a crowded ballroom under hundreds of critical eyes. Would she be pretty enough to attract the attention of anyone at all? Fortunately her brown eyes and shining brown curls were in vogue, brunettes being all the rage at the moment. What would she ever say to everyone? She was confiding this rapidly increasing list of worries to Lady Frances as the two awaited the arrival of the dressmaker at the Cresswells'. This was the final fitting for both of them before the ball, and Kitty had begged to be allowed to try on her gown at Lady Frances' in order to have the benefit of her opinion as well as general moral support. Naturally she wore the requisite white of one making her come-out, but with rose trimmings designed to bring out the enchanting color in her cheeks and emphasize the rich color of her eyes. Lady Frances, by her choice of dove-gray silk, claimed her position as a woman midway between maiden and dowager. She had been kept from further declaring her ineligible status—with a delicate lace cap—by the vehement protestations of both Kitty and the dressmaker.

"Madam is far too young for such a thing. A cap is only for someone who no longer has any possible claim to youth—not one as young and elegant as Madam. It would be a crime to cover up Madam's lovely golden hair with such a thing!" The seamstress was scandalized that anyone would welcome the advent of maturity.

Kitty, far less tactful, added, "Frances, if you wear that dreadful thing, no one will ask you to dance." When Frances finally made it clear that such had been exactly her intention, she was reminded in no uncertain terms of her promise to Lady Streatham to take care of Lord Streatham and Lord Mainwaring. This recollection, coupled with memories of other balls and other partners, caused her serious doubts about the wisdom of coming to London at all. Then she remembered Lady Streatham's merry face, her strictures concerning Lady Bingley and her cronies, and comforted herself with the thought that perhaps things would be different now that she was several years older, virtually her own mistress, and acquainted with more people than she had been before. At any rate, having stood up to something as threatening as Lord Mainwaring in a rage, she couldn't let the mere idea of dancing with him and other supercilious partners put her in a quake. This was a salutary recollection, as it brought to mind her first encounter with him. He had called her a bluestocking, and the remark, unjust though it was, still rankled. All thoughts of the matronly cap were banished and she resolved to get out the famous Cresswell set of baroque pearls to add to her éclat.

This settled, Frances decided to reward herself with a trip to Hatchard's to purchase *Waverly*, which had not been available in the country. Kitty was also fond of Scott despite her propensity for more frothy romances, and she was easily persuaded to accompany her. They set off in the carriage with Wellington. The little dog seized every opportunity for a ride, though he was still leery of the great amount of traffic in the city and much preferred sitting on the box next to John to dodging among the wheels of the throng of vehicles, avoiding the heavy hooves of cart horses or the wickedly quick ones of the highly strung prime bits of blood belonging to the Corinthians. From his perch he could sniff the gratifying variety of city smells and survey the scene with detachment while still attracting the attention of admiring ladies in passing carriages, who never failed to exclaim over his engaging countenance. All in all, he was in a fair way to preferring London to the country.

The tempting array of books catering to every taste and fancy banished all thoughts of the ball that evening from the minds of Kitty and Frances as they browsed happily among elegant gilt volumes. So engrossed was Frances that she failed to notice an exquisitely garbed elderly gentleman next to her, poring over a book of engravings of scenes from classical antiquity. As she stepped back to get a better view of the shelves above her, she bumped into him, rousing him from his absorption. "I do beg your pardon, sir." As she paused to frame a further apology, recognition dawned. "It's Monsieur le Comte de Vaudron, isn't it?" she hazarded, hoping that her memory served her as well as it usually did.

The gentleman regarded her quizzically for a minute before an answering smile broke. "*Cèst ma chère Fanny!*" he exclaimed, kissing her hand with Gallic fervor."

"How delightful to see you! But what are you doing in London, sir? I had thought you were still in Greece. Thank the merciful heavens you did not return to France as you were planning to when we last saw you." The questions and concern in Frances' face betrayed a warmth and fondness not usually present in her manner to those outside the immediate family.

The count laughed gaily. "Always the curious one, eh, my Fanny? I am staying with Lord Elgin. Originally I helped him to transport his precious marbles here from the Parthenon, but I have remained here to add my influential friends' pleas to his in order to make your so-stuffy government purchase them for England. Of course, it is very difficult. You English, the Cresswells and Elgins excepted, are not a cultured race. These treasures will be wasted on such a nation of shopkeepers, but at least they will be safe from barbarians and vandals. Not that I do not appreciate this nation of shopkeepers. After all, so far they have saved all Europe from *ce monstre* Napoleon—definitely a man of genius, but genius run mad with power. And I personally have cause to be grateful to these shopkeepers. Long ago I recognized that my own countrymen, whatever their talents in the more refined aspects of life, have no head for finance or politics, so I brought my money to your English bankers and businessmen, whose acumen now permits me to live like a human being—"

Frances interrupted this elaborate explanation to ask, "But what of your estates, your lovely château? Were they all destroyed in that revolutionary madness?"

"Ah, my child, who knows? News is so difficult to come by, and so unreliable. Whether they exist or not is a matter of indifference to me because they were no longer mine." Seeing Frances' look of horror, he hastened to reassure her. "I saw what that stupid Louis and the rest of his crowd were doing to the country. As you know, I never felt comfortable with the life of the so-called *ancien régime*. That is one of the reasons I left France—that and my wish to study the classical cultures. I left the management of the estate to my nephew Claude. He was a greedy young man and I knew he could be counted on to keep it productive. Soon I realized that he was beginning to consider my lands his own, so I merely formalized it by exchanging them for the family treasures he possessed. He cared nothing for historic tapestries, paintings, jewelry, furniture, but I loved them. He thought he had gotten himself a bargain, poor boy, but I have no doubt it's all gone, and he with it. The way he treated his peasants, I am certain he would have been one of the first to be consumed in the rage of the Revolution. Still, I do not wish such a horrible fate on anyone. Claude was not a particularly cruel man, just unenlightened and rather self-centered, as so many of those people were." He sighed and turned to her. "But, Fanny, tell me of yourself." A look of sadness crossed his face. "I was so very sorry to hear about your poor papa, but he and your mother were so very close, such a well-matched team of students, that I am certain, in spite of you wonderful children, his life must have been lonely after she died. He was a brilliant and amiable scholar, and so was she—perhaps the dearest friends I ever had.'' He fell silent. ''And how do you and Cassie and Freddie go on? You are all still my mischievous little devils, *non*?''

Frances answered as best she could, filling in the two years since her father's death. The appearance of Kitty followed by a heavily laden footman recalled her to her surroundings. Presenting Kitty, she bid the *comte* adieu, begging him to call on them in Brook Street at his earliest convenience. She wondered if he would be at Lady Richardson's ball, and hoped that she would have another friendly face and intelligent conversation to look forward to.

Frances did not like to ask, but the irrepressible Kitty suffered no such qualms. Extending a small white hand and dimpling up at him with her most enchanting smile, she inquired, ''Do you go to Lady Richardson's tonight? I am looking forward to it ever so much, as it's to be my first one.'' The *comte* assured both of them that he would not miss it for the world, and begged a dance from each of them.

''If your card becomes crowded, Mademoiselle Kitty, *naturellement* you will cross out my name and leave me to the dowagers, but if you become weary of inarticulate adoration, overblown compliments, or infatuated young bucks, I am at your service.'' His eyes twinkled. ''Now, let me escort you to your carriage.''

As Lady Frances mounted the steps back at Brook Street, she met Bertie Montgomery on the steps, exquisitely attired in a plum-colored coat, jonquil waistcoat, and fawn pantaloons, bearing a delicately shaded nosegay. ''Bertie, how lovely to see you!'' She smiled, realizing for the second time that day that she knew more people in London than she had imagined.

''Hallo, Fanny,'' he replied, presenting his offering. Her surprise and delight were ample reward for a harrowing afternoon. Bertie had spent the better part of his day trying to deduce what color gown Frances was likely to wear to the ball that evening. Fortunately, he was on excellent terms with Lady Streatham, he hastened to call at Bruton Street, where she was most happy to furnish him with the name of the modiste whose creation was to grace Lady Frances at Lady Richardson's that night. An even quicker visit to Bond Street established the color of her gown and allowed him to select an exquisite combination designed to enhance without overpowering her toilette.

It was more regard for an old playmate than obedience to Mainwaring's wishes that had then sent him posthaste to Brook Street to present it and enroll himself among her partners for the ball. Bertie had no idea how or why Lord Mainwaring had arrived at the conclusion that Lady Frances Cresswell was a prude, but he was determined that such a misguided opinion should not be allowed to take hold in his friend's head, much less spread elsewhere. In fact, by helping both Frances and Mainwaring, he was giving himself the pleasure of dancing with a partner whose grace could be counted on to put his own considerable skill in the best light. Moreoever, he could rely on her not to flirt with him or try to interest him in some pudding-faced daughter. It was an admirable situation. He could enjoy himself while indulging in the luxury of feeling exceedingly virtuous.

As Bertie sauntered off down Brook Street, having presented his posy and made his request, Lady Frances realized that she was well and truly committed to this ball. Even before crossing the threshold, she had no fewer than three partners. With the exception of Lord Mainwaring, they were all calculated to inspire confidence in even the most anxious of females. It came as a slight shock to discover that she was actually looking forward to the evening.

9

An elegant dinner at Lord and Lady Streatham's was a prelude to the ball. Arriving slightly later than she had planned after gratifying Cassie's and Freddie's request to see her in her finery, Lady Frances found the others already assembled. In addition to the family there were a few close friends of the Streathams', but she was acquainted with most of the company. Lady Streatham had tactfully placed Frances next to her husband, knowing that two such serious landlords could find much to discuss concerning the problems and particularities of their respective estates. Though Lord Streatham did not particularly enjoy London society, preferring the more relaxed atmosphere of country entertaining, he was a genial host and excellent conversationalist who welcomed the opportunity to discuss something other than the latest scandal of Byron's or the fashion in bonnets. Sensing a kindred spirit, Lady Frances relaxed and allowed herself to be drawn into a completely unfashionable discussion of the proposed Corn Laws and their undoubted disastrous effects on the farmers. It was thus that Lord Mainwaring, glancing around the table, had leisure to study Frances when she was most at her ease. Bertie Montgomery's revelations concerning her had surprised him and sparked his interest—not that he found her in the least attractive, but he prided himself on his ability to assess people accurately at his first meeting, and it piqued him not a little to be told he was wrong. Grudgingly he admitted to himself that her animated face and graceful gestures were not those of a prude, nor was her attire. The dove-gray silk, ornamented only by a flounce at the hem, was a perfect foil for the magnificent baroque pearls that had been the pride of Cresswell women for generations. Her hair, though simply done, shone a rich gold, which, coupled with her honey coloring and dark brows, made her appear less insipid than most blonds of the pink-and-white variety. The pearls and the silk gave a luster to her skin and made her eyes under their thick dark lashes more intensely hazel. The tasteful simplicity of her costume gave her an air of quiet elegance which, if not at the height of fashion, was not that of a prude.

However, snatches of her conversation confirmed his opinion of her as a bluestocking. He smiled with inward satisfaction as he caught the latest, ". . . the poor harvest I expect this year will drive up the price of corn and make the lot of the small farmer more difficult unless something is done to stop the Corn Laws, which make it impossible to buy cheap foreign corn, or eliminate the burden of taxes . . ."

His dislike of blue women did not stop him from voicing his total disagreement. "And how do you propose, ma'am, to finance the debt which we have incurred during this costly campaign against France, if you eliminate the tax? Besides, the Corn Laws were proposed to help your poor farmer."

Startled by the entrance of another party into her *tête-à-tête*, and stung by the condescension in Lord Mainwaring's tone, Frances raised an eyebrow and responded coolly, "I am referring to the small farmer, sir. Of course I'm not such a nodcock as to think we can completely do away with taxation. I meant merely that it must be redistributed to release the poor farmer who is suffering from the added burden of expensive grain. You don't seriously consider that it is the small farmer, who must devote much of his land to pasturage, that benefits from these Corn Laws, do you?"

Thus challenged, Mainwaring forgot that he would be wasting

his well-considered arguments on a mere slip of a girl and replied with some heat, "No, but I am more concerned with our fledgling industries—our gunmakers and steelworkers. Your farmers still have a market for their produce, but what will the gunsmith or foundry worker do with the decline in his market? Or would you tax him instead of the farmer?"

"Of course not!" Frances could not keep her annoyance at being viewed as a naive girl out of her voice. "But I would rearrange taxation so that those who can pay it are taxed. The American colonies spoke out against such an arbitrary and ill-conceived system, and so ought we."

"So we have a Jacobin in our midst!" he taunted.

"No, sir, you do not. I am not against a system of taxation. I merely ask for one that has been well-thought-out, not one that has been rushed through Parliament in response to the interests of a small group of people. But I do admire the Americans for one thing, and that is their originality in devising an entirely new political system based on soundly reasoned principles. It takes creativity and great courage to do so. However much we, and perhaps they too, may regret the separation between us, one must give them credit for it."

At this point Lord Streatham deemed it prudent to intervene. "Come now, both of you give over. You both talk a good deal of sense, but this is not the place to do so. You must empty your heads so that you can mind your steps later in the ballroom and render your conversation light enough to allay the suspicions of even the most fashionable members of the *ton*. It wouldn't do to *think* at a ball, you know," he added, shaking his head and quizzing them both. "I can see, Frances, that you must dance first with me so that I can get you off your high horse and to the weather, Kitty's chances of success this Season, or something equally likely to make you sound benignly insipid." Frances laughed, and recognizing the justice of his remark, accepted his offer with pleasure.

Lady Richardson's ball had already been dubbed a "dreadful squeeze" by the time Kitty, Frances, and the Streathams ascended the wide marble staircase to the brightly lighted ballroom above. For an instant Frances felt a knot in the pit of her stomach as the music, elegant dresses, sparkling jewels, and hundreds of chandeliers brought back memories of another Season, but this vanished as Lord Streatham, who, guessing her disquiet, patted her arm as he led her and his wife into the throng. Not allowing her to chance to do more than glance at the beautifully dressed women, masses of candles, and banks of flowers, he swept her onto the floor into a set that was just forming. Though neither he nor Frances was enamored of the social scene, Lord Streatham and she were both graceful enough that they enjoyed the exercise of dancing, and Frances, who loved music as well, soon forget herself completely as she gave herself up to the pleasure of executing the steps in time to it. Thus she appeared at her best—graceful and unself-conscious— to those dowagers and dandies who were scrutinizing every face new to the London scene. Not being a "diamond of the first water," nor decked out in the first stare of fashion, she did not attract a great deal of attention, but that which she did attract was approving.

Frances hardly had a moment to look around for Kitty before Bertie Montgomery came to claim his dance. Having ascertained from Lady Streatham that Frances waltzed, and having assured himself from her performance that she would do him credit as a partner, he resolved to demonstrate to anyone interested in observing that Lady Frances Cresswell showed to advantage in the ballroom. While he guided her expertly around it, he kept up a running commentary on the famous and infamous members of the *ton* to be seen there that evening. Did she see the elegant gentleman in the corner haughtily surveying the scene through a gold quizzing glass? That was Lord Petersham, tea connoisseur of the most exquisite sensibility and possessor of a different snuffbox for every day of the year. Mr. "Poodle" Byng, minus his omnipresent canine companion, thank heaven, was to be seen in the alcove chatting with Lord Alvanley. Now, Alvanley had his own peculiarity, being so fond of cold apricot tarts that he ordered a fresh one prepared daily and set on his side table so that he could indulge his fancy whenever it came upon him.

Frances had heard outrageous tales of extravagance, but, from her rational perspective, had put them down to the natural wish on the part of the local gentry to depict London as the scene of every absurdity and folly. Truly, it seemed they were not far wrong. The amusement in her eyes deepened as every whirl of the waltz faced them toward yet another person who had tried to win the fickle interest of society by carrying some personal fetish to an extreme. "And you, Bertie, I can see you are on the best of terms with all of them. What are you noted for?"

"Nothing at all," he replied airily.

"Well, I think it must be for your nicety in dress, for you do look quite fine, you know."

Bertie turned quite pink with pleasure and said he supposed he might be known as a fellow who possessed the happy knack of choosing and keeping a good valet and tailor.

"As well as possessing exquisite manners and a warm heart," she added, smiling.

He again flushed vividly but said simply, "I would do anything for a true friend of mine."

When the waltz ended, he restored to her to Lady Streatham and went in search of refreshment for both of them after their exertions. "Enjoying yourself, my dear?" Lady Elizabeth queried, noting with pleasure the flush in Frances' cheeks and a distinct sparkle in her eyes. Frances, however, merely nodded while her companion continued. "Mainwaring asked me to secure your next waltz with him if he were not here to claim it when you finished with Bertie." She glanced toward the end of the ballroom, where his lordship was escorting Lady Jersey to a gay-looking group of people.

"Oh, no!" Her ladyship looked surprised at Frances' vehemence. Then Frances explained candidly, "I don't think that's advisable in the least. He and I always seem to be dagger-drawing."

Lady Elizabeth dismissed this unworthy thought. "That's as may be, but his reputation as a severe critic of the female sex is well-known, and it will do you no end of good socially to be seen as his partner for the waltz." Bowing to unanswerably superior social wisdom, Lady Frances acquiesced.

The truth of the matter was that earlier Lady Elizabeth had seen Mainwaring propping his broad shoulders against a wall as he eyed the assembled throng sardonically. He had just finished telling himself that, having done his duty and danced with Kitty, he was free to go in search of diversion more to his taste, when Lady Streatham strolled by. He was fond of his cousin, so he had invited her to stand up with him. "How the devil did you get Streatham to accompany you to London?"

"Brute force," she confided ruefully. "And he possesses naturally fatherly instincts which have been roused both on Kitty's and on Frances' behalf."

"Frances!" his lordship echoed in astonishment.

"Yes." Lady Elizabeth explained: "She had a most dreadful time of it with that silly Lady Bingley. And who would not have been bored to distraction by that set? So she has come to think of herself as a misfit. Well not a misfit exactly, but certainly as someone who doesn't quite belong. It was only her great fondness for Kitty that brought her. I'm sure she would be happier by far in the country."

Suspecting what was coming, Lord Mainwaring glanced to where Lady Frances was expertly performing the quadrille with the Comte de Vaudron, and remarked that the lady in question did not seem to be having any difficulty that evening.

"But, Julian, you could do her such a world of good just by waltzing with her. You know how everyone will ape your every move—though why they should is more than I can understand." He grinned appreciatively. "And if it is seen you consider her a partner worthy of your notice, she will truly take."

"Oh, very well, Lizzie," he responded, no proof against the pleading in her eyes. "But I see Sally Jersey waving to me, and you know that one ignores 'Silence' at one's peril." He strolled off in response to a coyly beckoning finger.

"My dear Julian, how perfectly delightful to see you in England again, but whatever are you doing here, my friend? This is hardly your usual fare."

"True, alas, Sally," he agreed.

"Come." She laid a jeweled hand on his shoulder. "Dance with me and relieve this insufferable tedium."

"Bored, are you, Sally?" He manuevered her expertly around a panting red-faced gentleman and his equally red-faced partner.

She smiled mischievously at him. "Not anymore, Julian, not anymore." The mischief disappeared and the sparkle in her eyes became more pronounced as she asked, "What of Vanessa Welford? Are you still dancing attendance on her?" Her partner's dark eyebrows snapped together but she continued throatily, a wealth of meaning in her voice, "You can do much better than that, Julian, you know."

"Ah, but, Sally, do I want to?" The words were spoken softly, but there was no mistaking the tone. Completely silenced, she allowed him to return her to her friends, where she once again became the center of a laughing group.

Julian had no wish to become one of Sally Jersey's *gallants*, and highly resented her calm assumption of her absolute power over all men. The idea of dancing with someone who did not like the world where Lady Jersey and her sort were queened was becoming more attractive to him by the minute as he sauntered toward the spot where Frances and Bertie were chatting gaily. "Hallo, Bertie, do you mind if I deprive you of your companion?"

"Not in the slightest, old fellow," Bertie responded punctiliously, but the quizzing look in his eye was not lost on Julian. Mainwaring turned to his companion. "Lady Frances, may I make amends for my earlier conduct this evening by asking you to stand up for a waltz with me?" he invited. She raised her eyebrows at his calm assumption that a waltz with him was such a handsome means of rectifying his earlier attitude toward her, but she thanked him prettily enough and allowed him to lead her to the floor.

He was an excellent dancer, moving with the agility of a natural athlete. The strength in the arm circling her waist, the masterful guiding of her steps, made this an entirely different experience from her friendly *tête-à-tête* with Bertie. She found it slightly disturbing, but told herself that it was doing her no end of good socially. Another glide and she admitted to herself that it was not only good for her reputation to waltz with Lord Mainwaring but also a delightful sensation. After several minutes of silence the marquess decided he had seen all of the top of Lady Frances' golden head he wanted to see. He had been slightly piqued at her unenthusiastic acceptance of an invitation that would have cast any other woman in the room into transports. "Am I forgiven for annoying you?" he asked, looking quizzically down at her.

Frances, who had been completely absorbed in the music and

the motion, came to with a slight start. "Oh, certainly, sir. But naturally you could not expect anything but an argument when you disagreed with a 'bluestocking.' " This was spoken blandly enough, but there was a wicked twinkle in her eyes.

Looking at her more intently after what appeared to be a deliberately provocative remark, the marquess realized with a slight shock that she was laughing at him! No, he decided, she was laughing at both of them, and inviting him to laugh with her. This was a rather novel sensation for Lord Mainwaring. Ladies young and old, proper and improper, had smiled at him, simpered at him, looked at him with soulful intensity, but none of them had ever regarded him purely with amusement. He found it irresistible and smiled his own very attractive smile in return.

At least Frances thought it was attractive. It brought warmth to the dark blue eyes which were apt to look hard. The whiteness of his teeth gleamed in a face tanned by years in the tropics.

Rising to her bait, he could not resist teasing her in turn. "I had not thought that someone of your serious tastes would frequent such frivolous scenes as this."

Frances, accustomed to the constant teasing of Cassie and Freddie, was not in the least disconcerted. "Judging from the surprised and delighted look on the faces of our hostess and several other ladies, I assume you don't frequent them much yourself."

An appreciative gleam shone in Julian's eyes. "Touché, Lady Frances." The marquess's enjoyment of this bantering was not lost on the assembled company, and his partner was subjected to careful scrutiny, some of it jealous, some of it intrigued, depending on the sex of the particular observer.

Intrigued himself, Julian continued, "And how do you like London? I gather it has been some time since you have been here."

Ignoring the last part of the question, she replied rather archly, "I keep myself tolerably amused, for there are diversions to be found here that appeal to even the most serious of minds, sir. Why, just tomorrow I have planned an extremely edifying tour of the Tower and an evening at Astley's Amphitheater."

"Astley'sAmphitheater!" He was astounded.

"Cassie and Fredcrick," she confided. "I'm afraid I've been accompanying Kitty about so much that except for giving them lessons, I have neglected them sadly."

"Lessons? You don't mean *you* teach them," he demanded incredulously.

"And why ever not? I know far more Greek, Latin, and history than the local curate, and I am a *much* more amusing teacher," she added defiantly.

His smile flashed again. "No, don't get on your high ropes again, my girl. I merely meant that a London Season is considered more than sufficient occupation for any young girl, much less handling an estate, much less instructing two energetic youngsters."

"I'm not just *any* girl, Lord Mainwaring." A corner of her mouth quivered in a half-smile as she added, "Nor am I young."

"Now, that's doing it much too brown, my child. I'm more awake on all suits you know, and you look like a green girl to me."

She retorted, "Well, I'm not. I've been attending to the management of the estate since a few years after Mama died so Papa could continue with his work."

Lord Mainwaring looked down at the girl—for she really was little more than a girl—dancing with him and began to wonder just how many other surprising talents she had. Considering the weight of the responsibilities she bore, he thought that her whimsically uttered words were far truer than she appeared to think them. She certainly was not "just any girl," but what that did make her, he wasn't quite sure. She appeared to possess the intellectual confidence of a much older, more worldly woman, but if Lady Streatham was to be believed, her apprehension of the challenges of the Season and life in the *ton* was that of any unfledged young woman. That being true, he supposed he owed her the sanction of his social support. He could not say exactly why he felt the urge to assist Lady Frances, except that as someone who had complicated affairs of his own to deal with, he sympathized and felt compelled to help smooth over as many difficulties as he could.

Neither Lord Mainwaring nor Lady Frances had been looking forward to Lady Richardson's ball, but as they rolled home in their separate carriages, each one was occupied by more pleasant thoughts of the evening than either one had anticipated.

10

It would be too much to say that Frances was besieged by
admirers after her appearance at the ball, but she did have
several callers. The first was the Comte de Vaudron, whose
exquisite manners were put to a severe test the minute Higgins
ushered him into the drawing room. Here he encountered Aunt
Harriet, whose stiff "How de do" and basilisk stare were hardly
encouraging. Fortunately his quick eye and Gallic genius for
conversation connected the collection of orchids blooming in
the window with this dry, spare little woman, and through a
combination of adroit questioning and some happy
reminiscences on the horticultural wonders of Greece, the
Mediterranean, and his French possessions in the Caribbean,
he soon had her happily discussing the various soils of these
locales and the exacting climatic requirements of her own
blooms.

It was thus that Lady Frances, descending from a morning
session of lessons in the nursery, was astonished to discover
the two of them together in the window bending over one of
Aunt Harriet's particular favorites. So intent were they in their
discussion that they did not hear her enter, and were both quite
startled to find her regarding them amusedly when they turned
around to resume their seats.

"Ah, *chérie*, the belle of the ball," began the *comte*, bowing over her hand.

"Don't be absurd," Frances reproved, but she looked pleased all the same.

Aunt Harriet's attention was fairly caught. "Frances, the belle of a ball?" She gave her niece a sharp look.

"No, Aunt Harriet, though I did have a better time than I expected."

"*Mais non*, Fanny, how can you say that you were not a belle when outside of Kitty, Lady Streatham, and Lady Jersey, you were the only one with whom Lord Mainwaring danced the entire evening? He enjoyed himself too."

"Oh, Monsieur le Comte," interrupted Frances.

He held up a graceful hand. " 'Uncle Maurice,' please, but Fannie, *ma chère*, you may not pay attention to what the *ton* thinks or says, but me, I know that it is no small triumph to partner Lord Julian Mainwaring and to amuse him while doing so."

She sighed. "You may be correct, but that doesn't concern me. What does concern me is that I have spent so much of my time attending to dress and balls and my own affairs that I have neglected Cassie and Frederick dreadfully. So I have promised to take them on a surfeit of excursions this week. We're on our way to the Tower directly, I'm afraid. Would you care to join us, Uncle Maurice?" Frances invited him.

"*Mais, certainement*," he accepted, rising to greet the twins as they burst into the room.

"Cassie! Freddie!" Frances brought the two of them to a screeching halt. "This is Uncle Maurice, a dear friend of Mother and Father's. He has agreed to accompany us to the Tower."

The twins did not appear to be entirely gratified by this change in plans, but the *comte* speedily dispelled their doubts. "*Mes enfants*, please tell me if you do not wish me to join your outing, but I hope you will let me come because I do confess a wish to see the room where those two poor princes were so foully murdered." This very natural interest convinced them that Uncle Maurice was a "right one," and they enthusiastically added their invitations to their sister's. There was a brief scurrying for bonnets and coats while the carriage was brought round to the door.

As they rolled along toward the Tower, with Wellington in his usual position on the box, Freddie turned to the *comte*. "Uncle Maurice, sir?"

"*Mais oui, mon ami.*"

"You *are* French, are you not?"

"*Assurément.*"

"And you are a count, aren't you?"

"That, *mon ami*, depends on who is ruling France. Soemtimes I am Monsieur le Comte and sometimes plain *citoyen*, but I find 'Uncle' a far more honorable and amusing title than all of these."

"But what I mean, sir is: did you see anyone guillotined, or did you barely escape with your life?" Freddie asked in a hopeful tone.

The comte shook his head apologetically. "*Non*, Freddie, I regret to inform you that I was in Greece with your mother and father when the Bastille fell, and I have been traveling or in Great Britain the rest of the time, so I missed everything, even the Terror. I am afraid to say that my life has been extremely dull."

Fortunately for the comte's reputation, Lady Frances interrupted. "That's not at all true. Tell them about the time when you were captured by Greek bandits."

The twins' eyes widened expectantly. "Oh, please tell us, do," they breathed.

"Let us save that for another day. Here we are at the Tower, and one can't have too much blood and adventure in one day, you know—bad for the digestion." The twins looked doubtful; both were possessed of stomachs that would have done a goat proud, and both had an insatiable appetite for exactly such stories of gore and daring, but it wouldn't do to press their new friend too much.

The myriad of attractions to be explored at the historic spot put an end to all further discussion. Cassie and Frederick gazed at the yeoman warders in their Tudor uniforms, listened to the croaking of the sinister ravens on the green, and pictured all those who had laid their heads on the block there: Anne Boleyn,

Sir Thomas More, Sir Walter Raleigh, Lady Jane Grey. They followed an ancient woman who unlocked the vaults containing the crown jewels. Cassie was particularly captivated by the great golden orb reputed to contain, according to her elder sister, a piece of the true cross. Freddie, on the other hand, scoffed at the pile of useless jewels, preferring the golden spurs worn at coronations. They emerged from the gloom to peep at the lions in the Tower menagerie, but gave them scant attention in their haste to see the highlight of the visit—the room where the two little princes had been imprisoned before their mysterious and unfortunate end. They listened in fascinated horror as Frances recounted the tragic tale with all its grisly overtones. She was an excellent storyteller and her small listeners were spellbound. Even the *comte* was captivated. It would have been difficult to improve on the delights of the day, but when the *comte* treated them all to ices at Gunter's, their cups were filled to the brim. "I say, Fanny, London *is* a great place. Why've we never been here before?" Cassie asked. Freddie, his mouth too full of ice to say anything, nodded his head in fervent agreement.

The only member of the party not entirely satisfied with the day was Wellington. His winning expression and engaging manner, which never failed to win him friends and admirers wherever he went, had not done the least bit of good with the grim-faced yeoman at the Tower. "The Tower bain't be no place for dogs. Hit's han 'istoric monooment and that bain't no place for dogs," he stated stubbornly. Wag his tail and smile though he would, Wellington could not get him to abandon this un-reasonable position, so he waited rather glumly with John Coachman on his box, regretting that he would not be able to brag to Nelson about seeing such a bloody spot. Fortunately John was a friend, and his companionship lessened the indignity and boredom of it all to some extent.

They arrived back at Brook Street to discover that Bertie had called but had promised to return. He was ushered in not much later, to find Aunt Harriet tending her orchids and Frances writing instructions to be delivered by John to the housekeeper back at Cresswell. Bidding him a barely civil "Good-Day," Aunt Harriet made a swift exit, leaving him to gaze after her in a slightly bemused manner. "Lucky thing you ain't countin' on her to introduce you to the *ton*," he observed.

"You are right, of course, but she never meddles, you know. And if I need to display the respectable nature of our establishment, she is always available to stare down the impertinent."

Bertie was in total agreement there. He had come to say that thinking she might like to hear Catalani sing, he had procured a box and wondered if she would join him, Lady Streatham, and Kitty the next evening at the opera. Guessing that he had no real love for this type of amusement, she was touched by his generosity. "Bertie, it is too kind of you! I am assured you can't like to hear one of those 'dashed females screeching in Italian.' " Bertie looked slightly conscious at this perspicacious observation, but remained silent. She continued, "I hope that you may be well-rewarded for your magnanimity and that the prettiest opera dancers will be onstage later in the evening."

"Fanny!" He was scandalized. "You *mustn't* say such things!"

"I know, Bertie, but you're like a brother to me."

He replied with some heat, "But dash it, Fan, a gently bred female ain't even supposed to *know* such things." He continued, fixing her with a minatory stare, "And if she does, she certainly ain't supposed to let on—not to *anyone*!"

"I suppose you are right, Bertie," she sighed. "But it would make so much more sense if gently bred ladies paid more attention to these opera dancers. If they did, their husbands wouldn't need the dancers in the first place."

This piece of logic completely overset her companion. "I am not at all sure I dare escort you tomorrow," he sputtered.

"No, Bertie," she said soothingly, "I was just thinking aloud, and I promise not to do it again. I shall behave with the most rigid propriety, truly I shall."

"Well, don't think aloud. Better yet, don't think at all," he cautioned.

She laughed and held out her hand. "What a good friend you are. And I thank you kindly for arranging such a treat for us all."

Frances enjoyed Catalani's singing immensely the next

evening, though privately she wished the prima donna had demonstrated a little less histrionic and a little more dramatic talent. Catalani shared her attraction as a curiosity, at least for Kitty and Lady Frances, with someone else. Kitty had been begging Bertie to point out all the notables, a task for which he was admirably suited. He was happy to oblige, but seemed deliberately to ignore one astoundingly beautiful dark-haired woman in the box opposite. She was ablaze with diamonds and scantily attired in a dress of vivid green satin which clung to every curve of her voluptuous figure. This she displayed to the delight of several gentlemen crowded around as she reclined seductively in her chair. "But, Bertie, who is that?" Kitty demanded, nodding behind her fan in the woman's direction.

"Don't look!" Bertie almost upset his own chair in his frantic attempt to distract her. Kitty was taken aback at such a reaction from the ordinarily phlegmatic Bertie. "Take no notice of her, Kitty. That's Lady Vanessa Welford."

She was puzzled. "But if she's a lady, why shouldn't I notice her?"

Bertie ran his fingers rather desperately under his elegantly tied cravat, which suddenly seemed to be strangling him. "Well, she's a lady, but not much of a *lady*, if you see what I mean," he hazarded hopefully.

The familiar sound of the name which had been nagging her memory suddenly jogged it back to tea at the dowager Marchioness of Mainwaring's. "Oh," she exclaimed as she leaned forward to get a better view. "That's Uncle Julian's mistress."

Bertie was now certain that his valet had, in a fit of murderous rage at the number of cravats ruined that evening, tied this one too tightly on purpose to strangle him. It definitely seemed as though he had to gasp for breath, but at last he did manage to force out a good "Ssh!"

Though Kitty's remark had seemed to thunder in his ears, it had in fact gone no further than Lady Frances', but she was eager to discover just what type of woman did attract a man reputed to have such exacting standards for feminine attractiveness. Undoubtedly Lady Welford was magnificent. Her raven hair contrasted with seductive ivory shoulders and a tempting red mouth, but Frances took exception to her self-satisfied expression and guessed that she would not improve upon acquaintance, at least not acquaintance with another female. She told herself that it was far better to be appreciated for oneself and the less-tangible personal attractions of intelligence and character than to be admired for purely physical attributes. She had certainly educated herself on this premise, paying more attention to developing her mind and her values rather than a sense for fashion or the other feminine arts of attraction and dalliance. However, for one brief moment as she observed the magnetic woman across from her, so secure in her beauty, so confident of her power to win love and admiration, she questioned the wisdom of her choice. No matter that she told herself that a few years would prove her attractions to be the more durable ones. For once she would have preferred to have men love her beauty to distraction and women envy it to the same degree than to be respected for good sense. But such treacherous thoughts were gone in an instant as she again gave herself over to the pleasure of Catalani's rich voice and the fineness of the music.

11

B ertie Montgomery was not the only one who took it upon himself to introduce Lady Frances to some of London's fashionable haunts. In keeping with his impulsively formed resolve to smooth her social path, Lord Mainwaring decided that a drive with him in Hyde Park would be just the thing to set her feet firmly on this path. His lordship was a man of decision. Having settled upon a course of action, he executed it immediately, and the next day saw him knocking on the Cresswell's door while his magnificent grays stamped impatiently. Higgins ushered him in at a slightly inauspicious moment as Aunt Harriet, in a black humor at the inexplicable dropping of blossoms from a particular favorite, came bustling out of the drawing room without the least looking where she was going and collided solidly with him. "Oh, *do* get out of the way, you beast." It was a minute before Mainwaring, somewhat taken aback by this abrupt address, realized that as the collision and remark were simultaneous, she could not be referring to him. He looked down to see the culprit—Nelson—brushing affectionately against her skirts. "Oh!" Aunt Harriet recovered herself and directed a quelling stare at his lordship.

"And who are you, sirrah, to come barging in like a great looby?"

Mainwaring took her measure instantly and replied meekly, "Mainwaring, at your service, ma'am. I do apologize. I had not realized you were quitting the room. I shall be more careful in the future." Though he had introduced himself, Mainwaring had not the slightest idea of the identity of the tartar whose gaze had lost some of its ferocity at this graceful speech.

He was rescued by Lady Frances, who appeared just then in the doorway. Seeing her aunt and guest eyeing each other warily, she hastened to introduce them, mentioning to Aunt Harriet as she did so the great number of out-of-the-way places Lord Mainwaring had visited. Her aunt, never one to miss an opportunity to learn about or procure more specimens to add to her collection, looked speculatively at him, but before she could ask any useful questions, Lady Frances forestalled her. "How nice to see you, Lord Mainwaring. I hope I haven't kept you. Higgins tells me you came in your curricle. I hope your horses have not been kept waiting too long."

"No, ma'am, thank you. I drove here hoping I could convince you to come for a drive in the park."

Lady Frances may not have agreed with the *ton*'s unquestioning adulation of Lord Mainwaring, but she recognized an honor when it was offered, and was gratified. Regretfully she answered, "It is too kind in you and I would love it of all things, but I promised Cassie, Freddie, and Ned that I would take them to see Lord Elgin's marbles. It is the most unfortunate thing, and I do truly appreciate your offer."

"Don't refine upon it too much. Perhaps you will like to another day." Mainwaring's words were gracious enough, but there was a hard light in his eyes and he looked to be a little put out. In point of fact, he was. People of any sort, especially young females, rarely received his invitations with anything but excessive gratitude. The fact that he usually scorned such gratitude did nothing to lessen his pique at Frances for refusing him, and refusing him in favor of a parcel of brats at that!

Correctly interpreting these signs, Lady Frances experienced a tingle of satisfaction at having pierced his arrogance. She swiftly banished this ignoble thought, asking instead, "Would you like to go with us?"

Cassie and Frederick, who had now appeared and had seen from the expedition to the Tower that grown-ups could enhance an expedition, chimed in, "Oh, please do come along, sir."

Julian couldn't remember when his mere presence, regardless of social position or fortune, had been of material importance to anyone. He was oddly touched by the genuine invitation he could read in three pairs of eyes. Before he knew what he was about, he was not only accepting a place in a schoolroom outing but also offering Freddie a ride next to him in his curricle, with a promise of the return trip to Cassie. His second surprise came when he realized that, in a reversal of the usual way of things, he was highly gratified at the approval he saw in Lady Frances' eyes. It was certainly all very odd.

During the ride to Lord Elgin's mansion in Park Lane, he had ample opportunity to become acquainted with the loquacious Freddie. The conversation centered chiefly around the various points and capabilities of the "prime bits of blood" drawing the carriage, but in the course of the discussion Mainwaring learned a great deal about the Cresswell household. Freddie artlessly confided that Lady Frances, though an excellent horsewoman, usually left the selection of her horseflesh to her groom, which Freddie thought was a great deal too bad. "I know she has a superior eye for a horse, and I've asked her times out of mind why she doesn't choose her own. After all, I could help her. But she says that horse fairs and Tattersall's are no place for a lady. Can you believe such sad stuff? Fanny doesn't say that running Cresswell or teaching in the schoolroom is no place for a lady, so I don't understand such a paltry attitude in this case."

By describing some of the ugly customers who turned up at the fairs, and the purely masculine nature of the clientele at Tattersall's, the marquess was able to restore Lady Frances' credibility with her younger brother. "After all, Freddie, choosing a good horse is a tricky business. In addition to being able to recognize a thoroughbred from ear to hoof, it requires a good deal of discussion about the price. There is not much time for social niceties and polite conversation in this sort of business, so it is best that men who are less likely to be offended by plain dealing take care of the entire business. Don't you agree?''

Freddie listened intently to this description of the male world. The idea of purely masculine society appealed mightily to him. Cassie and Fanny were great guns. They never fussed if one tore one's clothes or got them dirty. In fact, Cassie was as likely to do this as Freddie. But they couldn't share all his interests the way brothers would, he confided. This rather wistful comment brought back a fleeting memory of the marquess' own childhood and the scrapes and adventures he had shared with his brother. He felt the wish to see that Freddie was given an opportunity to enjoy male companionship. The thought developed no further than that because they had arrived at the building Lord Elgin had built next to his residence to house the marbles he had brought back from Greece.

The twins had not been at all sure they would find these ''old statues and stuff,'' as Freddie scoffingly referred to them, nearly so interesting as the Tower, but they knew that their sister had been there with their parents when Lord Elgin first began to send them home, and that she was longing to see them. So they had gone with as good grace as possible in two eleven-year-olds dragged along to look at antiquities, and were agreeably surprised. Once again Frances' talent for narration held them enthralled as she identified various figures on the friezes and described the battles and contests among the various gods and goddesses, who turned out to be no less bloodthirsty and conniving than the monarchs who had given such an infamous history to the Tower. Freddie was extremely taken with the war horses that charged with such strength and fury, while Cassie marveled that the delicately streaming draperies were carved out of marble and not the gauze they resembled. Even though she had been quite young, Frances was able to remember and describe the magnificent temples that Pericles had had built on the ruins of Persian buildings high on the Acropolis. She told of the magnificent columned porch of the Parthenon and explained where various pieces they were now observing would have been. Her pictures of life in Periclean Athens were so vivid and the recreation of the mythology so gripping that even

Mainwaring, hearing snatches of her monologue from the other end of the room, moved slowly toward the little group to catch more. He was naturally familiar with most of what she was saying, but he was caught by the colorful language and animated delivery and found himself thinking rather wryly that it was a pity such histrionic talent would never appear onstage.

The door at one end of the room opened to admit none other than the Comte de Vaudron. He was welcomed joyfully by the twins. "I thought it would not be long before you paid them a visit," he remarked to Frances, including the entire collection with a graceful sweep of his hand. In answer to the questions with which Cassie and Frederick were besieging him, he continued, "One at a time, *mes enfants*. I am here because I originally helped Lord Elgin rescue these works of art, and now I am helping him to convince your government to buy them from him so that everyone will have a chance to admire them." He led them off to look at some of his particular favorites, telling them as he did so about the careful crating and shipping of these priceless pieces and the difficulties in transporting them from Greece to London. The details of this saga were almost as interesting as Frances' stories, and the twins listened eagerly.

Meanwhile, Mainwaring had joined Frances as she examined the flowing draperies that had so captivated Cassie. "I agree with you," he said, correctly interpreting her expression. "It is a pity the grace and simplicity of such artists should have been ignored for so long."

"Yes, and their beautiful sense of architectural proportion, and the lightness of their interiors as well," she added. Then, as she realized that he had voiced her own thoughts, she asked, "But however did you know what I was feeling?"

He replied with some amusement at her astonishment at what was merely a shrewd observation: "I could have guessed, knowing who your father was, that you would have shared this admiration for the culture. But having observed the elegance and simplicity of your own taste, I know it to be so."

"But how, after such a brief acquaintance, can you know what my tastes are?" she pursued.

His amusement deepened. "My dear child, the design of the

library at Cresswell, the Adam decorations in Brook Street, and the uncomplicated lines of your style of dress all show you to be an appreciator of classical simplicity. Besides, you are not a fussy person. Anyone who has spent the least amount of time with you would know that.''

She was surprised that a man reputed to pay so little attention to his fellowmen should be so perceptive, but remarked, ''I see you are determined to make me a bluestocking, sir, and would have me making an intellectual feat out of something as mundane as decorating my house and my person.''

He answered with unwonted seriousness, ''No, not in the slightest. It is the very consistency of it all that proves you are not a bluestocking. Bluestockings try to stun the world with their erudition, and they usually pay a good deal of attention to the current tastes of the *ton* when selecting an area in which to excel. You, on the other hand, have shaped your own tastes after your own reading and learning, else they wouldn't all contribute to what is more a style of living than an aesthetic preference.''

Frances was gratified and not a little touched by this sympathetic reading of her character. She remained thoughtfully silent for some time until the children and the count rejoined them. Remedying her earlier omission, she introduced Julian to the count, who recognized him with pleasure. ''Ah, Julian Mainwaring, I hear great things of you from my friend Charlton. I am delighted to know you, *monsieur*.'' Mainwaring, disclaiming any real political or diplomatic expertise, discovered that the *comte*'s was more than the conventional flattery. ''I agree with your opinions, my boy. The world may say that history is shaped by battles and the valor of its leaders, but I believe more and more it will become a question of economics. It is the businessman and not the generals who will shape history from now on. The countinghouses and the Exchange will be the true battlefields, and England will need men such as you, who are experienced in these things, to lead her.'' This approbation was not lost on Lady Frances, and she wondered if she had not been a little foolish in taking on such an opponent at the Streathams' dinner.

They bade good-bye to the *comte* and headed home, this time with Cassie sitting proudly next to the marquess. She was less voluble than her brother, but by no means less enterprising, and by the time they reached Brook Street, had managed—Mainwaring was still not sure exactly how—to extract an invitation to Astley's Amphitheater. She had barely been lifted down from her perch before she was sharing this delightful prospect with her brother and sister.

Lady Frances was well aware of her small sister's cozening ways and strongly suspected that the marquess, clever though he was, had been skillfully maneuvered into this position. She sent the children inside, then turned to him, extending her hand. "Thank you, sir, for joining us. It was very kind in you, but you mustn't let Cassie inveigle you into what would be very poor entertainment for you."

The marquess had just been wondering about this himself, but her words put him on his mettle. "By no means. It has been an age since I went. I enjoy good showmanship and beautiful horseflesh as much as anyone. I don't pretend to know a great deal about children, so I do hope you will accompany us. Actually, I suppose Cassie and Freddie would be happy to enlighten me if I didn't know how to go on, but I don't feel I have quite your talent for making an outing memorable."

She smiled ruefully. "All you have to do is invite them. It is I, their sister, who must resort to stratagems to keep them amused and in line." All the same, she found herself looking forward to the entertainment as much as Cassie and Freddie.

12

The marquess was as good as his word, but having considered the claims of Ned and Nigel, decided it would be extremely impolitic of him to exclude them merely because Cassie had had the originality and temerity to instigate this amusement. Until now, he had paid scant attention to Ned, who was as quiet and studious as Kitty was gay, and he felt a trifle guilty for having overlooked the lad. This seemed an excellent opportunity to become better acquainted. Nigel, he knew, was a lively, friendly boy who could be counted on to enjoy anything and anyone. Besides, Mainwaring did owe Lady Streatham a debt of gratitude for taking the burden of Kitty's Season off his hands. So it was quite a large party that was ensconced several evenings later in a box at Astley's Royal Amphitheater. The mere spectacle of the theater itself, with its huge chandelier illuminating the largest stage in London, was enough to take the children's breath away. Even the irrepressible Frederick could not find words sufficient to the occasion. He gazed in awed silence as Philip Astley, resplendent on his white charger, led the circus parade. The children's eyes grew rounder and rounder as wonder succeeded wonder. It seemed impossible to believe that a horse could dance a hornpipe. That he could

improve upon this exhibition by lifting a kettle from the fire
to make a pot of tea was beyond all belief. They held their
breaths as John Astley rode round and round the arena on two
horses before dancing on their backs. There were conjurers and
trapeze artists, but nothing could outshine the horses and the
magnificent equestrian feats of the Astleys themselves.

Glancing at Frances, Lord Mainwaring could see she was
enjoying it as much as the others. He found her unconscious
enthusiasm refreshing after the boredom so assiduously
cultivated by most Londoners. He still could not refrain from
inquiring, "Are you enjoying yourself?"

She turned to him, her face alight with pleasure, and
exclaimed, "Oh, ever so much! I came with Mother and Father
when we returned to England twelve years ago, and I have been
wanting so to come back ever since. But the twins were born
and Mother died the next year so I have not until now had the
chance. But it is just as wonderful as I remembered it!"

Mainwaring reflected that if her mother had died so soon after
and that if even a few of the anecdotes concerning Lord
Cresswell's legendary absentmindedness were true, she must
have had very little time in her life for amusements of any kind.
The thought of this, coupled with the very real pleasure he
derived from witnessing her simple enjoyment, made him
resolve to provide her with an amusing time in addition to
smoothing her path socially. It had been a long time since he
had been with people who were simply having a wonderful time,
unconscious of everyone else around and wholly involved with
what was happening onstage. Even Ned, ordinarily so quiet and
reserved, was exclaiming pointing as excitedly as everyone else.
The natural ebullience of Nigel and Freddie appeared to have
done the lad some good.

"I can't wait to get home to practice. I bet I could stand on
Prince's back like that . . . with a bit of practice, of course,"
Freddie boasted.

"With practice, of course," Nigel jeered. "You know you
couldn't do it the way Mr. Astley does, without holding the
reins."

"I'm sure I—" began Freddie.

Frances interrupted him. "Well, it isn't as easy as it looks, I can tell you. I had John Coachman balancing me on top of my pony for hours on end after I first came here, but to no avail. I did well enough when he let go, until the pony moved, and then I slid off his back as if it had been greased. I landed with a crash, tore my dress, covered myself with dirt, was stiff and disgraced for weeks." The children were highly diverted at the idea of the immaculate Lady Frances covered with dirt.

But Freddie was not to be put off. "Thank you for your advice, Fanny, but you *are* a girl, you know," he said with lofty superiority, "and girls aren't as expert with horseflesh as men are." The marquess recognized echoes, though improved upon by the speaker, of his own conversation with the boy, and smiled to himself. He had no doubt at all that such an opinion would find little favor with Frances.

He was entirely correct in his suspicions. "Freddie, you insufferable prig!" Both Cassie and Frances rounded on him. "You know that both of us ride as well as you do."

"And," Cassie continued triumphantly, "Fanny can drive horses and a phaeton and you've only tried the pony cart once around the park at Cresswell."

Freddie deemed it wise to withdraw from such an unequal contest and retired to the background with an air of injured dignity.

At this moment Frances became aware of their host, who was sitting back, arms crossed over his chest, regarding the scene with a great deal of amusement. "I do beg your pardon. I can't think how I came to be so ill-bred."

"I can," he replied, smiling. "Deliberate provocation." He turned to Freddie. "Next time, my boy, you should be more subtle in your attack and take on your opponents only one at a time."

Freddie grinned shamefacedly. "I'm sorry, sir, to act so childish." He threw a challenging look in his elder sister's direction.

"Not at all," replied his lordship. "It was a salutary lesson. I can see that I should have had sisters. With such treatment, a fellow could never come by a high enough opinion of himself to become 'arrogant.' '' He quizzed Frances wickedly as he made his last remark. Try as she would, she could not keep a becoming blush from suffusing her face. Whether this was a result of having her insulting reference to him thrown back in her face or her sudden realization that the marquess had a singularly attractive smile, Frances was not at all certain.

The schoolroom party labeled it a highly successful time, and the marquess was pleased to see that Nigel and Freddie were questioning Ned as to his collection of tin soldiers and that Frances looked relaxed and free of the slightly wary look she had worn at Lady Richardson's ball.

13

After spending so much time among the schoolroom set, Lord Mainwaring looked forward to a respite from such fatiguing company in the welcoming and flattering arms of Lady Vanessa Welford. She was far too clever to let her true feelings show, but she had been vexed by his absence. She knew that he had his niece to escort to Lady Richardson's ball, to which Lady Welford had not been invited. She schemed a great deal to maintain her air of respectability, and it was a source of constant irritation to her that some hostesses still refused to include her on their guest lists. Unfortunately, it was just those ladies who held the most influential positions in society. Though she had not been at the ball, Vanessa knew very well that Mainwaring had danced with his niece, Lady Sally Jersey, Lady Elizabeth Streatham, and Lady Frances Creswell. His niece and cousin were an obvious duty. Sally Jersey would equally obviously be unavoidable, and Lady Welford knew Mainwaring to be immune to that flirtatious lady's charms. But Lady Frances Cresswell was not so obvious. This roused her curiosity, and because she was attracted to Lord Mainwaring, her jealousy. It was not actually jealousy, but it was considerably stronger than mere curiosity. Had she been a less-fashionable creature, one whose existence extended beyond the ballroom, opera, theater, and Bond Street modistes, she might have been even more curious about his latest expeditions to Lord Elgin's or Astley's Amphitheater. It was fortunate for her peace of mind that she was not, that she did not move in such circles, or that she was not acquainted with anyone who did, or she might have been more alarmed than she was.

Lady Welford and Mainwaring were in his carriage en route to see Kean at Drury Lane when she began to question him subtly about the ball. She had heard it was a sad crush. Did Kitty enjoy herself? Was she a success? Had he even been able to dance with her amongst all the younger men aspiring to her hand? Had the rest of the company been very dull and respectable? They must have been if he had been forced to dance with Sally Jersey and some hitherto unknown young lady whose name escaped her.

"Lady Frances Cresswell, perhaps," he hazarded with a dangerous glint in his eye. Lord Mainwaring did not relish anyone taking a proprietary interest in his affairs.

"Yes, that was it." She nodded, the diamonds at her throat sparkling in the light of a passing streetlamp. "I have not ever heard her name. Who is she, Julian?"

His reply reassured her. "She is a neighbor of Kitty and Ned's who was kind enough to come to London during Kitty's first Season, as she knew Kitty to be a little apprehensive."

"Oh, she is quite a bit older, then?" Lady Welford's sources had implied that the lady in question was young, but someone who was this much a mistress of her affairs and who lent support to a young girl must be a spinster of some years.

Lord Mainwaring could have undeceived her, but he did not relish the tone of the conversation. "I had not thought to ask the lady her age," he answered blightingly.

"Oh, Julian, do not be angry," she pleaded, tracing the strong line of his jaw with a caressing finger. "I was only thinking of you. I know how you detest all those women who constantly throw out lures to you, whether they are the girls or their mamas."

The marquess was not so easily hoodwinked and he did not believe her for an instant, but in the interests of a peaceful evening he appeared mollified as he caught her hand and kissed it lingeringly. "Your solicitude overwhelms me, Vanessa, my dear," he murmured, gazing intently at her.

Vanessa, responding to the attraction of those dark blue eyes, failed to detect the undertone of sarcasm in his voice. She sighed contentedly and leaned back luxuriously against the squabs, revealing, as she did so, rounded white shoulders and a daring décolletage.

Kean was performing his much-celebrated *Richard III*, but Mainwaring, who considered him a shade on the melodramatic side, though admittedly an inspired actor, had come to the theater for other purposes than watching the famous man rave and roll his eyes. He was certain that he would encounter Lord Charlton there, and he felt that the delicacy of the business for which Charlton had approached him required the discretion of a seemingly chance encounter. His surmise was correct and he came upon Charlton in the gallery. They exchanged a few desultory remarks on Kean, the general public's opinion of his intensely original interpretation of Shakespeare, and their own slightly more critical views before Julian remarked casually, "Speaking of dramatic and theatrical natures, I saw Prinny the other day."

"Oh? And how is he? I haven't seen him this age." The other man's tone was equally casual, but there was a wealth of unspoken questions in his eyes.

"He's fine as fivepence. And he is slowly abandoning the idea of a purely Chinese theme for his Pavilion for an Indian motif, and wanted to consult me on decorations and architecture. You know the plan Repton submitted to him years ago was in the Indian style, but he hadn't the money at the time. Now he seems to think he has, and has urged Nash to make his alterations in that style. What a damned extravagance! But his pioneering use of cast-iron construction is something I would like to encourage, considering the plight that industry will be facing without the war and demand for artillery. We naturally turned from Indian art to India, to the world in general, and affairs in Europe in particular. He seems to be losing all his enthusiasm for Alexander as the world's enthusiasm for the Tzar grows. Poor Prinny, he doesn't like others to be more popular than he—as though that would be difficult. At any rate, as well as being a notable diplomat—or meddler, however you see it— Alexander is much more slender and fair than Prinny. He is also an absolute monarch and Prinny is inclined to be jealous of all that power. He seemed to welcome the chance to throw a dash of cold water on the flames of Alexander's enthusiasm for his much-vaunted Holy Alliance.''

Lord Charlton voiced his approval. "Very good, my boy, and I do thank you. I know it must have been a crashing bore to listen to those never-ending plans of his.''

"No trouble at all, George. Besides, one must give him credit, you know. Prinny is really quite an amusing and artistic fellow. It's a great deal too bad he happens to be a prince as well.''

Having concluded this satisfactory interchange, they proceeded to their respective boxes. It was with some difficulty that the marquess entered his, owing to the number of admirers crowded around Vanessa. Lady Welford might have lost her heart to her latest flirt, but she had certainly not lost her craving for masculine attention. She laughed and flirted, flashing her magnificent dark eyes, which seemed to promise anything and everything to whomever her glance lighted on. Her more rational self also dictated that it would be a politic thing to encourage other *cicisbeos,* despite her interest in the marquess. Seeing her constantly surrounded by males would make him proud to have won a prize so desirable to others, and it would keep him from becoming sure of her affections. When that happened, men were all too often known to ignore their mistresses as thoroughly as they ignored their wives. It would do Mainwaring good to be forced to compete with other men for her attention. And last, if by some incredible chance he did leave her, she didn't want to be caught without anyone to pay her court. It thus behooved her to cultivate as many admirers as possible. Hearing the door to the box open, she turned to see Mainwaring. Extending a swanlike white arm to him, she cooed invitingly, ''Do come back and sit down, my lord.'' She pulled a chair for him close to her, creating a sense of intimacy, as though they were the only occupants of the theater. She looked so lovely with diamonds sparkling at her smooth white neck and in her dark hair, her brows arched delicately over eyes alight with the flattery she'd been receiving, and a faint flush suffusing her beautifully sculptured neck and arms. Julian wondered at himself that he remained so unmoved by all this beauty, that he could mentally note and catalog all these features without feeling the least desire for her. He supposed he had been thinking too much about his conversation with Lord Charlton and all its political ramifications. He dismissed his lack of feeling as only natural in someone who had switched in an instant from playing a vital role in world politics to being reduced to flirting in a box at a play. He watched the rest of the act in thoughtful silence while his charming companion continued to laugh and chat with her eager swains.

As he escorted her in his carriage back to Mount Street, the marquess reflected rather cynically on the flatness of the evening. With the exception of the encounter with Charlton, it had been like so many other evenings: dressing to be seen and admired; selecting a place to be seen and admired; and then being seen and admired, as though there were nothing more to life. Unconsciously he compared this evening to the one at Astley's and the pleasure every person in the party derived from the skill and daring of the performers. Everyone had been in high spirits that owed nothing to a selfish craving for attention, but to a zest for living and enjoying each other. That last thought caught him up short. I'm not only becoming cynical but also entering my dotage, he admonished himself.

Vanessa had ordered an intimate supper in her boudoir. Certainly she had done everything to create a romantic atmosphere: peach satin draperies and upholstery coupled with the warm glow of a few strategically placed candles enhanced the warmth of her skin, lent her dark eyes an air of mystery, and hid any possible wrinkles. The food was exquisite, the wine a perfect complement to the dinner and the evening. Her conversation, consisting chiefly of the latest *on-dits*, was both amusing and provocative. But somehow, the very skillfulness of her creation robbed it of all romance for Mainwaring. The perfect setting was more a credit to her skill as a woman of the world than to her heart and its supposed passion for him. Or, if passion did exist, he reflected cynically, it was more for the money and position he represented than for his personal or mental attractions. The evening was anesthetic to his senses. He did not even bother to protest when she draped her soft arms enticingly around his neck, though he did not feel in the mood for lovemaking. I think too much, he told himself. Deliberately emptying his mind of all possible thought or observation, he gave himself up to her skillful seduction.

Sometime later he slipped out of her house and into the fresh night air. He was glad he had sent his carriage home as he sauntered along savoring the coolness of the breeze that ruffled the leaves on the trees in Berkeley Square and cleared his head. The entire evening had all been so predictable, so . . . so very . . . "flat"—that was the word. Even the passion had been practiced rather than experienced. How can I feel so thoroughly jaded at thirty-five? he wondered. It must be time for a change of scene, a change of climate. As soon as Kitty has had her Season and I have found a man to look after Camberly properly, I shall get away. It's been some time since anyone has visited the plantations in Jamaica. I ought to take a look at them for myself. Somewhat cheered by this, he entered Mainwaring House, where Kilson was waiting for him. The sight of that old ally's battered face with its reminders of the adventures they had shared further improved his temper, and he was able to fall into a deep sleep untroubled by additional disquieting reflections.

14

In contrast to the marquess, Lady Frances was finding London progressively exciting. Lady Streatham had most graciously taken her around with Kitty and introduced her to a variety of fashionable and intellectual delights she had not before encountered in the capital. If someone had told her before she left the country that she would spend an entire morning shopping in Harding, Howell, and Company's Grand Fashionable Magazine, she would have laughed at the absurdity of it. Yet she heartily enjoyed wandering from one department to another admiring the taste of the fittings and the glass partitions that separated them. When it came time to go, she was astonished at how quickly the time had passed while she strolled around looking at everything from furs, fans, silks, and laces to jewelry, clocks, perfumes, and toiletries. Always slightly inclined to scorn fashion and the hours people spent at modistes' and milliners', she was surprised to discover the artistic satisfaction to be found looking at beautiful silks and damasks, exquisite laces and gaily colored ribbons, not to mention the challenge in envisioning how to display them to their best advantage. She realized that to many, the pursuit of fashion was a form of aesthetic pleasure which, in addition to exercising their artistic and creative sensibilities, brought the additional reward of being regarded with envy and admiration by those around them. She purchased a handsome shawl of Norwich silk and some ribbons to brighten up a bonnet that had somehow always lacked the style she liked. Kitty found a beautiful corsage of silk flowers to add some color to the delicate pastel hues of the requisite attire of a young unmarried woman this Season. Lady Elizabeth discovered some magnificent beading at an excellent price, so all three ladies voted the excursion exceedingly satisfactory.

Lady Frances' more formal artistic tastes were stimulated and gratified when she was invited to join Lady Elizabeth on an excursion to the Royal Academy's exhibition at Somerset House. "I simply must go so that I shall be able to tell people that I have seen it," Lady Elizabeth declared. "Besides, Lawrence's portrait of my dear friend Georgiana Beaumont is being shown, along with his portrait of the Prince Regent, so you see it is imperative that I at least take a peep. Critics insist that Lawrence's portrait of Prinny is 'the finest portrait of the heir apparent that has yet been painted,' but I am not the least interested in paintings and have no artistic tastes whatsoever to help me understand or criticize them. Music, I enjoy and understand, but painting, especially portraiture, does not speak to me. Mainwaring says that you have an excellent eye, and Bertie praises your aesthetic sense excessively, so I do hope you'll come with me and tell me what to think or say, should someone ask me."

Frances could not help feeling gratified at both the wording and the invitation, though she suspected Lady Elizabeth of improving on Mainwaring's and Bertie's admiration of her aesthetic sensibilities. Still, it was very flattering to have them remarked on at all. "I shall do my best, ma'am," she replied. "But don't depend too much on me to articulate what is thought to be the most fashionable opinion. I do not in general admire Lawrence, and certainly do not agree with so many nowadays who consider him the equal of Gainsborough and Reynolds. Lawrence encourages social pretensions, painting the flashy exteriors of his patrons—the way they wish to be seen—instead of trying to reveal the personality underneath. Still, with those two great portraitists gone, he is the best of those that remain. I confess I am more interested in Turner."

"Turner!" exclaimed Lady Streatham. Though she knew little about this unusual artist, she was nevertheless surprised that he should appeal to Lady Frances Cresswell. "I shouldn't think you would care for his work in the slightest. I remember seeing *Snowstorm* at the exhibition some years ago. It was all sky and violence, far too emotional for someone of your quiet elegance, I should think."

Lady Frances was oddly upset by this remark. Did she appear so cool and unfeeling, then? She knew her natural reserve was interpreted at best as dignity and at worst as shyness. But perhaps it was also interpreted as indifference. Could it be true that Mainwaring's description of her as a prude—a remark she had interpreted as one made solely to provoke her—was in fact the articulation of general opinion?

Lady Elizabeth, noticing an unwontedly thoughtful expression creep into Frances' eyes, wondered what in her remark could have prompted such serious reflection. She promptly strove to banish this during the drive to Somerset House by chatting gaily of Freddie's and Nigel's latest antics. "I hear from Nigel that Mainwaring took the schoolroom party to Astley's. How did you ever accomplish that? If he even notices the existence of children, which is highly unusual, he ordinarily doesn't pay the least attention to them."

The serious look vanished instantly, and Lady Frances laughed. "It was not my doing. Cassie was riding in his curricle on the return from seeing Lord Elgin's marbles, and I believe she merely asked him. Lord Mainwaring never had the slightest chance. Once Cassie has set her mind to a thing, she will brook no refusal."

It was Lady Elizabeth's turn to look thoughtful. If she had been surprised to hear of the marquess's party at Astley's, she was astounded to learn of his expedition to view the marbles. He must be interested in Frances in some way to allow himself to be saddled with such lively children twice in one week. She had pushed him to waltz with Frances simply to ensure her acceptance in the *ton* and subsequent enjoyment of the Season.

Now she wondered if she might not have unwittingly done more than that. Julian rarely put himself out except for a few select relatives and friends. For those few, he would do anything in his power, or beyond it, to secure their happiness, but he had a hearty dislike of obligations to anyone else, and was brutal in squelching expectations before they arose. She immediately resolved to visit the dowager with this piece of information, and perhaps the two of them could puzzle it out. That lady had a way of selecting the most reliable gossipmongers and expertly separating mere conjecture from fact so that she unerringly arrived at the truth of the matter. Lady Elizabeth very much wanted to test out her speculations on that reliable sounding board.

Somerset House was a sad crush, so they had very little opportunity to study anything at great length. The portrait of Georgiana was seen and admired, though Frances thought privately that it could have been any face atop the magnificent gown and jewels, so little did the painting reveal of the sitter's character. However, she kept this particular opinion to herself. She did not hesitate to voice her annoyance that most of the paintings with true artistic merit had been "skied" high above the portraits that would capture the attention and commissions of the fashionable viewers, so that it was only with great difficulty that one could see them. "The way to recognize a person with true aesthetic sense," she confided to Lady Elizabeth as they left, "is to identify those with severe eyestrain and a crick in their necks." Still, she had enjoyed herself very much and was glad to have a sensible companion to view them with her.

Such had been her entertainment in London that Lady Frances began to feel quite guilty for having ignored her responsibilities. It seemed an age since she had given any serious thought to the affairs at Cresswell, and she had not even executed the business for which ostensibly she had come to London in the first place. She kept meaning to send a note around to Mr. Murray, once her father's publisher and now hers, but somehow each succeeding day brought with it a new amusement of some kind. One day she and Lady Streatham had taken the children to a balloon ascension at Vauxhall Gardens. Then, remembering her promise to Aunt Harriet, she arranged for a picnic party, consisting of the same group, at Kew Gardens, as well as another trip to the hothouses of the Botanic Society. These excursions were followed by a trip to Sadler's Wells, where the famous Grimaldi amazed them with his acrobatic feats, the absurd expressions on his mobile face, and his skill in juggling a seemingly incredible number of objects. Last, there was a visit to the British Museum to see two helmets. One had been dug up from the ground where the Battle of Cannae had been fought in 216 B.C. The other was completely covered with feathers and had been brought back from the South Seas by Captain Cook. Cassie was interested in these curiosities, but her twin was entranced. Freddie could talk of nothing else for days, and immediately discarded the prospect of a promising career at Astley's in favor of exploring the world with Cook. Even Cassie's "He's been dead these past thirty-six years, you gudgeon!" could not dampen his enthusiasm, and he resolved to consult Lord Mainwaring on a captain who could be considered a suitable successor to the immortal Cook.

In addition to these various expeditions, Frances spent a great deal of time conferring with Kitty and Lady Streatham about the ball to be given for Kitty at Mainwaring House. In reality, there was little conferring to be done. Lady Frances simply provided an appreciative audience as Kitty, alive with enthusiasm, rapturously described the masses of flowers ordered to transform the ballroom into a fairy garden; debated the rival merits of lobster patties, jellied eel, iced champagne and ratafia, *gâteaux*, and marrons glacés; and boasted of the quantitites of red carpet that had been ordered and the enormous troop of linkboys pressed into service for the gala occasion. "Truly, Frances, I believe it will be the most elegant event of the Season," breathed Kitty. "At first I didn't care for Mainwaring House in the least. It was so formal and grand that it seemed cold after dear old Camberly, but I do admit it is a most impressive edifice, and the ballroom is magnificent. Lady Elizabeth and Kilson seem to know just how to go on, and Lord Mainwaring"—Kitty still could not feel comfortable referring to anyone as imposing as the marquess as "Uncle Julian"—"is sparing no expense."

Lady Frances had attended enough balls to feel that one was very much like another, differing only in scale of grandeur and expense, but she was happy to see Kitty so excited and pleased.

It was thus some time before she was able to visit Mr. Murray at his establishment in Albemarle Street. His enthusiasm for her new idea of a history written with more emphasis on biography and a livelier narrative style, which would lend vitality to important episodes instead of turning them into a dry series of dates and names to be memorized, was most encouraging. He advanced several suggestions of his own, which caught her imagination and made her eager to try them out on her own. "It is a revolutionary approach, Lady Frances, but it just might appeal," he remarked thoughtfully.

"Oh, I feel certain it would, Mr. Murray. I would never dream of suggesting it if I had not found this storytelling method to be most effective with Cassie and Freddie. They are both bright enough but would far prefer to be out-of-doors in search of adventure instead of trapped in a schoolroom. And, being only their sister, I find it more difficult than an ordinary tutor would to capture and hold their attention. I must say that I have met with remarkable success," she admitted candidly.

"Very well, then, continue with your project. I look forward to seeing the final product," he encouraged her as he escorted her to her carriage.

That task accomplished, Lady Frances felt exonerated from her guilty feelings of frivolity and at liberty to give herself up to the pleasures of the metropolis without further interference from an overactive conscience.

15

The marquess, having recovered from a bout of cynicism precipitated by the shallowness of the evening with his mistress, decided that a further restorative would be the encouragement of someone who was worthy of society's notice. If he had stopped to consider, he would have been amazed at how far he had come in so short a time from condemning the lady in question as a prude and a bluestocking to wishing to introduce her to the *ton* as someone worthy of its admiration. With this plan in mind, he drove around to Brook Street one afternoon to hold Lady Frances to the promise he had extacted from her on their visit to the Lord Elgin's marbles. Arriving at Brook Street, he discovered Freddie and Nigel intent upon cricket and witnessed the narrow escape of the drawing-room window from a misdirected hit. Assuring himself that he was merely looking after Frances' peace of mind, the marquess strolled over to where the two boys were arguing over the most effective method of improving one's aim. The truth of the matter was that Mainwaring was more interested in sharing his own cricketing skill than in the continued serenity of Frances. "A capital hit, Freddie, but rather glaringly abroad," he remarked, sauntering up.

"Oh, sir, how famous that you should come along just now! Could you settle a question, do you think?" Freddie inquired, outlining the basis of their disagreement.

"By all means, but here, give me the bat. It is easier to demonstrate than explain. You must grip it more this way and pay closer attention to the ball, marking with your eye exactly the direction you wish to send it—thus." The bat connected with a resounding thwack, sending the ball precisely to the spot indicated. If he had been concerned at all over the possible deterioration of his prowess on the cricket field, the marquess's notion was swiftly dispelled by the blatant admiration in the boys' eyes.

"Thank you ever so much! You are very good, sir, aren't you?" Freddie said, looking worshipfully up at him. Mainwaring was not a little touched by the lad's appreciation, and wondered at this unusual rush of feeling himself. I *know* I'm approaching my dotage, he concluded as he nodded to Higgins and allowed himself to be ushered into the drawing room, where a most unusual sight assailed his disbelieving eyes. Lady Frances was precariously balanced on a footstool by the window, engaged in earnest conversation with . . . a tree! For one dumbfounded moment Lord Mainwaring thought Frances had succumbed to her aunt's horticultural passion, until Nelson appeared inching his way cautiously along a branch, meowing pitifully.

Nelson had been blissfully sunning himself on the steps when the nasty overfed pug from the adjoining house had stumbled out for his morning shuffle. Being a city dog of impeccable pedigree, he had been highly insulted at the sight of a motheaten cat who had the colossal nerve to sit in the sun in this exclusive neighborhood. He had voiced his disapproval immediately and vociferously. Nelson was more startled than frightened by the vehement yipping, but he had not stopped to consider this as he scrambled up the nearest available tree. When he reached the first branch, he stopped to look down and was immediately disgusted with himself for having fled from a canine that would have made a mere mouthful for Wellington. In fact, the pug was so fat he wouldn't have been able to move fast

enough to pose any real threat to Nelson. Staring at the ground
that was beginning to sway under his horrified gaze, the cat
bitterly regretted his flight. Before he was completely overcome
with vertigo, something grabbed his tail and he leapt up
scratching and spitting, his fear of heights forgotten. The thing
that had caught at his tail withdrew, and then, to his intense
relief, he heard the comforting tones of Lady Frances reassuring
him, and he inched carefully toward her.

Mainwaring strode across the room to help lady Frances and
her burden off their perch. His eyes, brimming with amusement, laughed down into hers. She smiled mischievously up
at him. "No doubt you thought my wits had gone begging when
you came in, but Nelson has one bad eye, which makes him
very upset at heights. He already scratched James, the footman,
so I was summoned to reassure him."

"I understand perfectly, ma'am," he assured her gravely,
but his lips twitched suspiciously. "After this heroic rescue,
are you in fit condition to go for a drive in the park with me?"

She laughed. "What a poor creature you think me. I should
like it of all things," she thanked him. "But I must fetch my
bonnet and pelisse. I shan't be a moment."

Julian, well-versed in the ways of women, was surprised when
it was just a moment later that she reappeared in her white satin
pelisse, tying the bow of a matching twilled sarcenet hat.

It was a fine day and Frances was content after a morning
of tending to estate business and the rescue of Nelson to sit and
watch the passing scene as the marquess skillfully maneuvered
his powerful grays through the traffic on the streets. In fact,
there was no less traffic when they arrived in the park, but it
was traffic of a more modish kind than the carts and mail coaches
they had been forced to dodge en route. It was the fashionable
hour of five o'clock and the park was crowded with beautiful
thoroughbreds and elegant ladies taking the air in carriages of
every hue and description, attended by gorgeously liveried
footmen and coachmen. They saw the "diamonds" of the day:
Lady Cowper, the Duchess of Argyll, and Lady Louisa, holding
court among the gentlemen who clustered thick about them. The
Marquess of Anglesea, accompanied by his lovely daughters,

all superbly mounted, trotted sedately by. Lady Frances even caught a glimpse of the Prince Regent and Sir Benjamin Bloomfield. All in all, it was an animated and colorful scene that she surveyed, deciding as she did so that the fresh air and magnificent horses made this fashionable promenade infinitely preferable to the ballroom.

Having negotiated the streets and worn off some of the restiveness of his horses, the marquess was at leisure to study his companion, who was looking quite lovely in the new white pelisse, which accentuated the delicate flesh on her cheeks and the opalescent clearness of her complexion. The startched lace collarette and plume of feathers on her bonnet framed her face charmingly and enhanced the delicately molded features. However, her face wore a slightly abstracted expression that puzzled him. When she did not reply to his question as to whether or not she planned to attend Lady Harrowby's Venetian breakfast, which Kitty was anticipating with enthusiasm, he became concerned. "Lady Frances . . ." he began.

She started, and turned to him with an apologetic look in her expressive eyes. "I do beg your pardon, Lord Mainwaring. I was not attending."

"I am well aware of that," he responded dryly. "What serious concern was exercising your thoughts so thoroughly?"

A conscious look spread over her face as she admitted rather shamefacedly that she had been deliberating over a letter she had received that morning from Dawson, down at Cresswell. "You see," she confided, wrinkling her brow thoughtfully, "Squire Tilden is selling his prize bull and approached Dawson about it." She saw amusement creep into his eyes, and one corner of his mouth twitched, but having given herself away, she contiued determinedly. "Our bull is very old. I am surprised he made it through the winter. We must think about procuring a new one. Squire Tilden's is certainly a fine specimen, but I am sure he comes very dear, and I do not anticipate a good harvest this year, so I wonder if it is wise to purchase it." Turning to him, she added contritely, "I don't know why you are so kind as to take me driving with you. Well, I mean, I do know why you do it. You do it because you are helping me become more fashionable and more sought-after in the *ton*, but

I don't know what motivates you to do that. Whatever does, I am excessively grateful for it, but I don't like you to put yourself out from such a hopeless case. I am ever so sorry to be prosing on about country matters, but you *did* ask.''

He interrupted this tangled speech. "My dear girl, don't refine upon it. Where else would I encounter a lady who would discuss prize bulls with me?" This won a chuckle and almost erased the wrinkle between her brows. Seeing that it remained to some degree, he became more serious. "Besides, I am glad you mentioned it. If the price of the bull turns out to be a burden to Cresswell, you may sell him to me. Camberly does not have one and my income is from such a variety of sources that a poor harvest will not affect it to the degree it does yours."

She was silent for a moment, considering the proposition, trying to decide whether it was motivated by a true need or some unfathomable wish to help her. "Very well, but I am convinced you are doing this to be kind, and I do not want to be given any special favors, for that will make it more difficult for me to judge the true consequences, and therefore the real wisdom of my decisions." He thought wryly that most of the women with whom he was acquainted cultivated favors to the top of their bent, and these favors were ordinarily in the form of jewelry or other extravagances. Here, on the other hand, was a woman who worried about being obliged to someone over livestock! Truly, he did not know as much about women, or this particular woman, as he had imagined. And somehow, her determined self-reliance made him wish more than ever to ease any burdens she might have. But he had driven her to the park with the express purpose of erasing such cares from her mind, not discussing them. Trying for a lighter tone, he pointed to a high-perch phaeton whose driver and canine companion closely resembled each other in their tightly curled locks and disdainful surveillance of the assemblage.

"That miserable dog needs a salutary dose of Wellington to wipe that supercilious sneer off his face. Why, Wellington could dispose of that fop of an animal in no time flat.'' Frances laughed. "And he would certainly enjoy putting him in his place. He seems to have taken exception to every canine on Brook Street. With the mongrels, however, he has established fast friendships. The stable dog is his greatest crony, and the pug in the adjoining house was his bitterest enemy even before he scared Nelson up the tree. Ever since Wellington pulled Nelson from the pond, he has looked upon that cat as his personal responsibility, and he highly resents anyone or anything who upsets that miserable animal.''

They finished the drive in companionable silence—a new experience for both of them.

As he escorted her to the door, Mainwaring took Lady Frances' hand in his and smiled down at her. ''I feel certain that you won't believe me when I tell you I enjoyed myself.''

''No, I do not,'' she replied forthrightly. ''I saw the shock on your face when I told you about the bull. It is not exactly the topic of a fashionable conversation. But you seem to be such a friend, and I cannot dissemble with my friends.''

He looked at her intently, an unreadable expression in his dark blue eyes. ''That is precisely why I enjoyed the drive.''

She thanked him for the outing and the conversation. Then, as she entered the door Higgins had held patiently during this interchange, she remembered yet another debt of gratitude she owed him. ''I saw you coaching Freddie today. I do so appreciate that. I truly do try to give him all that a father and mother could, but I am afraid I do have my limits. I did help him with his cricket, but with his batting only. I can only pitch, you see. I have no affinity for batting,'' she apologized.

A swift smile illuminated his features and warmed his eyes. ''I can see that you are in need of some coaching as well, then. I shall be happy to oblige,'' he offered.

''Thank you again.'' She smiled shyly and, at last, to Higgins' intense relief, entered her elegant hallway.

16

Higgins brought tea, and for some time Lady Frances sat stroking a subdued Nelson and reflecting on the outing. She was at a loss to explain the marquess's attentiveness when she was neither a relative to whom duty owed such consideration, nor was she the sort of ripe beauty to whom his own personal tastes would attract him. It was a puzzle in which she suspected Lady Elizabeth Streatham played a major role. She recognized that that amiable and energetic lady felt herself honor-bound to give Lady Frances an enjoyable Season. Having observed at first hand that redoubtable female's forthright but effective methods, she felt reasonably certain that it was she who had coerced Mainwaring into partnering her at Lady Richardson's ball and inviting her to drive with him in the park. Both of these activities were implemented in the most public places of the *ton* and thus served to attract a maximum amount of fashionable attention, thereby ensuring the rapid establishment of a favorable social reputation. On the other hand, the two other times he had honored them with his company had had nothing to do with Lady Streatham. In each case, his escort had been demanded by her irrepressible brother and sister. Frances had no illusions about the difficulty of resisting the blandishments of either one of the cozening pair, but then, she was fond of the children. If Kitty's impression of Mainwaring was to be trusted, his lordship was not. Still, no one had asked him to help Freddie and Nigel with their cricket. Whatever his motives, he had provided her with no little enjoyment and a feeling of easiness, even pleasure, in his company. It was not surprising that a man as attractive as the marquess would have developed a charming manner, but it was more than charm that made her look upon him as a friend. After their unfortunate initial encounter, he had treated her as he would have treated any one of his friends, discussing politics and estate matters with her as if she were another man, instead of a young woman whose mind should have been filled with fashionable *on-dits* and social repartee. Beyond teasing her the tiniest bit, he never indicated by tone or gesture that he considered it unusual for her to have the interests she did. Heretofore she had encountered either criticism of a woman's participating in traditionally male preserves or condescension. Above all, he shared her sense of humor. Even those such as Sir Lucius Taylor, who did take her seriously, rarely saw the humorous aspects of life that she saw. She was grateful for Julian Mainwaring's attention, but she certainly expected no more of it now that he had danced with her and driven her in the park. Why, for most women in the *ton* that could have been considered the apex of existence.

Mainwaring's attitude not only perplexed Frances but also agreeably surprised two veteran Mainwaring watchers—the dowager Marchioness of Camberly and Lady Elizabeth Streatham—who discussed this interesting situation one day over tea. Though Lady Elizabeth had visited her at the dowager's "kind request," she recognized a command when it was given and knew that her role would be to share all her privileged information in return for the honor of drinking tea with her formidable relative and agreeing totally with that lady's interpretation of the information Lady Elizabeth divulged. In truth, Lady Elizabeth was longing to speak with the dowager, who, whatever she might lack in firsthand knowledge of the goings-on in the ballrooms, promenades, and drawing rooms of the *ton*, made up for it with a natural sharpness of perception and a wealth of experience that had refined this into a nearly infallible ability to predict the outcome of almost any social encounter.

Lady Streatham had barely untied the bow of her bonnet when, tapping her ubiquitous walking stick, her hostess demanded sharply, "Now, Elizabeth, what's all this I hear about Mainwaring and the Cresswell chit?"

"Well . . ." Lady Elizabeth stripped off pale lemon kid gloves. "He has danced with her at a ball where Sally Jersey and Kitty were his only other partners."

"That would have been Belinda Richardson's squeeze." The dowager nodded sagely. "Very well done of you, Elizabeth."

"But I did not force him by asking him to do so. You know Julian. That is the quickest way to make him do what you least wish him to."

The dowager nodded again. "But he enjoyed it, didn't he? He laughed with her and conversed with her later. It's a rare person, least of all a female, who makes Mainwaring smile as he apparently did."

Lady Elizabeth was not a little put out that the dowager, who had only her social spies to rely on, seemed to be so well-informed and so perfectly capable of arriving at her own conclusions without her guest's assistance. "I certainly can add nothing to what you have already discovered," she replied with some asperity.

"Now, Elizabeth, don't fly up into the boughs. I didn't ask you to tea to find out about the ball. Anyone could tell me about that and the drive in the park, but my observers do not ordinarily visit Lord Elgin's marbles, nor do they habituate Astley's Amphitheater. Now, what on earth possessed Mainwaring to go to either of those places, and with a pack of children besides? You know both Lady Frances and Mainwaring. What do you think? Is he caught at last? From all accounts, she isn't his type, but why ever else would he allow himself to be dragged along on nursery outings when he don't even like children? Do tell me, Elizabeth, what is Lady Frances Cresswell like?"

Mollified, Lady Elizabeth tried to express Frances' style as best she could, but found herself at a loss to put that young woman's unique charm into words. Concluding that physical description was the easiest, though the least informative for Lady

Frances in particular, she began. "Decidedly, she is extremely elegant. She has style, but because she is reserved and does not put herself forward, one doesn't recognize it immediately. She's of average height, with features that give a sense of character despite their delicacy. She is reserved, but not at all shy, meaning that she converses elegantly and easily without revealing anything about herself. Her hair is dark blond and her eyes, which are definitely her best feature, are large and hazel, but often take on the color she is wearing."

"Humph!" The dowager was unimpressed. "She don't sound like Mainwaring's style in the slightest. He has always chosen well-endowed women of the world—ripe' uns, every one of 'em."

Lady Elizabeth was miffed at this brusque dismissal of the portrait of her friend. "That's as may be, but I haven't heard that he ever wanted to marry one of them, or even to be seen very much with them."

"Aye, you have a point there," conceded the dowager. "But I have heard that she manages her own estate or some such nonsense. If she's Cresswell's daughter, I don't know as I would believe that. He had a lot in his brain box, but practicality wasn't his long suit. I can't picture any daughter of his being able to take care of herself, much less an entire estate and two lively twins besides."

"Not at all," her informant assured her. "Frances is the most unusual girl. Without one's precisely knowing how she does it, she contrives to get the children and the staff to do exactly as she wishes, with the minimum amount of fuss. She doesn't look to be the 'managing' sort of female at all, but she must be. I gather from Kitty that she did call Mainwaring to task about the agent at Camberly, and there was a rare set-to over that." Lady Elizabeth paused, contemplating the scene with relish. "I only wish I had been there," she commented regretfully. "To continue: when I forced him to call for Kitty at the Cresswells' and he could not avoid saying how-de-do to her, he looked as black as a thundercloud, but I made the two of them act like civilized human beings to one another."

"That I can well believe," her hostess remarked dryly. "Mainwaring was always strong-willed. What with his father dead and no one but that flighty mother around, there was never anyone to oppose his least little wish. Do him good to be sent the right-about now and then. I like a girl with backbone. How about her mind? Mainwaring may have mistresses that are beautiful dull-wits, but he won't tolerate that in his friends."

Lady Elizabeth lowered her voice confidentially. "You couldn't guess it for the world, because she is so charming, but Lady Frances is excessively well-educated. I believe her father taught her not only French and Italian but also Greek, Latin, and mathematics besides. At first, something Julian said made me think he considered her a bluestocking, but John says that didn't stop him from bluntly interrupting the quiet discussion he and Frances were sharing at the dinner party before Lady Richardson's ball. John reports that Julian monopolized her from then on, arguing about the economy, of all things! Julian, of course, because of his uncle's affairs, knows a great deal of such matters, but John says Frances is remarkably well-informed, and she gave as good as she got."

A speculative gleam appeared in the dowager's sharp black eyes as she absorbed this revealing bit of information. "You may have something there, Elizabeth. Julian has never really had a friend. That silly brother of his was certainly no match for him, and by the time he went to Eton he had developed a tough, self-reliant streak that made everyone a little uneasy with him. Of course there's Bertie, but how can one have a friendship with someone who reserves his most serious conversations for his tailor? Julian can be perfectly charming when he wishes, but he usually doesn't come across people who interest him enough to win his attention or his friendship. Maybe an intelligent woman who cannot be brushed off as nothing but an attractive appendage, a mere titillation of the senses, is precisely what he needs. It certainly is time he settled down. And now that he has inherited the title, he must do so and get himself an heir with all speed." Her eyes softened, and she continued almost as though to herself, "But above all, he needs a friend. He is the sort of man who prefers to go it alone, but even such a man as that needs one very special friend. For a man like that it takes a special woman. Once he has found her, though, he will never need anyone else. He will be to her what

Alistair was for me—everything: friend, lover, protector, critic, and admirer. And she will be very lucky indeed,'' the dowager concluded, looking reminiscently into the fire. For a moment she seemed to have forgotten Lady Streatham's existence, but the sound of a passing carriage recalled her and she looked up sharply. ''Bring the gel to visit me someday, Elizabeth. I want to meet her. And now I am tired and I must rest. Please ring for Minter and tell her I want another shawl and some pillows.''

Lady Elizabeth bade the old lady adieu and rode back to Bruton Street in a most thoughtful mood indeed. She agreed wholeheartedly with the dowager as far as it went, but the dowager had been solely concerned with the marquess. Much as she liked and admired Julian, Lady Elizabeth was now more interested in Lady Frances' happiness. The girl had moved her somehow. Perhaps it was because she herself was so happy with John and wondered how she could have lived had she not met and married him. Perhaps it was because she felt that she alone understood and appreciated Lady Frances' excellent qualities— knew and appreciated their fineness and uniqueness—even better than Lady Frances herself did. And, unlike anyone else, she had been able to see the kind and impulsively generous, loving nature beneath the reserved exterior. She wanted this loving nature to be awakened and made to flourish. It would take a special man to appeal to Frances' keen intelligence, her integrity, and her sense of humor, but such a man would be able to arouse the passion and enjoyment of life that Lady Elizabeth knew existed, even though it lay dormant, unaroused by the beefy squires and dissipated macaronis that seemed to populate Lady Frances' world. She needed someone who was man enough to enjoy and challenge her. Lady Elizabeth had decided long ago that Lord Julian Mainwaring was such a man. And having decided this, she was wasting no time in fostering the acquaintance—an acquaintance that she fully intended to develop into the first true love affair for either Lady Frances Cresswell or Lord Julian Mainwaring.

17

B lissfully unaware that her fate was being skillfully manipulated by two experts in the field of intrigue, Lady Frances went blithely about her business. Her second visit to her publisher was as gratifying as the first. He highly approved of several chapters she had given him and offered not the slightest criticism of style or content. This visit did, however, cause a slight deterioration in her developing friendship with the marquess and thus a slight setback to the Machiavellian plans of his female relatives.

Having bid a cordial good day to Mr. Murray, Lady Frances had just stepped out into Albemarle Street. As Aunt Harriet had taken the carriage to pick up two highly unusual rosebushes from a horticultural crony, Lady Frances had been forced to take a hackney to Albemarle Street. She had very properly been accompanied by James, but, not having been able to convince the hackney coachman to wait, he had been forced to go some ways off to procure one. It was thus that Mainwaring, driving back from a satisfying morning at the Royal Exchange, was astounded to see Lady Frances Cresswell alone and unattended in a neighborhood not at all the normal haunt of a fashionable lady. Mainwaring himself was not a rigid stickler for the niceties of *ton*-ish behavior. He certainly was not at all interested in the rigid propriety of most of society's grandes dames and had occasionally found it inconvenient in the extreme, but he thoroughly understood the minds of those who controlled social opinion. They *did* subscribe to such propriety and would have instantly condemned Lady Frances had they seen her. He could not have said why he cared so much that Frances not run the slightest risk of incurring their censure, but he did. He was not about to allow her to behave in a manner that would ruin her chances in the select society in which they both moved.

Consequently, his "Lady Frances, whatever are you doing alone in this vicinity!" which assailed that startled lady's ears was tinged with concern.

Recovering from her initial surprise, Lady Frances looked up to see him frowning down at her in a most discouraging manner. The frown and the tone of Mainwaring's voice were more indicative of his apprehension for her own good reputation than of disapproval, but Lady Frances, already guiltily aware of what the *ton* would think of an authoress, especially one who had the temerity to meet her publisher, heard only the severest censure in his tones. Annoyed that he should have discovered her in such a situation, and more annoyed that he seemed to think her answerable to him for her conduct, she put her chin up and greeted him defiantly. "Good day, my lord. And may I ask whatever are *you* doing here?"

Mainwaring, who had immediately realized the infelicity of his tone, tried for a gentler one in hopes of mollifying her antagonistic response. "It is not at all the thing, you know, for a young lady to be in this neighborhood and alone."

Well and truly roused by this piece of condescending solicitude, Lady Frances had to exercise the strictest control to keep her temper in check. How dare he tell her what to do! She would have resented such censure from anyone, but from someone she barely knew, who surveyed her with a superior air from his elegant curricle, it was intolerable. She did not acknowledge the more personal hurt she felt, that someone with whom she had trusted her friendship thought so little of her that he should immediately leap to such an unflattering conclusion instead of relying on her judgment. In spite of all her resolution, the anger quivered in her voice as she answered, "I am not such a greenhead, my lord, as to have come here unescorted, but my footman has gone in search of a hackney. I had business to conduct here, and surely you would not have a lady sully her drawing room with trade?"

The set of her jaw and the martial light in her eye would have told a less-perceptive man than Lord Mainwaring that he had deeply offended her. He was slightly taken aback at the intensity of her anger, which resulted more from her sense of betrayal than from her taking exception to his criticism. In an attempt to retrieve his position, he offered her a place in his curricle, but his calm assumption that this magnanimous gesture would instantly repair any damage done to her social standing merely served to antagonize her further, and she coldly declined.

Fortunately, before the situation could deteriorate further, James arrived with a carriage and helped his mistress as she regally climbed into it without so much as a backward glance at the now furious Mainwaring.

The marquess would have been hard pressed to say whether he was more furious with himself for badly managing the affair, or with Lady Frances for her prickly independence and her refusal to let anyone assist her in the least. His actions had been motivated by the best intentions, but somehow Lady Frances had contrived to make them appear an intolerable insult and he was just as hurt as she that she should have so little faith in his judgment or actions. These reflections did nothing to improve his temper during the drive to Mainwaring House. His face looked like a thundercloud as he descended, throwing the reins to his tiger, and strode into the hallway. Kilson, relieving his master of his many-caped driving coat, sagely refrained from making any remark. Privately he tried to recall when he had ever seen his lordship in such a taking, and decided that only a woman could have made him angry enough to wear such a black look. He knew that Mainwaring, having dealt with chicanery and insulting behavior in every corner of the world, was too experienced and too much in control of himself to be overset by any man. Kilson was well aware of his lordship's liaison with Vanessa Welford, but he could not believe that a woman who catered only to the more basic aspects of Mainwaring's nature could arouse such anger. Lady Welford was too predictable to have done such a thing. Clearly it was another female. And Kilson knew of no better source of information on that head than Kitty's Alice.

Upon being approached by the great Mr. Kilson himself, Alice was practically speechless with the honor, but in defense of her reputation as confidante, she rose nobly to the occasion and confided to her august interrogator that she suspicioned it was Miss Kitty's great friend Lady Frances Cresswell who had overset his lordship—that lady being the only one, besides the dowager and Lady Streatham, mentioned by Kitty in connection with his lordship. Kilson knew as well as, if not better than, the dowager his master's taste for voluptuous females. The news that a young lady whom he recalled as being a mere slip of a girl was taking up so much of his master's time gave Mainwaring's seasoned henchman pause for thought. If Mainwaring preferred ripe beauties, he also preferred those whose sophistication made dalliance with them a much more comfortable and predictable affair than it was with those who were young enough to retain romantic notions and thus make unreasonable demands. That his lordship was paying even the slightest attention to someone who was more elegant than alluring, was unmarried, and only twenty-two besides, meant that the situation was serious indeed. In all the years he had been with his lordship, Kilson could not remember his having enjoyed a woman for a companionship other than the type supplied by his mistresses. The single exception to this was the dowager, for whom he retained a deep, though well-concealed fondness and respect. Kilson completed his inspection of the wine cellar, where he'd gone to mull over this revelation in privacy. As he slowly mounted the stairs, he resolved to keep a much closer eye on things. Years of sharing every sort of uncomfortable lodging and adventure with Lord Mainwaring had given him a great fondness as well as a healthy respect for his master. He had often wished that Lord Mainwaring had had a brother or cousin who possessed the same curiosity, the same keen mind, the same willingness to take risks that so endeared his master to him and made him stand out among men the world over. No man should be as constantly alone as Lord Mainwaring was, not that he was without friends, but none of them ever seemed to be a true companion who could share the same view of the world he had. It had been Kilson's dearest wish that such a companion would appear. Until now, it had not occurred to him that such a companion might be female, but the more he considered it, the better such an idea seemed, and he began to devise ways in which he could learn more about this Lady Frances of whom Alice seemed so sure.

The object of these reflections, having failed to quell his ill humor by tossing off a glass of the best brandy and immersing himself in some complicated business correspondence, gave up and strode over to Gentleman Jackson's, hoping to work off his ill humor through physical exertion. There he was welcomed enthusiastically by the noted pugilist, who was often heard to remark that his lordship had excellent science and was certainly wasting his talents in diplomatic circles. The physical exertion and the reassuring male sporting atmosphere, whose simple codes offered a direct contrast to the complicated patterns of polite behavior imposed by the *ton*, restored his good humor in part. He decided to improve it further by dropping in at Brooks's. Apparently the exertion at Jackson's had not dissipated his ill humor as much as he had thought, for Bertie, encountering him on the steps, greeted him with an inquiring look. "Hallo, Julian. Whatever has put that murderous scowl on your face?"

"Hallo, Bertie," his lordship responded, not a little put out that he was still annoyed by such a trivial incident. As Bertie's inquiring look showed no signs of fading, Mainwaring sighed and confessed, "Very well, if you must know, it's that high-handed friend of yours. She's too independent for her own good."

Comprehension dawned in Bertie's eyes, but he agreed in a conciliatory tone, "Yes, she never would be led by anyone else. But whatever does that have to do with you?"

Mainwaring related with some acerbity the entire encounter. "Well, you do have a point, Julian. She undoubtedly was wrong, and not a little stupid in being there—especially unattended by more than her footman—but I don't blame her for being annoyed at your interference in her affairs. You should be the first to understand her resentment. You're too accustomed to running your own show, Julian. You forget that she might be as little inclined to take anyone's advice as you are.'' Bertie's look seemed to suggest he was recalling an incident when he had been foolhardy enough to do just that. Mainwaring grinned ruefully, acknowledging the accuracy as well as the justice of his friend's observation.

18

L ord Mainwaring was saved by his grandmother from having to debase himself with a call of apology to Lady Frances. Curious about the young woman who seemed to be occupying an unusual amount of her grandson's busy life, she took matters into her own hands and invited the elder daughter of her dear friend Lady Belinda Cresswell to tea. Taking a more active role in the matchmaking, she instructed Julian himself to drive the young lady. She had also invited Lady Streatham and Kitty, who, having spent the morning together running up bills on Bond Street, came separately in the Streathams' carriage.

It was an unusually fine day and Mainwaring took advantage of the opportunity to drive Lady Frances around the park before proceeding to the dowager's. For some time they rode in silence while Mainwaring tried to phrase an apology for his interference in her affairs that would convey his sympathy with her resentment at this interference while at the same time maintaining the correctness of his original censure of her conduct. Judging correctly that an abject apology might mollify Lady Frances temporarily, but would in the long run weaken her confidence in the strength of his character or judgment, he decided to forgo any apology in favor of offering assistance. Still, he hesitated, searching for just the words, asking himself at the same time why he should care in the least what he thought of her or she of him. "Lady Frances," he began tentatively, and then continued with more assurance, "I have some experience in the business world and would be more than happy to put that and any personal connections I might have at your service should you have any affairs you would wish settled."

Recognizing this offer for what it was—a very handsome and practical offer of assistance and an assumption of some of the responsibility for the unpleasantness of their last encounter—Lady Frances was both surprised and touched. She turned to him with a grateful smile, "Why, thank you, my lord. It is very kind of you." Mainwaring was unprepared for the relief he felt at her ready acceptance of his peace offering, and found himself thinking what very fine and expressive eyes she had.

Frances knew that her own bristly independence had been at least as much responsible for their contretemps as Mainwaring's interference, and she offered her own form of apology by admitting the true nature of her business. "Ordinarily I would accept your generous offer, because though I may be a green 'un, I am not fool enough to insist on doing myself what someone else can do better. But in this instance I am afraid I can't. You see"—a slightly conscious look crept over her face—"I was conferring with my publisher."

"Your publisher!" her companion echoed in thunderstruck tones. "No doubt we can expect to see ourselves pillored in print soon in *Society Unmasked*, by a Lady of Quality."

Lady Frances laughed, but she had recognized the suspicious look at the back of his eyes. "Oh, no, I am not *that* sort of female who preys on society in order to satisfy a craving for power or notoriety. This is, I am afraid to admit, a project that is far more in keeping with a 'bluestocking' than a 'lady of quality.' "

Julian cocked a quizzical eyebrow.

"You see," she continued, "I have always felt that people go about educating children in a way designed to set up their backs in the least amount of time possible. They stuff their brains full of dry, disassociated facts and expect them to repeat them in the same disembodied manner. Then they are astonished when children fail to do so. Yet children can remember and repeat a story quite easily, and the more adventurous the tale, the more readily they remember it. What is history, what are wars, kings, queens, scientific discoveries, but great adventures? I have written a history book in this style and taken it to Mr. Murray, who was my father's publisher. He had already published some of my tales for children, but nothing so ambitious as this, and he felt he needed to consult with me personally before doing so." Here Frances paused to draw breath and look anxiously at Mainwaring.

His face softened and he smiled at her enthusiasm. "An excellent idea. If your book is half as enthralling as the two expeditions I was privileged to join, I predict an enormous success. You certainly have no competition."

She turned pink with pleasure. "I had thought that if the author were identified as 'F. Cresswell, child of the noted classical scholar Lord Charles Cresswell and product of this excellent educational scheme,' it might win further approval."

The bland tone of this suggestion did not deceive his lordship, who caught the wicked gleam in her eye and smiled appreciatively. "What a wily creature you are," he teased.

"Oh, no, my lord, merely practical," she assured him innocently.

"Eminently so, believe me."

By this time they had arrived at the dowager's and the door was thrown open by her stately if aged butler. Lady Frances glanced apprehensively at her escort, but he smiled reassuringly and took her arm in a firm grasp to conduct her to the drawing room, where the dowager awaited them ensconced in an enormous chair by the fire and flanked by Kitty and Lady Streatham. "Come in, my child, come in. Excuse the fire on such a lovely day, but my bones are so old they need all the warmth they can get. Come, let me get a good look at you, my dear. Don't be shy. I was so fond of your mother—liked her more than my own brats. You have the look of her, but not quite so pretty, I think. Belinda Carstairs was one of the most beautiful girls I've seen in many a season—a real diamond she was—and gay as she was lovely. I missed her sorely when she married your papa and went off to those outlandish places. But who could help being happy for her? You rarely find such love as theirs except in literature. Those two adored each other. Once they met, the rest of the world didn't exist.'' She sighed and patted a chair that Mainwaring had placed next to her. ''Sit down and tell me about yourself. I hear you have charge of the estate now, as well as two rambunctious twins and that crazy Harriet Cresswell. She's a bright woman, Harriet, and she can be amusing, but tetchy—lord, she is tetchy, and always was.''

Frances, whose eyes were not a little misty at the mention of her beloved parents, smiled and sat down gratefully. ''Yes, ma'am, I have managed Cresswell really ever since Mama died.''

The dowager interrupted, ''Yes, I can imagine that Charles wasn't much good at it. He was a brilliant man, but he never could manage the practicalities of life. Belinda took care of those, in addition to sharing his intellectual passions. She was truly a remarkable woman. I hear you're not unlike her. But continue.''

The others, completely ignored, were left to their own devices. Lady Streatham and Kitty were quite happy to devour the abundant supply of cakes while gloating over their purchases from a successful morning on Bond Street. Mainwaring leaned against the mantel, content to listen to Frances' recital of family affairs. As her musical voice described her taking over the household at the age of twelve under the aegis of an elderly housekeeper, gradual assumption of duties connected with the estate, and finally, with the death of her father, undertaking the education of Cassie and Freddie, he began to appreciate more fully the enormity of the burdens she bore. Such responsibilities often proved too much for men of his own age, much less a girl of twenty-two. No doubt, he thought wryly, she would object strongly to being labeled a ''girl,'' but that was in fact what she was. He had never been one to seek frivolous amusements for himself or encourage them in his friends, but he found himself longing to immerse her in a whirlwind of totally self-indulgent frivolity. She had probably done nothing solely for her own diversion since the age of twelve. As he examined her more closely, he could detect the marks these years had left.

She had a charming smile, but it was gracious rather than gay. Her large hazel eyes fringed with long dark lashes were her most attractive feature, but there was a gravity in their expressive depths that was never completely banished even when she was most amused. And always she exhibited a certain awareness of her surroundings that belied a consciousness of what the children were doing, of things that needed her attention. Thinking of her in a variety of past situations, he realized that despite an excellent sense of humor, she was more often serious than not, and she never completely forgot herself. This seriousness he found oddly touching, and at the same time attractive. Her honesty and her openness made him trust her in a way he had never trusted a woman, and very few men. Her simple acceptance of responsibility for herself and her family, her down-to-earth approach to problems, kindled admiration—an emotion that was unusual in someone as capable as the Marquess of Camberly. And here he felt himself at a loss. Because he understood the reality of her responsibilities, because she accepted her duties as a matter of fact and without complaint, he wanted very much to relieve her of them while at the same time he realized that the best expression his respect for her capabilities could take would be to trust her to be as adept at solving her problems as he would be. After all, using Bertie's logic, he would look upon any assistance offered him as indicative of a friend's lack of confidence in his abilities, even if it stemmed from a purely generous impulse to ease the burden of a fellowman. He sighed ruefully and confessed to himself that he was at a standstill and could only hope for some chance to smooth her path without seeming to interfere.

A sharp "Ahem, Mainwaring, are you even in the same country with us, or at any rate the same room?" broke his train of reflection.

He grinned sheepishly."Ah, yes. Were you addressing me, ma'am?"

"I most certainly was, young man. Don't you know it is excessively rude not to pay attention to your elders? I was wondering if you planned to grace your own ball for Kitty."

He looked affronted. "But of course, ma'am. How can you think otherwise?"

"Well, knowing how independent you are, how little you care for social opinion, and how much you loathe such squeezes, I should be surprised if you did not contrive to be called away on some matter of urgent national business."

This forced an answering grin from her grandson. "I assure you, I know the duties of a guardian very well, and I am not such a ramshackle fellow as to run off on the big day. I have even made sure that she opens the ball with me, and now shall take advantage of the opportunity you have provided to secure the first waltz with Lady Frances." He turned to Frances with a quizzical gleam.

It was not for nothing, Lady Frances reflected a trifle bitterly, that Lord Mainwaring was in the diplomatic service. Even if she had wished to hesitate or refuse, she could not in such a public place and in front of someone who cared for him so dearly. It seemed that whether she wished to continue it or not, their misunderstanding was to be cleared up. With as good grace as she could muster when so obviously maneuvered into a situation that allowed no alternative, she smiled and thanked him.

"Lucky gel," the dowager, who had watched the scene with great interest, commented enviously and not without a trace of self-satisfaction. "Not only will he be the most handsome man there, he is an excellent dancer. After all, he had plenty of practice in Vienna, where, according to some, that was about the extent of the activity."

Julian's eyes twinkled wickedly. "If you weren't such a snob, Grandmama, forgoing all but the most rigidly select tea parties, I would ask you, but I know you detest these squeezes more than I." The twinkle became a speculative gleam as he saw her begin to consider his invitation seriously.

After a moment's hesitation she thumped her stick on the floor. "Dashed if I don't accept you."

Mainwaring bent over one frail beringed hand and said with real gratitude, "Thank you, Grandmama."

Here they were interrupted by Lady Streatham. "Do my ears deceive me? Did I actually hear you convince her to come?" Mainwaring nodded, "I must confess, you are the most complete hand, Julian." She turned to Kitty, exclaiming, "What

a triumph, my love! Now I know you are assured of success."
Then, noticing how tired the dowager looked, "We must be
going or my men will be sending out the Bow Street Runners."

Lady Frances bade adieu to the dowager, promising to honor
her request and provide her with intelligent conversation at the
ball. Kitty curtsied and thanked her prettily, and the whole party
left the old lady to some very interesting reflections of her own.

The drive home for Lady Frances and her companion was
equally pleasant. Mainwaring retrieved his position by
apologizing for asking her to dance in such a public situation.
"It was rather high-handed, but you are so busy, I wasn't sure
of having another opportunity before the big event."

"That's of no account, my lord," she replied, but he
recognized from the slight constraint in her answer that she truly
had felt manipulated.

"I am sorry," he continued. "Tell me what I can do to show
that I truly do apologize."

He had offered this more as a matter of form, and was rather
surprised when she tilted her head speculatively and began,
"Well, I . . ."

"Yes, go on," he encouraged, wondering what possible
request could cause her such difficulty.

She brought it out in a rush. "I was just wondering if you
would mind very much telling me what it was like at the
Congress in Vienna."

He burst out laughing. "No, don't poker up, my child. It was
just that you looked so apprehensive, I made certain you were
going to make some impossibly difficult demand. No, I don't
have the slightest idea what I thought it was likely to be, but
I felt sure that I would be traveling at least to the West Indies
to accomplish it. No, of course I shouldn't mind in the least.
It's just that most people are barely aware that it is going on,
much less expose any interest or curiosity." He began giving
her a rather general account of the proceedings, but soon
recognized from her questions that he was dealing with a very
informed listener. As he warmed to his subject, he realized that
she was helping him clarify his thoughts on some points that
had remained muddy for him until now. In fact, so involved
was he in trying to capture the exact scene, the precise

atmosphere, every machination, and every insinuation, that he was unaware of the slackening pace of the horses until they came to a dead halt in the middle of the park. This brought him up short and he finished with a laugh. "So, you see, it really did not challenge my mental skills as much as my social ones."

Lady Frances wrinkled her brow thoughtfully. "Hmm, yes, I can see it must be a little bit like running an estate—with more important consequences, of course. One thinks one will spend one's time evaluating and putting into practice agricultural principles and deciding how to make the wisest use of financial resources, when, in fact, all one's energies seem to go toward soothing ruffled tempers, exhorting the lazy or the uninspired, and listening to a steady stream of complaints that have more to do with neighbors' stupidity or carelessness than with estate management." Her sigh was not lost on her companion.

"Exactly," he responded dryly. "It is amazing how human vanity continually reduces the most lofty and inspiring situations to triviality."

She twinkled up at him, "Well, then, the Prince de Ligne's comment, '*Le Congrès ne marche pas, il danse,*' was not too far wrong. And, Lady Mainwaring's prejudice aside, you have returned an excellent dancer."

"Why, thank you, ma'am," he replied meekly. "And if I thought you cared for that at all, I might be flattered."

"Well, I should think you would be pleased," she remarked candidly. "My opinion is not worth anything in particular as far as fashionable tastes go, but I do recognize grace and finesse, which are to be found in not only the social world. And since you, with your diplomatic duties, are constrained to be constantly in the most exclusive social circles, it is no small thing that you are so adroit. Even Princess Esterhazy and Madame de Lieven must be impressed. Right there you are assured of success in all that you attempt."

He knew from the wicked sparkle in her eyes and the smile hovering around one corner of her mouth that she was quizzing him, but in spite of that and despite the triviality of the accomplishment, Julian felt a warm rush of gratification at her approval. I am becoming positively infantile, he told himself severely. Women have been flattering me more lavishly for years, to no effect, and this chit makes me feel grateful for a teasing remark. He smiled at her. "Enough of such world-shaking events. We must concentrate on the more important present, and I must get you home before Cassie and Frederick have completely torn the house apart."

She agreed ruefully. "Yes, they are a precious pair, aren't they?"

The carriage drew up in front of her house, but he did not immediately alight, turning instead to say, "Thank you for the drive. And don't forget that I do mean to have that waltz, even if my methods annoyed you."

It seemed odd to her that he should thank her for the drive, especially since he said it in such a way that made it more than a mechanical social response. Some of this puzzlement must have shown on her face, because he explained, "It's rare to find someone who can understand and share in my concerns. In fact, some of your questions have directed my thoughts toward other possibilities."

The puzzled expression was replaced by one of astonishment at this, but she merely replied, "I suppose 'bluestockings' do have their uses."

"Off with you, baggage. Since you never seem to forget an insult to your precious pride, don't forget that waltz I forced out of you." He handed her down and escorted her to the door being held open by Higgins.

The look of long suffering on Higgins' face had not been merely the result of having to hold the door open while the marquess and his mistress chatted. He had more disturbing matters on his mind, but was at a loss how to begin. He could hardly remember a time when he'd seen such a glow on his mistress's face, and now it fell to him to banish it with the worry of yet another problem. He was rescued from his dilemma by the timely entrance of Aunt Harriet bearing a bowl of broth. While Farnces had been gone, Frederick, who had thought of nothing but Astley's for weeks—so much so that his tin soldiers gathered dust—had at long last prevailed on a stableboy to let him try standing bareback on his pony. For several weeks the lad, who stood in awe of John Coachman, had resisted, but eventually Freddie's blandishments, supplemented by hefty offerings of sweetmeats, had had their inevitable effect and he had been won over into agreeing to stand in the stableyard holding the rein of Prince while his scapegrace young master did his best to imitate the famous equestrians. Freddie had been doing quite well and had managed several circles upright when a large fly was his undoing. For several seconds after his head hit the paving he lay motionless, but before the stableboy could decide whether to run away or run for John, he came to, grinning sheepishly. "Here, give me a hand. I shall be right as rain in a moment." Gasping with relief, the lad leapt to help him up, but this was easier said than done. As Freddie slowly returned to a vertical position, he was overcome with faintness. His head buzzed uncomfortably and the world receded into a blur. At this crucial moment John came around the corner with one of the carriage horses he had been grooming. After one look at Freddie's white face, he turned fiercely on the unfortunate stable lad. "Oho, laddie, and what mischief have you been letting young Master Frederick get into?" The miserable boy stammered out the tale as best he could, but before he was half through, John had picked up Freddie and borne him into the house. Fortunately Cook and the housekeeper were women of sense and in no time at all had him in bed and, upon the advice of Aunt Harriet, had sent the stableboy posthaste to summon Dr. Baillie.

All this had occurred not twenty minutes after Lord Mainwaring had handed Lady Frances into his curricle. The staff and Aunt Harriet agreed unanimously that the afternoon treat so rare in Frances' life was not to be spoiled until absolutely necessary, and by the time she returned, Freddie had been examined by the good doctor and pronounced a lucky young devil who was fortunate to get off with a mild concussion and a number of scrapes and bruises. "And so I hope he's learned a good lesson, though I doubt it," sniffed Aunt Harriet, concluding her tale. Her undramatic recital of the afternoon's events had calmed Frances' worst fears, but failed to allay them completely. "Very well, come see him if you must, but he's quite safe now and the less fuss there is, the better, to my way of thinking. And any bother at all is more than the scamp deserves."

Frances, seeing her little brother propped up against the pillows, pale but absorbed in the neglected tin soldiers, said to herself that Aunt Harriet was probably completely in the right, but another part of her, which had never fully recovered from the loss of her mother and father, felt desperately afraid that another one of her dearest companions was in danger. She managed, at least outwardly, to stifle such fears and was able to say in an admirably offhand way, "What a silly clunch you are, Freddie. Don't you know the Astleys spend years practicing with all sorts of special aids and tricks before they try such a stunt?"

She had hit the right note. Frederick, prepared to resist and resent an onslaught of sisterly tears of remonstrance as feminine silliness, was stricken with guilt at the thought of the worry he had caused by the stupidity of his escapade. But he managed to smile in his usual winning way. "I am most dreadfully sorry, Fanny. I was a regular chawbacon. I do promise not to do it again . . . leastways not without more practice," he amended truthfully.

"Yes," she agreed. "I should think your head will be too dizzy for you to balance with much skill for a considerable while. Wait until we return to the soft turf at Cresswell and then John and I shall help you."

"You're a great gun, Fan," said her small brother appreciatively. This tribute and the subsequent wince of pain as he shifted position went straight to her heart, and she left the room in some haste. The careless attitude she had so carefully maintained in front of Frederick evaporated as she closed the door to the nursery and fled to her own dressing room to collapse in a chair, drop her head into her hands, and think. No constructive, rational thoughts came, and she stared out of the window, fighting the conviction that she was naive and optimistic in thinking it a mere schoolboy mishap.

A light tap on her door broke into these unwelcome thoughts, and her maid came bearing an exquisite bouquet in a filigree holder. There was nothing at all unusual about the inscription on the card. In fact, there was rather less inscription than ladies ordinarily received, but something about the forcefully scrawled "Mainwaring" brought the faintest flush to her cheeks and left her slightly breathless. "Ain't it lovely, though, miss," breathed Daisy.

"Yes, thank you," agreed her mistress as she savored their scent. And then, "Heavens! The ball! Daisy, you must ask Higgins to send a footman round to deliver a note to Lady Streatham." She hastily wrote a note, briefly recounting the mishap and begging off the evening's festivities.

It seemed no time at all before Cassie appeared to inform her breathlessly, "Lady Streatham is below, Fan, and she's been telling me all about the time Nigel fell off his horse going over a jump. He was unconscious half a day but was right as a trivet in no time. Is she come to tell you to go to the ball? I think you should go. It will be the most famous thing. Ned has been telling Freddie and me about the quantities of flowers and red carpet and how everyone has been cleaning chandeliers and polishing for weeks. He says the ballroom looks like a palace and there's going to be ever so much food—jellies and cakes and ices. You must go. I can take care of Freddie. All he has to do is sit quietly. We can play jackstraws, and if his head aches I can read to him. Just tell me what you would do. I know where the lavender water is and I remember just how you put it on my face when I had measles last summer. Please, Fan, let me take care of Freddie," she pleaded.

By this time they had reached the drawing room and Lady Streatham was able to add her voice to Cassie's. "Yes, Frances, I think that's an excellent idea. Cassie seems a sensible girl. I'm sure she could do very well. After all, you did quite passably when you were left in charge of twin babies. I believe you were not much older than Cassie is now." She shot a conspiratorial glance toward Cassie, who was looking eagerly at her sister. "Besides, this is such a momentous occasion that Kitty and I are in far more need of you than Freddie is." After a brief hesitation, Frances capitulated and was given a hug and glowing look by her younger sister, who dashed off to inform her patient.

"Truly," Lady Streatham continued after the little girl had left, "he needs no care—just confinement to his bed. He'll probably fret less at that if Cassie is there than if you are."

"I suppose you are right," sighed Frances. "But that still does not put me in the mood for a ball."

"You may certainly disregard that, because you know perfectly well you arc never 'in the mood' for a ball," her friend teased.

Frances, forced to admit the accuracy of that observation, also recognized the necessity of her presence at the most critcal moment in her young neighbor's existence. "Very well," she said, and was rewarded with a quick, grateful hug from her ladyship, who declared that she must be on her way in order to keep Kilson from slitting his throat or someone else's. "He does very well organizing Mainwaring's affairs in some outlandish backwater, but he isn't up to London servants. Thank you again, my dear—see you this evening. You will see, everything will come about." And with a wave of her hand, Lady Streatham drove off.

Left alone, Frances wandered back into the drawing room and sat for the better part of an hour staring out of the windows and pulling absently at Wellington's ears. This, though highly gratifying to the little dog who lay on his back with a blissful smile on his lips, did nothing to relieve her mind. In her years as mistress of Cresswell, Frances had become accustomed to emergencies of every variety, from broken legs to pregnant maids, from sick horses to flooded fields. She had schooled herself to deal with them in a cool and rational manner. However, none of her family had been directly involved in these, and she had thus found it fairly easy to remain detached. Now it was a different matter altogether. Her intelligence told her there was nothing to fear. Little boys always had adventures that more often than not ended in disaster. Such unfortunate accidents were a requisite part of any young man's education. But her heart, which had suffered the great losses of a beloved father and mother, anticipated the worst in a manner that made a mockery of her rational approach of life's problems.

Before Lady Frances had been able to demoralize herself completely, she as interrupted in the middle of her visions of doom by Aunt Harriet. "Buck up, my girl. You really don't want to make a cake of yourself over this. If you weren't everlastingly letting your infernal sense of responsibility for the family's welfare cloud your senses, you would remember that you were no older than Frederick when you fell off your own pony. Not only were you dead to the world for an entire day, you broke your wrist as well.''

"You're right, of course.'' She smiled ruefully. ''If Papa were alive, I would be telling him it was nothing a good solid rest wouldn't cure.'' Giving herself a little shake, Frances jumped up. ''And I would be right! If I am not to be an antidote at Kitty's ball, I must get some fresh air and make sure that the dressmaker has done what I asked with the pink-and-white satin.''

"That's my girl. Run along now and I shall endeavor to keep Cassie from completely wearing out her twin with her ministrations.''

Wellington, who enjoyed a walk even more than having his ears stroked, leapt up determined to give his mistress an outing invigorating enough to restore her equanimity and make her positively glow with good health.

19

Wellington performed his duties so well that if Lady Frances, mounting the steps of Mainwaring House that evening, did not outshine all the accredited beauties, she certainly presented a picture of grace and elegance. The delicate pink in her gown enhanced her fine coloring and the sparkle of her mother's diamonds at her throat and in her ears was reflected in her eyes and brought out the warmth of her skin while lending sophistication to the simple line of her dress. Not even the most prejudiced observer would have singled her out among London's beauties as a diamond, but her assured and graceful manner was a refreshing contrast to those tricked out to absurdity in the highest kick of fashion.

If anyone were the cynosure of all eyes that evening, it was Kitty, standing at the head of the stairs with her uncle and the Streathams. The exquisitely simple white muslin, relieved only by cherry ribbons at the sleeves and hem, gave her the ethereal look of a fairy princess just awakened. Her wide brown eyes took in the glittering scene with shy fascination. A delicate flush just rising in her cheeks matched the ribbons in her hair and dress. Her toilette was completed by her mother's pearls, and a delicate nosegay made her truly radiant with youth and anticipation, becomingly timid, but eager to please and be pleased.

"Oh, Frances," she exclaimed breathlessly, "isn't it beautiful?" Her eyes clouded with sisterly sympathy. "Thank you ever so much for coming. I am so glad you were able to, and I do hope Freddie is doing better."

Frances answered with an assurance she was far from feeling. "Yes, a few days of rest and he should be quite the thing." She smiled fondly at her friend. "I am glad I came. You are looking fine as fivepence, Kitty. But I can see that I am not the only one to notice. I'd best let the rest of them meet you." Lady Frances moved along to give room to a hatchet-faced dowager leading a blushing son who could only gaze admiringly as he stammered his greetings.

Lady Streatham kissed Frances on the cheek while her husband pressed her hand and smiled at her warmly. "My dear, not only do you look lovely, but you appear as though you had nothing on your mind more serious than dancing—not that that is not serious business at a ball. Thank you again for coming."

Her husband added his reassurance. "You know Freddie should be sleeping now anyway, my dear. If you were at home, he'd only be begging you for stories instead of getting the rest he needs."

Frances smiled gratefully at him and found herself looking up into Mainwaring's tanned face, where she could read a wealth of understanding and approval in his dark blue eyes. "Now that you and Grandmama are here, our ranks are complete and we can rush to Kitty's defense as she takes the *ton* by storm." The sardonic tone was belied by the encouraging pressure of his fingers and the warmth of his lips as he bent over her hand. Inexplicably Frances felt more comforted and reassured by that simple gesture than she had by all the sage and carefully expressed advice offered by Aunt Harriet, Lady Streatham, and several others.

Before she had time to reflect upon this perverse state of affairs, she was accosted by Bertie. "Hallo, Frances!" he greeted her gaily. "I do hope you are saving the opening dance for me. Except for Kitty, of course, you are quite the finest lady here, and I shall be extremely puffed up if I'm allowed to do the pretty with you." He glanced quickly over his shoulder to ascertain whether he had spoken loudly enough for Kitty to hear, and was gratified to see her blush with pleasure. "Seriously, Fan," he continued in an undertone as he took her arm, "I'll be more than puffed up, I shall be spared a fate worse than death. That Dartington woman has been throwing her platter-faced daughter at me everywhere I turn."

"What, the duchess? But, Bertie, you ae to be congratulated! She will only take the most eligible *partis* for that girl. You are excessively fortunate. Willoughby has been trying to fix his interest for years." Frances tried desperately to keep a straight face, but Bertie's patent dismay was too much and she gave a gurgle of laughter.

"Dash it, Fanny," he complained in an injured tone, "it ain't funny."

"I know," she gasped. "But your face is. How good it is to see you! I can count on you to put things in the right perspective. Here I am worrying about a bump on Freddie's head when you stand in danger of being saddled with an antidote for the rest of your life."

"Give over, Fan. It ain't the least bit funny to be chased, and I mean *chased*, by that hag. My peace is entirely cut up. I can't walk down Bond Street or take a stroll in the park but what she's there. I shall have to get myself invited on one of your educational excursions just to save myself."

She smiled sympathetically. "You're too well-mannered for your own good. You need to give her a sharp set-down."

He nodded. "Several of them, I should think." He added gloomily, "But it takes such a devilish lot of work to think one up. Tell you what." He brightened. "You're good with words. You think of some during this set and I'll practice on you when there's a waltz." And, his equanimity restored, he led her gracefully through the opening quadrille.

To Lady Frances' utter astonishment, she was able to forget Freddie in the music and the steps of the dance. Bertie's diverting chatter was just what she needed at the moment. Knowing that his insouciance hid a very kind heart, she half-suspected that the story of Lady Dartington had been concocted on the spot to take her mind off more serious things.

When the set broke up, he led her over to the corner where Lady Streatham and the dowager marchioness were surveying the festivities with barely concealed satisfaction. "Haven't seen the place so crowded since you were puffed off, Elizabeth," the old lady chortled gleefully. "You and Mainwaring have done Kitty proud. Shouldn't wonder if this ain't one of the events of the Season." She nodded sagely and turned to a breathless Kitty, who was being restored to her chaperones by an eager young man.

"Oh, Frances, isn't it just like a fairy tale?" the girl asked when she had had a moment to catch her breath. Then, remembering that she was now a grown-up young lady, "But, of course, it is a sad crush, isn't it?"

"A terrible squeeze," Frances agreed, shaking her head gravely before quizzing her. "Are you enjoying it, then? I am so glad." Kitty barely had time for an enthusiastic nod before another swain appeared to lead her away.

Lady Streatham broke her own discussion with the dowager concerning Kitty's probable success, the possible choices she might have among the various eager young men, and a shrewd reckoning of their eligibility, to turn to Frances. "But are you enjoying yourself? Almost any young girl . . . well, any impressionable young girl," she amended, remembering the misery that had been Frances' first Season, "is bound to enjoy herself at her own ball if she is not an antidote and is elegantly dressed. It is the older, more critical, but still young ladies I worry about such as you." This was said with a meaningful look.

"Me?" Frances demanded in some surprise. "What can it signify, how I feel?"

"Really, Frances, for a bright girl, sometimes you are a muttonhead! Did it never occur to you to do something for the sheer pleasure of it? Must you do everything for a reason, and a reason that usually involves helping someone else?"

"Of course, but . . ." Frances was at a moment's loss as the truth of Lady Elizabeth's observation sank in. She shut her mouth with a snap.

"If you won't look after your own amusement, may I induce you to take care of mine?" a deep voice at her elbow interrupted some rather unpleasant revelations. She whirled around to meet the marquess's quizzical smile. "Come . . ." He held out a shapely hand. "Waltz with me. I have spent the entire evening thus far trying to get blushing young women to speak to me, pompous dowagers to be silent, blushing young men to speak to blushing young women, and no one has spoken two sensible words to *me* the entire evening." Lady Streatham had voiced her hope that Frances was having a good time. Her cousin was determined to carry this out. He had kept his eye on Frances' progress around the room, and seeing her free, had rather abruptly left a dashing young matron who had been casting languishing glances at him, to arrive in time to hear the end of Lady Elizabeth's remarks. He wholeheartedly agreed with her observations and thus ascribed the rush of warmth he felt when Lady Frances smiled at him to mere sympathy for one who bore too many responsibilities. If he had thought about it at all, he might have realized that this agreeable feeling could more accurately be ascribed to the way her hazel eyes widened with pleasure and seemed, along with an enchanting smile, to sparkle for him alone. But he did not stop to wonder any of these things, giving himself up instead to the pleasure of whirling around the floor with someone whose movements matched his to perfection.

His partner's feelings mirrored his as completely as her steps. It was true that she rarely did anything without a very good reason, but for the moment she was content to forget everything except the joy of gliding over the floor and the agreeable sensation of being expertly guided in the marquess's firm clasp.

For a time neither broke the spell, but the marquess, misinterpreting Frances' abstracted expression, demanded bluntly, "Are you still blue-deviled about that ridiculous brother of yours? Because you shouldn't be, you know."

She was startled out of her reverie, blushed, and admitted, "No, in truth, I wasn't."

He cocked an incredulous eyebrow.

"If you must know, I was thinking how much I was enjoying this dance." She looked impishly up at him. Decidedly it wasn't the standard answer for a society lady, but it was a gratifying one. Her eyes clouded. "I know I shouldn't worry about him, and ordinarily I wouldn't. After all, I did nearly the same thing myself once. It's just that I have lost two of the people I care most about in the world, and now, if the least little thing happens to any of the family, I fear the worst. It's silly to let a little thing like that overset one, I know . . .'' Her voice trailed off.

''My child, there's not the least need to excuse yourself.''

''But I detest such missishness, and fear that at the same time I am turning into the protective type of female I heartily loathe.''

''You need to inspire Freddie to teach Wellington equestrian tricks instead of essaying them himself. You know how that misbegotten mongrel adores horses and attention.''

''He's not a mongrel!'' Lady Frances rose instantly to her pet's defense. She smiled. ''But he *is* virtually indestructible. How clever you are. But enough of my affairs. We must be the only ones in the entire room who aren't discussing this ball or Kitty's chances of becoming an incomparable. And speaking of incomparables, who is that Adonis partnering her now? He looks to be so besotted as to be in danger of suffocating.''

Mainwaring glanced in his ward's direction. ''My God, now we are in the basket!''

She was puzzled. ''He seems perfectly unexceptionable to me.''

''That, my dear, is Willoughby's eldest.''

''What could be better—a title, an old name, and a fortune?''

''But he's barely dry behind the ears, and to make matters worse, he's a budding poet,'' he finished in accents of disgust.

''That's as may be, but I fail to understand your objections.''

He snorted. ''They're both babes in arms. He's as romantic as she is, and neither one of them has the least notion how to go on in the world.''

''Well, of all the queer starts!'' she gasped. ''And why, pray tell, did you come to Cresswell if not to convince me that it was in Kitty's best interests to be married and off your hands as soon as possible?'' A dangerous glint aappeared in the corner of her eye. ''Doubtless you worked yourself up then for no other purpose than to brangle with me.''

H had the grace to smile sheepishly. ''Will you forgive me if I admit you were totally in the right of it? She is a dear girl, but she does want some town bronze and definitely a mature and sensible man for a husband.''

She was mollified and impressed too by this handsome concession. Her mischievous smile as she magnanimously forgave him was so appealing that he decided there was a great deal to be said for humility.

The dance had long since ended, but the two of them, so engrossed in their conversation, might never have noticed it had not Bertie come up and said meaningfully, ''I'm ready now, so you must dance this next with me, as you promised.'' Frances laughed gaily, nodded a smiling thank-you to Mainwaring, and whirled off, leaving his lordship slightly miffed at the easy way she quitted him to share secrets with his friend.

I must be in my dotage, he thought. A chit with an unbecoming habit of arriving at and voicing her own opinions is on intimate terms with the friend I asked to take charge of her. I should be congratulating myself on my own cleverness at ridding myself of her with such aplomb. And I *do* congratulate myself, he averred with total lack of conviction.

A sharp voice at his elbow observed, ''I like that gel. She's got style and she's got sense—a looker, too.''

''A little too much sense for her own good, but . . . she does have a certain something.''

Unlike her grandson, the perspicacious old dowager marchioness had no difficulty in interpreting the cause of the slight frown creasing his brow. She chuckled gleefully and settled herself to await further developments. It was going to be a long time. Mainwaring had not the slightest inkling of how much Lady Frances meant to him. And, by the looks of it, the girl was no more aware of her feelings than he was. When and if they tumbled to their situation, the ensuing courtship would be even more interesting. The dowager hadn't enjoyed herself so much in years.

Meanwhile, on the dance floor Lady Frances finally broke in on her companion's thoughts. ''Out with it, Bertie. The suspense is killing me. The look on your face tells me that you have devised A PLAN.''

A smile of satisfaction spread across his features. ''It's quite

simple, really,'' he admitted modestly. ''I shall just tell her I
ain't the marrying kind, and if I were, her daughter ain't the
kind I would want to marry.'' Frances eyed him skeptically.
''Well, it's the truth, ain't it?'' he muttered defensively.

''Oh, I'm not challenging your veracity, merely your
optimism. I think you underestimate Lady Dartington's
determination and her desperation. A woman of her kidney isn't
put off by something as paltry as the truth. Let me see,'' she
ruminated. ''I shall tell her that Lady Streatham and I had had
you in mind for her daughter until we began to wonder about
your past.''

''Past!'' he exclaimed indignantly. ''I haven't got a past!''

''That's exactly why we've been wondering about it.''

Comprehension dawned. ''I must say, Fan, that's devilish
clever. Because the less you say, the worse she'll think it is,
and that old beldame is quite gothic. Even my mother thinks
she's hideously straightlaced, and the Mater's so rigid herself
it don't bear thinking of.'' He maneuvered her deftly back to
the corner where Lady Streatham and the dowager were holding
forth.

These two ladies looked slightly conscious as Frances
approached, but she was too busy trying to catch a glimpse of
Kitty to notice. They had been amusing themselves the past half-
hour counting the number of times Mainwaring's eyes had
strayed to whatever part of the room happened to be graced by
Frances and her partner at that moment. Naturally, Julian was
the perfect host, moving easily among his guests, chatting with
this dowager, helping along that young woman's reputation by
stopping to talk with her, giving his opinions on the probable
speed of Stapleton's new bays to a group of young bucks, but
this behavior seemed curiously mechanical to those who knew
him best. In fact, after his last waltz, he had seemed, for
Mainwaring at least, unusually abstracted.

He approached now as he saw Frances joining them. She had
laughed and chatted gaily enough all evening, but to him her
face looked pale and slightly drawn. He smiled kindly at her.
''Do me a favor and sit the next one out with me. I fear I am
getting too old for this frantic frivolity.''

''Doing it much to brown, my lord, for one who has just

returned from Vienna. I expect there might be some skills of yours that became rusty there, but dancing was not one of them.''

''No? Well, let's just say that I had enough of dancing and diplomacy to last a lifetime, and not nearly enough rational conversation. But do let me get you some refreshment.'' He disappeared into the supper room, his tall form towering above those around him. Unbidden, and certainly unexpected, the thought came to Frances that with his broad shoulders, severe dress, and air of command, he dwarfed almost everyone else in the room. She had never really paid much attention to what men looked like. She either liked or disliked them, but recognizing the attraction that a strong face, responsive dark blue eyes, and well-knit physique could hold was a novel sensation. Before she had time enough to explore and feel threatened by this sensation, the marquess had returned to ply her with a variety of delicacies and an absurd description of Kilson's struggles to adjust to the snobberies of London servants. She enjoyed it hugely, for he was a good storyteller, but some of the strain remained at the back of her eyes. He frowned slightly and offered to have someone call her carriage. ''You have done your duty here and I am persuaded you would feel much more the thing if you were to get some rest.'' She started to protest, but with so little conviction that he soon overrode her objections and summoned one of the footmen hovering at the side of the ballroom. ''I shall spirit you out so no one will know you have left. Besides, you have made your appearance, so if you are now missed, no one can fault you.'' She smiled gratefully and allowed him to lead her to her carriage.

Before handing her in, he adjured her to get a good rest. ''Are you still worried?'' She shook her head slightly. Not at all satisfied by such an equivocal response, he cupped her chin in his fingers and tilted it up. ''Now, look at me and tell me you promise not to fret yourself, especially since you know I shall call tomorrow to give that young would-be equestrian a severe talking-to.''

Frances looked into his dark blue eyes and read such a wealth of concern that she was too touched to reply. She nodded. ''That's my girl.'' He handed her into the carriage, but retained her hand in his strong clasp. "No more giving way to irrational fears. Promise me?"

She looked at him and for an instant as transfixed by the intensity of his gaze. "I promise." He squeezed her hand ever so gently before placing it in her lap, shutting the door and sending her on her way. She leaned back against the squabs. It had been quite a day. One that had forced her through a gamut of emotions: fear for Freddie, unexpected enjoyment of the ball, and now an odd feeling of some special bond, some private communication with Mainwaring. She didn't know what to make of it or of the attention he seemed to be paying her, and she wasn't at all certain how she felt about it. At the time, she had enjoyed the strength of his arms around her as they danced, sensing a special friendliness in the smile he seemed to reserve just for her, and had appreciated the attractive picture he presented as he moved among his guests. She hadn't thought much about it until he had held her hand and looked at her in such a way. Then she began to realize just how disturbingly attractive he really was to her. She felt slightly breathless and excited. Now it dawned on her that she had felt that way with him several times this evening. Whatever it is, it won't do, my girl, she admonished herself sternly. Men, particularly those of Lord Mainwaring's discriminating taste, aren't likely to feel anything for one such as you, much less heightened pulses. Best to forget it all. With this salutary thought, which somehow vanished as quickly as it came, she fell into a pleasant reverie that lasted until they arrived in Brook Street.

20

True to his word, Lord Mainwaring appeared in Brook Street at the unfashionably early hour of ten o'clock the next morning. He too had undergone some soul-searching the night before, and as he sauntered leisurely along, all his thoughts from the previous evening returned with a vengeance. Until the ball he had enjoyed Lady Frances' company for her quick grasp of a variety of subjects, her interested and intelligent comments, and her complete disregard for any of the flirtatious arts most women practiced assiduously on him. He admired her elegant taste and the quiet courage with which she shouldered enormous responsibilities, but he certainly had not felt anything more for her than admiration and a friendly wish to alleviate some of her responsibilities. Somehow, as they had been whirling around the floor, things had changed—so subtly that it had been some time before he was aware of the difference. She had felt so slight and graceful in his arms that her brief admission of her fears for her graceless brother tore at his heart. When she had tried to smile and quickly blink away the tears in her clear hazel eyes, he had wanted nothing more than to crush her in his arms and kiss the lips that would tremble in spite of her best efforts. He too had sensed that strong bond between them as he helped her into her carriage, and had tried ruthlessly to suppress these unwanted and most disquieting feelings. *You're returning to your salad days, my boy. You've been away from the charms of London and London beauties so long that when one of them looks at you gratefully you are knocked into the middle of next week. She's only one of a dozen pretty faces—and not the prettiest of them either.* But he knew he was wrong, that beauty had very little to do with it. *Botheration! The more you try to define it, the worse case you become.* It was almost with relief that he recognized Lady Jersey beckoning to him. That lively lady's naughty flirtation had soon banished all such unwelcome reflections.

Fortunately for his peace of mind, Lady Frances was not at home when he arrived. As a treat after her nursing of Freddie, she had taken Cassie to the Tower, as Cassie had been wishing to view the lions at greater length than they had the previous visit. Frances had come home the previous night to find the little girl reading to Freddie in a valiant effort to put her twin to sleep and keep herself awake. She had barely managed to keep from bursting with pride as she shushed her sister. "Be very quiet, Fan. I've just now managed to get him to sleep." She nodded importantly. "He was a little feverish, but I bathed his face with lavender water. I believe it is said a good night's sleep is the best thing for a fever." Frances had no trouble in identifying the source of this wisdom, having heard Aunt Harriet intone it repeatedly during her childhood illnesses.

So it was that Mainwaring had the patient all to himself when Higgins showed him into the nursery. Its occupant was sitting up in bed scowling at *Robinson Crusoe*. He glanced up fretfully when he heard Higgins cough, but on seeing his visitor, became instantly animated. "Sir, I did not expect to see you here!" he exclaimed in astonishment, but with such a look of unfeigned admiration that the marquess began to question his ability to measure up to the demigod status to which Freddie seemed determined to elevate him.

"Well, cawker, I came to see how you did. And since I think this, ahem, unfortunate incident is partly my fault, I've come to take your mind off any ill effects of your adventure and to keep your sister from feeling compelled to amuse you. I thought you might enjoy this. I found it rather well done." He handed the invalid the latest engravings of some "prime bits of blood" done in the manner of Stubbs.

"Oh, sir," Freddie breathed. "They're wonderful! They do look so real they seem to step right off the page, don't they?" Then, remembering his manners, he added shyly, "I do thank you. It's very kind of you to think of me."

"Not at all. As I say, I feel slightly responsible for putting the idea in your head. Besides, I know just how tedious recuperation can be. I once took a rather ugly gash one night in India from a dacoit who was trying to break into the shipping office. It wasn't all that bad, just across my arm, but it was deep, and out there you never know what complications will occur, what with their dreadful fevers and such. I knew that for my own good I should stay quiet, but I can tell you it was dull as dishwater lying there with nothing but my account books for amusement. However, I was right to do so, and I breezed right through it, unlike another poor fellow I knew. He cut his hand on a nail in a packing barrel he was unloading, contracted the most violent fever, and was gone within the day."

"Fanny said you had traveled, but I thought she meant around the Continent, you know, the Grand Tour and the Congress. She didn't tell me you'd been in India. Did you see any tigers? Were there lots of deadly snakes and spiders?" Freddie asked hopefully.

The marquess had purposely brought in his accident to amuse the boy, but he had underestimated the curiosity of an intelligent eleven-year-old starved for tales of masculine adventure. Before he knew it, he was regaling Freddie with one story after another, from Cape Town to Calcutta. It did him good in the rather stifling atmosphere of mid-Season social London to recall those free and easy days when his quick intelligence and athletic skills were more useful and more admired than his name and the size of his rent roll. And he truly enjoyed making Freddie's eyes shine with excitement as he drew exotic pictures of tiger hunts, ships battling monsoons, and hostile rajahs. Moreover, he was impressed with the thoughtfulness revealed by the boy's questions and felt a real sense of pride in being able to bring to him a world that was at once diverting and educational. He experienced a sense of usefulness that he had not felt in a long time. In fact, he couldn't remember when he had last sensed that he, as a person apart from all he stood for, was important to anyone. Having spent a rather lonely childhood as the second son of a father who concentrated all his affections and energies on his heir, Julian had never looked on children as anything but necessary encumbrances for other people concerned with carrying on family names and traditions. He was surprised how much he enjoyed Freddie's company. He was even more surprised, when Frances appeared, to discover that he had been there an hour and a half.

She had come dashing up the stairs in a most unladylike fashion to check on her little brother. When she saw him, arms encircling his knees, listening with rapt attention to a description of tracking a man-killing elephant, she screeched to a halt, but it was too late to keep from interrupting. "Fanny, look at this capital book Lord Mainwaring brought me! And he's been telling me the most bang-up things about India. They make the Greek bandits who attacked your trip to Delphi seem pretty tame, I can tell you."

She smiled at the marquess, shrugging apologetically. "I can see that my one claim to fame, my storytelling skill, has been completely cast in the shade. I can only warn you, my lord, that with fame comes responsibility, and you will now be hounded to death."

"Oh, Fan, come now, you know I don't *hound* you and I certainly wouldn't bother his lordship," protested her outraged sibling. "Besides," he added with his engaging grin, "I know how much store you grown-ups set by learning, and these stories are as good as a geography lesson any day."

"Freddie, my boy, you are incorrigible even when you are ill. I wish you'd gotten a stronger bump on the head. But, there, I only came up to check on you, not to give you a bear-garden jaw. I'll let Lord Mainwaring finish his tale."

As she closed the door behind her, Freddie whispered conspiratorially to his companion, "She's a great gun, and I do love her. She doesn't ever nag or worry. But sometimes it is nice to talk to a man. I mean, women don't have many adventures, do they, sir? Fan has set-tos with Snythe and frequently she has to give Farmer Stubbs a talking-to, but those aren't really exciting. About the most dangerous thing she ever did was to go tell a wicked-looking Gypsy king that his band couldn't camp on our lands because she didn't want them stealing the chickens. But you'd never find her doing anything as thrilling as hunting a tiger.''

Privately Mainwaring thought that Lady Frances Cresswell led a more hair-raising existence than most of his London acquaintances, but he realized the futility of explaining that to a bloodthirsty eleven-year-old. "Well, I do agree she is an excellent sister. You mustn't be too hard on her. After all, she isn't as old as I and she's been too busy looking after Cresswell and you two to get herself into as many ticklish spots as I have.''

Freddie was much struck by this novel view. He had never really stopped to consider that his sister might have wished to do something else besides managing the estate and bringing up him and Cassie. It suddenly occurred to him that teaching them Latin and geometry might be as dull and dry for her as it was for them. After all, they were only doing it for the first time and she was doing it for the second! Such drudgery didn't bear thinking of. Being a sympathetic lad, he was already concerned about the worry his accident might have caused her, but he had never stopped to think that the routine of daily existence at Cresswell might be as unadventurous for her as it was for him— more so because she wasn't constantly falling out of trees or tearing her clothes or getting caught trying to free the rabbits in Snythe's snares.

Mainwaring said good-bye to the patient, warning him that though his head might feel perfectly recovered to him in a horizontal position, any attempt to assume a vertical one would probably make him extremely unwell. Freddie grinned. "I may get into scrapes, but I'm not a complete bacon-brain, sir.''

"No,'' agreed his lordship. "But you certainly are an impudent scamp.''

The marquess stopped in the front parlor, where he found Frances sorting through a sheaf of bills and frowning over the price of feed. She rose, saying in her frank way, "How very kind of you to visit and to hit upon the very thing to keep him quiet.'' She would have gone on, but Mainwaring dismissed her thanks with a wave of his hand.

"I like Freddie. He's a bright lad and he has a great deal of spunk. Besides, if I hadn't taken you all to Astley's, he never would have gotten such a maggot in his brain in the first place.''

She interrupted, "Well, that is complete nonsense, because you know any child even halfway interested in horses feels compelled to experiment just as he did. After all, I had a very similar escapade and I am sure you did too.''

He smiled rather bitterly, she thought. "No, in a vain attempt to win my father's approval, I was a model child.''

"Thus your excessively adventurous existence in subsequent years,'' she teased.

He grinned. "You must admit that these 'excessive adventures,' as you so skeptically call them, served their purpose today. I told Freddie such a hair-raising story about complications attending a seemingly simple accident that I promise you he won't stir from his bed for days.''

The quizzing look in her eyes disappeared, to be replaced by one of shy gratitude. "How very good you are to us, and just when you've had to take on such irksome new responsibilities of your own.''

He stood looking down at her, but his thoughts were elsewhere, and there was a rather fierce expression in his dark blue eyes. "My lord . . .'' She claimed his wandering attention.

His eyes softened. "Did you have no male relatives?''

Somewhat taken aback, she replied, "No, but we had no need of them.'' She raised her eyebrows, and a distinctly frosty note crept into her voice. "Are you again questioning my capabilities? I assure you I have more sense than Papa's nearest relatives, distant as they are, all rolled into one.''

"Gently, my child. I have no quarrel with your obvious capabilities. I was merely thinking of you and the time you are forced to lavish on others when you should be spending it on yourself.''

"And what would I do with that time? Do as everyone else would have me do and flit from one social event to another, flirting with all and sundry to catch myself either someone who spends his entire time and energy choosing and changing clothes or some beefy squire who does nothing but hunt and is a great deal worse than I at managing Cresswell?''

He took both her hands in a firm clasp. ''Don't fly into a pelter. I would, if I could, give you time to ride or to write without eternally having to stop and cope with some problem. I would wish you free from worrying about the twins' education so you could visit all the museums, attend all the lectures, and enjoy all the concerts and plays that you wish.''

She glanced at him in some surprise. He truly was thinking of her, and showing an understanding that no one had ever shown before. Such sympathy quite undid her, and tears pricked at her eyelids as she gazed down at her hands in his. He raised them to his lips, forcing her to look up at him. ''Don't wear yourself out, my girl. You take things so much to heart that *your* health is in far more danger than Freddie's.'' He pressed a warm kiss on each hand, gave her an encouraging smile, and was gone, leaving her in a daze.

Finally she shook her head and returned to her bills, but try as she would, she could not focus on the figures. She kept seeing, instead, the concern in his eyes, hearing the understanding in his voice, and feeling the pressure of his lips on her hands. She tried to recapture her equanimity by explaining away his concern: he is so accustomed to running everything, to being admired and flattered, that he can't bear the thought that he might be responsible for some mishap. All this attention is to keep you from thinking the same thing. Now that he's done his duty and called on you, he'll think no more about it. But try as she would to put it down to arrogance, she kept remembering his sympathetic reading of her life and inter- pretation of her dreams.

21

Contrary to Lady Frances' prediction, Lord Mainwaring continued to demonstrate his interest in the invalid and his family. Ostensibly, he came to see Freddie, maintaining that he didn't trust such an adventuresome spirit for a minute, but he managed to inject some enthusiasm into Cassie, who was at the same time concerned for her twin and ever so slightly jealous of all the attention he was receiving. As she later confided with great pride to her sister, "He came and asked Higgins if I were free to drive in the park, just as if I were a grown-up lady. And he has such a bang-up pair and drives so well that simply everyone was looking at us." Freddie took this in good part, though he would have willingly traded all his tin soldiers to Cassie for the honor of driving with his hero.

Even Aunt Harriet had a good word to say for him. "He brought some excellent cuttings that his gardener had sent, as well as some fine fruit from the hothouse at Camberly, and how he talked that uppity gardener out of them is more than I can tell."

Despite his attention to the other Cresswells, his real concern was for Frances, and he made sure that every day she got to the park for some fresh air and adult conversation. His earlier impressions were confirmed and he found her informed and interested in a wide variety of subjects. Their discussions ranged from Prinny's evolving designs for his Pavilion to the constant bickerings at the Congress of Vienna to crop rotation. Lady Frances was rediscovering the joys of intelligent companionship, a component of her life that had vanished with her father's death. How delightful it was to be able to share ideas and worries with someone who could understand them and offer a perspective different from her own. It was rare that she could talk with neighbors about anything more theoretical than breeding horses, and even then, they looked askance at any ideas more recent than the previous century. Here was someone who was ready to try new things, who had an inquiring mind that he stimulated by constant reading and travel. This adventurous outlook, as much as the information he had gathered from a vast array of experiences, excited her interest and her own curiosity, making her realize how much of her own personal development she had been neglecting for the past few years.

They had just considered in great depth the relative merits of a free, relatively informal exchange in international politics so beloved by Castlereagh. Having thrashed out the pros and cons to their mutual satisfaction, they were driving along in companionable silence, enjoying the fineness of the day, when the marquess suddenly turned to her, remarking, ''Freddie tells me that you are always having some set-to or other with Snythe.''

This was dangerous ground, and Frances considered for a moment before venturing mildly, ''Well, he isn't the easiest person to rub along with.''

''Meaning . . . ?'' he prompted, raising one dark brow.

She saw that he was not going to let her escape with generalities, but remembering the great exception he had taken to her previous criticism, she trod warily. ''He doesn't know how to get along very well with your tenants or mine.''

''To be exact, he bullies those who stand most in need of his advice and makes unwelcome advances to their daughters, while behaving most obsequiously to the other, more respectable elements in the district.''

''He is the most odious toad of a man it has ever been my misfortune to meet!'' she responded, her eyes kindling at some unfortunate memories. Yet she was impressed at his accurate reading of the man's character and his grasp of the situation.

"And what would you have me do with such a man? Turning him over to local justice will merely serve to exacerbate the situation. He will become a more intolerable bully and a more groveling toad than ever."

She looked up in some surprise. His solicitation of her opinion, for which he had taken her to task a few months earlier, was unexpected. A man as accustomed to command and as sure of himself as Julian Mainwaring was not given to asking advice—especially from women who had only a particle of his experience and were much younger besides. She half-suspected him of mockery, but one surreptitious glance out of the corner of her eye assured her that he was serious.

In fact, she would have been even more astonished to learn that the man she had just labeled as self-assured was, at that moment, at a loss. He was trying to decide what it was about his companion that made him find her so charming. She was no more than pretty, and he was a man who could, and did, demand nothing less than overwhelming beauty in his mistresses. In spite of her air of quiet elegance, she was not at all fashionable, nor did she care to be. She had not the least notion how to carry on a flirtation. In fact, she was far more likely to ask him about improving her stock than she was to admire the cut of his coat, the truly legendary quality of his horseflesh, his rig, or his skill in managing both. No, she had none of the standard qualitites of the women he usually admired, but somehow she made him feel more appeciated for the qualities that were uniquely his than the most flattering of his mistresses. He liked the frank way she looked at him when talking to him. The questions she asked revealed how closely she listened to what he had to say and how much she respected his judgments. Only a very few of his closest and oldest friends recognized how carefully he considered before forming them. And none of them felt close enough to quiz him in quite the manner that she did. In a way, this teasing was complimentary because it showed that she believed him aware enough of her high opinion of him to recognize that her criticisms were purely ironic. It was an intimacy that no woman except his grandmother had shared with him. He found it endeared her to him and touched him at the same time. In spite of their early differences, she had come to value his opinion and to trust him as a friend. Oddly enough, he found this trust more gratifying than many greater honors he had achieved over the years.

Her thoughtful reply interrupted his speculations. "Yes, I know it is difficult, especially as he is someone who bitterly resents criticism and is so relentless in bearing a grudge. What if you were to send him to one of your establishments in India or the West Indies? You could allow him to think of it as an advancement, a chance to make his fortune, when in reality you would probably be throwing him among a group of people who are as conniving as he and would make short work of him. They certainly wouldn't allow him to bully them as the poor people around Camberly and Cresswell do."

Mainwaring was much struck by her perspicacity and the soundness of her suggestion. "A very good idea. You have an excellent sense of people. I wish it were you I could send to oversee my affairs."

"A fine mess I should make of them if I can't even keep an eleven-year-old from making a fool of himself." Nevertheless, she flushed with pleasure at this unexpected praise.

They found themselves in such charity with each other that they were both surprised and sorry at how swiftly the time passed. It seemed they had been gone no time at all when they completed their tour of the park and returned to Brook Street. In fact, they had been out the better part of two hours. Higgins was the only member of the household to note this, but its significance was not lost on him. "I can't recall when Miss Fanny took such pleasure in anyone's company, excepting her dear father's, of course," he confided to Cook. Though she had been in name, as well as fact, the head of Cresswell for some years now, and had been managing the household in a highly efficient and satisfactory manner, she was still "Miss Fanny" to her loyal servants.

Kilson and Higgins were not the only ones observing with interest the growing intimacy between Lady Frances Cresswell and Lord Julian Mainwaring, Marquess of Camberly. In the opulently decorated house in Mount Street, Lady Vanessa

Welford was beginning to be seriously annoyed at the turn of events. She was aware of precisely the amount of time her lover was spending in Brook Street, exactly the number of drives during which Lady Frances was his companion, not to mention the dances when she had been his partner, and she was not the least bit pleased. She would never have stooped to ordering her servants to spy on him for her, but Polly, her abigail, soon discovered that the number of dresses thrown her way because her ladyship ''couldn't bear to be seen another time in that old rag'' increased in proportion to the number of reports she brought of the marquess's doings. And a certain footman noticed that Miss Polly acted far more interested in him if he were able to tell her precisely where Lord Mainwaring's equipage had seen that day.

The friendship between Mainwaring and Frances had even come to the attention of some sharp-eyed members of the *ton*, who were not behindhand in putting this intriguing tidbit to the best possible use. Thus at Lady Billingsford's card party, the marquess's mistress was forced to appear conveniently hard of hearing when Lady Stavely confided to her bosom friend Edwina Hamilton in tinkling tones clearly audible throughout the room, ''I do believe Mainwaring must be looking for a wife. He seems to have changed his preference for older, ahem, 'sophisticated' women to those who have a number of childbearing years left. Lady Frances Cresswell is a delightful girl. I would be happy to see her so well-settled, and it does seem as though he's trying to fix his interest there. My dear, he's her constant companion, they say.''

Lady Welford, a determined smile pinned on her face, never stopped to consider that Lady Stavely's good opinion of the girl she would never have noticed two months ago had less to do with the delightfulness of Lady Frances than with the fact that until the advent of Lord Mainwaring, Lord Stavely had been Lady Welford's most devoted escort. Fuming inwardly, she managed to continue her hand, ignoring the knowing looks cast in her direction. She maintained her equanimity with aplomb, but took her leave as soon as it was possible to do so without occasioning further comment.

She spent a restless night pacing the floor, working on various ploys to heighten the marquess's dwindling interest. But no sooner had she conjured up one scheme than she discarded it as being too obvious or too desperate. Morning found her no closer to any plan of attack and a good deal more frustrated. Of course, the sleepless night had not improved her countenance, and it seemed to her, after nearly an hour spent contemplating her reflection in the mirror, that she had never looked more hag-ridden. Wrinkles and gray hairs, which had never dared show themselves before, now popped up all over. By the time her maid appeared with her morning chocolate, she was in a thoroughly bad humor, which she alleviated only slightly by giving the poor girl a regular tongue-lashing for having let it become lukewarm. The arrival of a new walking dress of a muslin so fine it made only the barest pretense of covering her limbs restored her humor somewhat, as did the arrival of a huge bouquet from a callow youth who had seen her at the opera the previous evening. She had no intention of allowing him to dangle after her, but the intensity of the infatuation was gratifying nevertheless.

Several hours later, a testimony to the art and artifice of her abigail and the expert hands of a wonderful new French hairdresser, she was at last able to face herself in the mirror again with satisfaction. The elegant visage looking back at her was encouraging enough to send her off to display her charms in the park. The flimsy walking dress, trimmed with deep flounces that made it cling even more, was further enhanced by a bonnet of straw-colored satin, matching parasol, green kid sandals, and a green sarcenet pelisse that she left open to reveal the full effect of the muslin dress. And she was able to console herself with the thought that though she lacked the youth of Lady Frances, she certainly was quite at the top of the mode, something which even the most enthusiastic of Frances' admirers could not say of that young lady.

Fortune, so noticeably absent the previous evening, was smiling on her today. She had not gone ten steps into the park when she encountered Mainwaring cutting through on his way to Mainwaring House. "Julian," she trilled, shrugging the pelisse open further. "How delightful to run into you. I haven't seen you this age."

The marquess did not look best pleased at this encounter. "Hello, Vanessa, you're looking exquisite as usual," he greeted her, edging in the direction of Grosvenor Square.

Not about to let such a golden opportunity escape her, Lady Welford slipped her hand through his arm and leaned her ample charms tantalizingly close. "Do walk with me a little way," she invited, gazing meltingly up at him and fluttering dark lashes.

He was fairly caught, but managed to stifle his annoyance with a semblance of good humor. "Very well, but I can't spend too long, as I am taking tea with my grandmother."

Lady Welford knew very well what that old tartar thought of her grandson's latest flirt, and she also knew that she demanded punctuality. Sighing inwardly, she determined to make the most of the little time she had. Try as she would to win his lordship's attention with her most amusing stories and her most scandalous *on-dits*, she could see that his thoughts remained elsewhere. She eventually decided to abandon her verbal attempts to attract his interest in favor of a more physical approach. She had just draped herself more voluptuously along his arm and tilted her gaze even more seductively up at him when they rounded a bend and came face-to-face with Lady Frances in charge of a schoolroom party.

Freddie had adhered so scrupulously to Mainwaring's strictures that he had recovered rapidly and was soon pronounced well enough to venture out-of-doors. Cassie, in-spite of her drive with his lordship, had been frantic to get out and enjoy the beautiful weather. Thus at the soonest possible moment, Frances had taken them for a leisurely turn around the park. In addition to the twins, she had invited Ned, who was often left to his own devices while Kitty made her social rounds. He provided a quieting influence on the twins' high spirits that was especially useful at this stage in Freddie's recuperation. Naturally, Wellington was not about to allow any one of the Cresswells out without his valiant escort. Who knew what horrible mongrels might be lurking in the bushes? And even Nelson, his courage bolstered by the fineness of the day and the size of the expedition, overcame his fear of London traffic enough to join them. Frances had her hands full trying to convince Wellington not to chase after Mr. Poodle Byng's carriage to challenge the right of his canine companion, that supercilious cur, to respect from all other dogs. Cassie, Freddie, and Ned were in whoops at the absurdity of Mr. Byng's turnout. Thus they were a sizable, miscellaneous, and noisy group that approached Lady Welford and the marquess.

Confronted with the source of her ill temper, who was, furthermore, at a distinct disadvantage, Lady Welford seized the opportunity to eliminate the recipient of so much of the marquess's time and attention. As Lord Mainwaring helplessly ground his teeth and made the unavoidable introductions, she smiled indulgently at the younger woman and remarked with ill-concealed condescension, "Small wonder we see so little of you in society, Lady Frances, when you have all these claims on your attention. Of course, with these responsibilities and your bluestocking propensities, it is no wonder you haven't the time to be fashionable."

For a moment Lady Frances was speechless at the unexpected intensity of the attack. She was simply astonished by the animosity she saw in the other woman's eyes, and totally at a loss to explain it. However, she was not about to be snubbed by one such as Lady Welford. Gazing limpidly up at her opponent, with the faintest of smiles she explained, "But you see, I would so much rather be *respectable* than fashionable." Her deceptively mild tone was not lost on anyone as she continued, "I've heard so much about you, Lady Welford. I am glad I had the opportunity to meet you, but Freddie has not been well. I am sure you will forgive us for hurrying him home. Come, children. Good day to you, Lord Mainwaring, Lady Welford." With that she turned her back on both of them and shepherded the group along in the opposite direction.

An unbecoming shade of red suffused Vanessa Welford's features. Eyes narrowed, she hissed furiously, "Why, that impudent little nobody! How dared she! How dreadfully ill-bred of her!"

"Quite the contrary, Vanessa," an icy voice interrupted. "She showed considerable restraint in the face of one of the most vulgar and uncalled-for setdowns it has ever been my dubious privilege to witness.'' If Lady Welford's eyes flashed, her companion's glittered like chips of ice. The set of his jaw and the line of his dark brows were truly alarming as he hurried her to the edge of the park. Catching the attention of a passing hackney, he hailed it and handed her in, instructing the coachman as he did so, ''Take Lady, ahem, *Madam* Welford wherever she wishes to go.'' With that, he handed the man a heavy purse, slammed the door, turned on his heel, and strode furiously back into the park, leaving Vanessa staring after him, prey to the most unpleasant reflections.

Despite his hasty pace, Lord Mainwaring could catch no sight of Frances as he headed angrily back through the park in the direction of Mainwaring House. The disagreeableness of Vanessa's reflections was nothing compared to the turmoil of emotions besieging the marquess. The foremost was anger— anger at himself for allowing her to entrap him as she had that morning, for not rescuing Frances from an unpleasant situation even before Vanessa's insulting remarks, for not retrieving the situation after those remarks. There was blind fury at Vanessa for reading more into his relationship with her than there was, for putting him in such an impossible situation, and for behaving with such gratuitous cruelty. Anger was his instant reaction, but it was followed by a stronger, more complicated sense of unhappiness. The impression that remained with him the longest and the most bitterly was the shock and betrayal he had read in Frances' eyes. It had been almost immediately replaced by the anger that produced her effective reply, but for a brief moment her eyes had revealed the hurt of a loyal pet whose master has turned on it without cause or warning. Julian was tortured with remorse for being the unwitting instrument of such pain, and he wished with all his heart that he could have taken her in his arms then and there and kissed it gently and reassuringly away. And last of all, he was cynically grateful to Vanessa for having shown him at the same time how little he cared for her and how much he valued the friendship and good opinion of Lady Frances Cresswell.

By the time he arrived back at Grosvenor Square, the anger had burnt itself out, leaving him subdued, but with a corroding sense of loss and disillusionment. Kilson was totally mystified. "I ain't never seen himself look like that beforc in all the years I have been with his lordship," he confided later to Alice as he tried to fathom the cause. He nodded sagely. "If you ask me, this bears some watching."

22

"**B**ut, Fanny," protested Cassie, struggling to keep pace with her sister's angry stride, "I thought this was supposed to be a *restful* outing."

"It was," Frances snapped, slackening her pace somewhat. The twins exchanged puzzled glances and hurried along, eager to reach the privacy of the schoolroom, where they could sort out this unusual show of temper.

After bidding a hasty good-bye to Ned, they raced upstairs. "What do you think, Freddie?" his sister demanded. "I just asked her a question and she snapped my head off."

He considered a moment. "I'm not sure, but I think it had to do with Lord Mainwaring's being a friend of that lady. P'raps Fanny thought if he was a friend of that lady's he wouldn't be her friend. And I must say, I don't blame her. I wouldn't like a special friend of mine to be friendly with someone like that. You want to watch out for people like her," he confided darkly. "She has mean eyes. I think she's a bad 'un. We'd better warn Fan to keep a weather eye out for her."

"She doesn't seem to like Fan much either, though I can't think why," observed Cassie. "I wish there were some way we could keep that lady away from his lordship. Maybe we could ask Neddie to keep an eye out, and if she shows up at Mainwaring House, he could discourage her," she added, warming to the plan.

"Nah," scoffed her twin. "Don't be a bacon-brain. Ladies don't call on gentlemen."

"Much you know," she retorted. "Ladies that wear dresses like that do!"

This unexpectedly superior worldly knowledge awed Freddie into silence, but his busy brain was scheming ways to keep his friend the marquess out of the clutches of someone who was so clearly a bad 'un.

Meanwhile, Higgins had stopped Frances in the midst of her angry flight. "The Comte de Vaudron is in the front parlour, my lady."

"Thank you, Higgins," she managed as she stomped upstairs in a most unladylike fashion. Actually, the *comte* was just the person she needed at this particular moment. A combination of the sophisticated man-of-the-world and paternal adviser to her and the twins, he would be able to offer her the exact amount of wisdom and sympathy that the situation warranted.

"*Ma chère Fanny*," he exclaimed, rising to bow gracefully over her hand. His quick glance apprehended the state of affairs and he drew her to the couch, inquiring gently, "*Mais, ma petite*, what has put you in such a pucker? A young lady moving in the highest circles in the *ton* should be *aux anges* instead of wearing a face like a thundercloud."

The sympathetic look and calmly supportive manner almost overset her, and she wished with all her heart that she could climb into his lap and burst into tears, as she had so many years ago in Greece when her pet bird had flown away. "It is nothing, really, *monsieur*." She pushed aside a stray lock of hair, grimacing at her overwrought state.

" 'Uncle Maurice,' please. And I know you, Fanny. You are of such good sense that you do not fly into a pelter over nothing. Come, tell me about it."

And as she had done so many times before, she found herself confiding in him. He sat silent during the entire recital, raising a speculative eyebrow here and there, but otherwise making no comment. When she had finished, he stared thoughtfully into space for some time, wondering exactly how conversant Frances was with his lordship's amorous affairs.

She broke in on his thoughts. "Am I that much of a quiz, then? Is that truly what they say of me?"

He snorted. "*They* don't say anything at all about you, my dear."

"But," she pursued, "am I so dowdy, then?"

"You are always *très elegante, ma chère*," he replied slowly. Then, recognizing the seriousness of her concern, he added, "But *un peu sèvére, n'est-ce pas*?" He hastened to reassure her, "But, my child, with all you have to think about, how could you be anything else?"

"It isn't fair," she protested. "Why is it that women of lively intelligence and high values are labeled prudes, while someone such as Lady Welford, with only her beauty to recommend her, wins admiration and attention?"

The picture suddenly became abundantly clear to the *comte*, but he managed to phrase his answer in the same vague generalities used by Frances. "I can see that for all your intelligence, you are not very clever about people, *mon enfant*, and about *les hommes du monde* in particular. Everyone wants to enjoy himself. No one wishes to worry, to think seriously and question deeply. Thus they are attracted to those who make them enjoy life, make them forget any cares or responsibilities. Now, someone such as Lady Welford devotes all of her energies to making people, men in particular, do just that. She makes them forget anything except how beautiful she is and how important she makes them feel, and the pleasure she can bring them. Ah . . ." He held up an admonishing hand. "I know that you will say this is hypocritical, and you would be entirely correct. But there are other people who enjoy life in a less-cynical and manipulative manner. They delight in life, relishing everything from playing with their children, to attending concerts of ancient music, to giving balls and parties, to gardening, and they are loved and enjoyed wherever they are, whether or not they are beautiful or fashionable. Your Lady Streatham is such a one who has this *joie de vivre, non*? And there are others who cultivate this most supreme of all social talents. I know you scorn those who live in the lives of social butterflies, but you must look upon the *ton* in the civilized way we French do. To us, this social intercourse is an art to be cultivated, as much as proficiency at watercolors or the pianoforte. To dress oneself beautifully, to bring wit and intelligence to conversation, is to bring pleasure to other people. Just because one is a skilled conversationalist does not mean that one must confine one's conversation to superficialities. And selecting clothes that are exquisite or hair styles dressings that are appropriate, particularly to oneself, are as much expressions of one's personality and aesthetic philosophy as collecting Dutch masters or antiquities.'' He could see she was much struck, and pressed his point home. "And this is not self-indulgent or frivolous. Quite the contrary, it shows an awareness and a concern for the enjoyment of other people.''

Frances sat quietly, her brow wrinkled in thought. Unpleasant as it was to face, she admitted that she did allow herself to become immersed in the seriousness of her responsibilities, to the exclusion of enjoyment. To others she must seem dull and prudish. She raised troubled eyes. "And how would you have someone who knows nothing of this change?''

The count's eyes twinkled as he thought: I knew we should soon get around to this. But he kept these reflections to himself as he continued blandly, "I would first have that person go to a modiste of my acquaintance, who is exceptionally skilled at designing creations that are accurate reflections of the wearer's true personality. These modistes today, bah! They are clothes-mongers who pay no attention to the person they are dressing. They cover fat dowagers with ruchings and flounces. They overwhelm delicate ladies with bows and elaborate corsages. In short, they fit their patronesses to their fashions, instead of the way it should be. Once a woman is elegantly garbed in something that makes her feel beautiful, without changing her into a doll dressed up in what fashion dictates, then she is confident and relaxed enough to pay attention to others, to share her wit and conversation in a way that amuses.''

"Do you think your strategy would work for someone like me?'' Frances asked shyly.

With just the correct mixture of surprise and interest he reassured her. "You, *mon enfant*? But it would be the most delightful thing! And certain to prove the efficacy of my system.'' He held up an admonitory hand. ''But even though you could be assured of success, I couldn't guarantee to make you into an incomparable or even a diamond . . . at least not overnight. Even *I* don't dictate society's whims to that extent. But you don't want that, do you?'' He asked this with deceptive innocence, having a very good idea of exactly what she did want.

The sparkle reappeared in Lady Frances' eyes. ''That would be capital, *monsieur*. Thank you ever so much.''

''*Mon enfant*, we shall begin at once,'' he began with Gallic enthusiasm. ''But, please, no more, '*monsieur*'—'Uncle Maurice,' as I once was for you.''

Frances smiled. ''*Eh, bien, mon oncle. En avant.*'' If the energy and gaiety in her voice were a trifle forced, no one but an uncle, and one well-versed in the ways of the world at that, would have noticed this unnatural exuberance.

He gave a conspiratorial wink and replied, ''We shall visit my friend immediately, as soon as you are ready.''

Frances dashed upstairs to assure herself that Cassie and Freddie were at their lessons, which, hearing her on the stairs, they were perusing diligently when she entered the schoolroom. ''I am just going out with the Comte de Vaudron. You can finish that chapter on Caesar without me, but I shall ask you to tell me all about it when I return.''

The twins nodded and kept their expressions of earnest scholasticism until they heard the carriage roll away. ''Now, where do you suppose Fan is going in such a hurry?'' Freddie wondered.

''At least she no longer seems so angry,'' his twin volunteered. ''I hope she won't remain angry, because she's not nearly as good a friend when she is. Remember the last time she got really mad, I mean, really, really mad at Snythe? Why, she even snapped at Wellington and Aunt Harriet,'' Cassie reminisced.

Meanwhile, Lady Frances and the Comte de Vaudron were en route to the establishment of the count's friend Madame Regnery. Modiste to many of France's most aristocratic families, Madame had discovered her name on the list of the enemies of new republic just in time to make a hairbreadth escape in a linen draper's cart. Since coming to England, she had worked long, arduous hours to establish herself. Forced to inhabit the smallest of shops on South Moulton Street, which, if not directly on fashionable Bond Street, was at least within hailing distance of this mecca of the *haut monde*, she had had a difficult time of it. Those of her former illustrious customers who had not succumbed to La Guillotine were in no circumstances to patronize her. The English, an unadventurous race altogether, lacked the imagination to try someone new. Moreover, they were naturally suspicious of a novelty that also happened to be French.

Thus, the sight of such an old and still solvent patron as the *comte* was a very welcome one indeed. Madame hastened to him, hands outstretched in greeting. "*Monsieur le Comte! Il y a longtemps, n'est-ce pas*? But," she broke into prettily accented English, "I can see your companion is English. What may I do for you today?"

"*Eh bien*, Henriette, you may do nothing less than effect a transformation," he replied, bending over one work-worn hand.

"A transformation? But of whom? Surely you don't mean of this young lady? But she is already so charming."

Here Frances broke in. "*Mais non, madame.* I do not wish to be merely '*charmante.*' That is what one says of someone neither pretty enough to be a diamond nor ugly enough to be an eccentric or an heiress. In short, it means one is mediocre or, at the very least, excessively dull. I no longer wish to be either."

The count interrupted this impassioned diatribe, the bulk of whose significance was slightly lost on Madame. "What Mademoiselle would like to be is fashionable, *à la mode*, in a style that is particularly her own."

Comprehension dawned. "Ah, I understand," Madame replied, wrinkling her brow speculatively. "It should not be so difficult. *Mademoiselle est d'une taille elegante.* She carries herself with style already. She does not need all those laces, flounces, ruchings, and ribbons with which these young ladies ornament and obscure themselves. Bah! Such stupidity! One looks very much like another, and they all resemble a milliner's window. Mademoiselle has intelligence, character, and, I think, a subtle charm which is enhanced by simple design, *n'est-ce pas*?'' She cocked a birdlike head in Frances' direction.

''I believe so, *madame*. At any rate, that is always what I have preferred,'' Frances began timidly.

''*Eh bien*. Marthe, bring the gossamer silk at once,'' demanded the little lady. ''We begin with a ball dress because that is where one makes the greatest impression on the most people.''

The faithful Marthe appeared bearing a shimmering roll of material which sparkled gold and emerald according to the light. ''Oh, how lovely!'' breathed Frances involuntarily as she caught sight of it.

Madame wore a satisfied smile. ''You are quite correct, *mademoiselle*. It is most unusual. *Un ami* . . . a dear friend gave it to me just before I left. It was something they had just begun to work on at Lyons when . . . when . . .'' She broke off.

Frances held out her hand. ''But surely something such as this is far too precious for you to waste on someone who has no claim to fame, fashion, or great beauty.''

The seamstress smiled through the tears she could not hide. ''Mademoiselle sadly underestimates herself. But in any event, I would much rather adorn a heart as warm as yours than the most-toasted incomparable in London.''

The next hours were, for Frances, a blur of laces, satins, gauzes, plain and printed muslins, ruchings, and flounces, the chatter of French and deft fingers pushing, pulling, fitting, and sewing. She emerged somewhat dazed, her wardrobe increased by an exquisite ball gown from Madame's special material, a carriage dress with a white satin pelisse, a walking dress of jaconet muslin over a peach-colored slip, two morning dresses, and another evening dress of an unusual rose satin slip with silver spangled gauze over it giving a most ethereal look. ''I cannot thank you enough, *madame*, for having created costumes that fit me and the type of person I am,'' began Frances. But Madame was not yet through. While Frances was bemused by the selection of trimmings to embellish her choices, Marthe had been sent to fetch Monsieur Ducros, hairdresser to many of the ladies of Versailles. Frances was not at all certain she wanted the transformation to extend quite so far. "But I don't think . . . that is, I like the simple style I have now. It is not fussy, and that, you know, is of paramount importance when one leads a country life," she objected.

"Mademoiselle does have beautiful hair," agreed Monsieur. "But," he added severely, "she does nothing to show off its true beauty. As to the care . . ." He shrugged with true Gallic expression. "Why, the time you spend brushing it now is twice the care this new style would require."

"Very well," sighed Frances. "Never let it be said that I didn't do my utmost to be worthy of one of Madame's creations."

It would not be entirely accurate to say that Lady Frances Cresswell emerged from Regnery's establishment transformed into a diamond of the first water and bearing no earthly resemblance to the serious young woman who had entered some few hours before. She remained Lady Frances, but it was a different Lady Frances—one whose curls caught the light, softened her face, and gave it a slightly mischievous look. She was elegant as ever, but, wearing a new bonnet and a walking dress Madame had happened to have at hand, she somehow looked lighter, more carefree. The dress of primrose sarcenet under matching jaconet muslin with puffs down the sleeves and trimming at the hem was more elaborate than her usual style and lent an interesting air of fragility and delicacy. The ruffled parasol completed her toilette. The *comte* walked round and round, examining every detail. At last he stood back, his face breaking into a smile of paternal pride and satisfaction at his own cleverness. "Ah, *madame,* you have not lost your genius. And you . . ." He included Ducros in an expansive gesture. "You are more talented than ever. Thank you. Now, come, my child, we must show the rest of the world that you are a woman of exterior, as well as interior, beauty and taste." He bowed and escorted Frances to the carriage.

Though no one stopped to stare as they made their way home, their reception on Brook Street was highly gratifying. The twins, who had become more curious the more they discovered that no one in that establishment had the slightest idea of their elder sister's whereabouts, had been watching for her return from the drawing-room window. Higgins had barely closed the door behind Lady Frances and the *comte* when they came clattering downstairs, closely followed by Wellington and Nelson. The cavalcade screeched to a halt at Frances' elegant parasol and lemon kid slippers. "Fan!" Cassie exclaimed. "You look . . . you look beautiful!"

"Slap up to the echo," her twin agreed heartily.

Frances didn't know whether to feel flattered or insulted at the disbelief in their voices.

They walked around her, Cassie remarking in puzzled tones, "But, Fan, whatever for? I thought you detested dressing up. And at any rate, we thought you were pretty before." Wellington sniffed the new parasol but gave over as soon as he had established that it was too new to have acquired any interesting scents. Nelson examined the flounces with equal curiosity.

Frances was touched by their loyalty, but said in a rallying tone, "Well, now that I've been so thoroughly inspected and met with your approval, will you let us come in?" She smiled and led the way into the morning room. "Monsieur le Comte has, in addition to asking that we call him Uncle Maurice, invited us on a very special outing." Immediately all eyes were riveted on him. "He has invited us and Aunt Harriet to go with him to the botanic gardens at Kew. We shall pack a lovely picnic and make a real expedition of it. I thought we would ask Kitty and Ned to go with us as well."

"May we take Wellington and Nelson?" begged Cassie, seconded by Freddie. "Yes, please, Fan, may we? It's been so long since either one of them has been in the true country. I think they're becoming a bit tired of all the London traffic." Freddie remembered his manners. "But, I say, sir, it sounds like a bang-up idea. Thank you."

"Yes, thank you ever so much," added Cassie as the twins dashed out the door to tell their aunt of the forthcoming treat. "Aunt Harriet, Aunt Harriet, Uncle Maurice has invited all of us, even Wellington and Nelson, to the gardens. Aunt Harriet, Aunt Harriet . . ."

Frances turned to the count. "Thank you for giving us all something to look forward to."

He bowed over her hand, his eyes twinkling. "I shall be watching future events with interest myself," he replied somewhat enigmatically.

23

The Comte de Vaudron had no intention of concluding his campaign with the mere transformation of Frances' appearance. He was too much a man of the world to let it ride without laying further plans. He knew that no man, no matter how well-versed in fashion and the ways of the *ton*, could effect a change in someone's social reputation as well as a woman could, so he made his way as quickly as possible to someone who had been making and breaking reputations for forty years—the dowager Marchioness of Camberly.

She was delighted to welcome a visitor who brought, along with news of the latest scandals, memories of a past in which she had lived close to the edge of scandal herself. "Maurice," she sighed as he bent over a beringed hand. "You look as distinguished as ever. How delightful to have you back in London."

He smiled. "I wish I could say how delightful it is to see you queening it over all of them in your old haunts, but you insist on remaining a recluse."

"Well, to tell you the truth," she responded in a conspiratorial whisper, "I find that I hear just as much of what is happening if I remain here entertaining a few select friends who visit me.

It's much less fatiguing than the eternal dressing and promenading, and it's far more entertaining because one sees only whomever one wishes."

He smiled fondly. "But, my dear Marianne, it is so much more boring without you for those of us who continue to dress and promenade."

"Be off with you, Maurice. You always were too charming for your own good." But the dowager looked pleased in spite of herself. Not being one to waste time with mere civilities, she inquired, "You know how glad I am to see you, but as you are not one of my regular callers, more shame on you, I surmise you have some special object in visiting me?"

"*Mais certainement*, Marianne, I do. Though you maintain you have left the *ton* for a more peaceful existence, I know that you retain as much influence as ever in that select little circle of reputation-making matrons." She raised an eyebrow but made no comment. He continued, "There is someone very dear to me, whose life would be a great deal happier were her path to be smoothed for her by someone such as you."

The dowager did not look enchanted with the idea. She rarely put herself out for anyone. It ruined her image as a crotchety and demanding old town tabby. "And who might this person be?" she inquired somewhat coolly.

"Don't get on your high ropes with me, Marianne. She is someone worthy of your sponsorship in every way—beauty, intelligence, and a handsome fortune." The *comte* paused for effect before adding the clincher to his argument. "And, I believe, she has just had a most unpleasant encounter with that haughty grandson of yours."

The dowager rose instantly to Julian's defense. "He's a good lad who's awake on every suit. If he's a bit high in the instep, it's because someone deserved it."

"That's as may be," rejoined the *comte*, equally hot in the defense of his favorite. "But in this case it wasn't Lady Frances Cresswell, but Vanessa Welford who deserved to be made uncomfortable."

The dowager's interest, piqued already, was fairly caught at the mention of these two names. "You always were a deep 'un, Maurice. You didn't come here just to get me to put a few good words about this gel in a few well-chosen ears. Now, cut line.''

The count poured out the entire story of the encounter in the park and the subsequent trip to Madame Regnery. ''But, Marianne, you know as well as I do that a fashionable appearance is only the start. One must be known to be all the crack, and that's where you come in. If you tell a few of those friends of yours that Lady Frances Cresswell is all the rage, she will be.''

A look of amused comprehension appeared on the marchioness's face. It turned to satisfaction as the tale progressed. ''It seems, Maurice, that you and I can be of the greatest help to each other.'' As the count looked totally blank, she explained, ''I met my grandson in Bond Street this afternoon. He had just been sparring in Jackson's and seemed to have derived singularly little satisfaction from this exercise. In fact, he looked as blue-deviled as I can ever remember having seen him. He was perfectly polite to me, but his replies were completely at random—really quite unlike him. I've seen him furious at women times out of mind. I've known him to despise them, but I've never known him to be in such a rare taking as he was today. Mark my words, your Frances is having a most unusual effect on my grandson. And it's about time someone got beneath that well-controlled shell of his. I'll play your game, Maurice, and if I'm right, and she means as much to him as I think she does, we'll win more than social cachet for your Lady Fanny.''

''Ah, Marianne, I knew you wouldn't disappoint me. Still the same sharp observer of human nature. What a pity we're too old to intrigue on our own behalves. We could teach this namby-pamby generation a thing or two.''

She smiled mischievously up at him. ''Too true. But be off with you now. If we're to pull this thing off, I must get to work at once.''

Well pleased with himself, the count bade good-bye to the marchioness and sauntered over to White's to set the second half of his strategy in motion. He stopped to exchange greetings and news with several old friends in the card room, but his eyes strayed to another part of the room, where Bertie Montgomery was listening attentively to a furious debate over the rival merits of two newly discovered opera dancers. ''Come now, Forsyth,'' admonished one buck. "She may have the figure of a Venus and legs beyond compare, but her face ain't much. It don't hold a candle to Aimée's."

"There you're fair and far out," argued Forsyth. "Aimée ain't pretty. She's too flashy by half. Mouth's too wide and her nose ain't nearly so pretty as Babette's."

"But her eyes, man," the enthusiast protested. "Have you ever seen such eyes? A man could drown in them."

The *comte* expertly detached Bertie from this group without his being aware of it and led him out of earshot. In no time he had this young man's entire attention and allegiance to his cause, through a time-honored method of flattery—the appeal of an older man-of-the-world, to someone much younger and less sophisticated, for aid and advice. The count mounted his attack with a gambit certain to succeed. "I come to you directly, *mon ami*, because a certain lady has named you as one of her oldest and dearest friends." Bertie gave a start of surprise and opened his mouth to blurt out some indiscreet remark. The count forestalled him. "But of course we both know the identity of the charming lady to whom I refer—the daughter of an admired friend. I had hoped . . ." Here the count, with his unerring sense for the proper dramatic touch, sighed gently. "I had hoped that, once in London, she would forget her duties and cares and give herself over to the delights of the Season. To some degree she has. Little by little she has begun to forget here familial responsibilities and certain other serious concerns of her own. I have seen her more often at balls, the opera, the theater, and have been satisfied. I started to relax my vigilance, but now something has occurred that might make her think that her original reading of the *ton* and all its amusements—as vain, silly, useless, harmful even—was the correct one." Bertie, who had been frowning earnestly as he followed the thread of the count's narrative, looked up in some alarm. "The Lady Vanessa Welford," was the count's somewhat cryptic response to the look of inquiry directed at him.

Mysterious as this reply was, it appeared to be enough for Bertie, who remarked with a conscious look, "Oh, ahh."

"Just so. I have done my best to counteract this unfortunate episode by immediately escorting my young friend to a clever modiste who, with her usual skill, has recreated my young friend's look. But in order for this new image to succeed, it must be carried off with assurance. And that is where you, as an arbiter of taste among the younger set, can help. All you need to do is observe several times, in such discussions as the one I interrupted, that Lady Blank seems to be all the rage. That should be sufficient for young bucks as impressionable as those.''

Bertie, who had turned quite pink with pleasure at the count's confidence in his influence, assured him earnestly that he would do his utmost.

Well-satisfied with his choice of conspirator, the count bade him adieu and hastened off for a well-deserved hour of relaxation poring over the latest arrivals at Hatchard's. He had not gone far before he caught sight of Lord Petersham. ''The very man,'' he chuckled slyly to himself. He was especially cordial in his greeting as he resolved to introduce this avid connoisseur to Lady Frances at the earliest possible moment. Her elegance of mind and manner, her excellent conversation, refined taste, and well-informed mind were certain to appeal to this rather eccentric peer who, depsite his eccentricities, was an acknowledged judge of beauty and style. The encounter was highly successful. Petersham looked forward to meeting someone who had lived and been brought up among the aesthetic dictates of classical antiquity. Well-pleased with his morning's work, the *comte* gave himself up to the pleasures of Hatchard's.

24

On the other hand, the objects of the *comte*'s machinations, Lady Frances Cresswell and Lord Julian Mainwaring, were having an encounter as disastrous as his had been successful. After passing a more sleepless night than he ever remembered having endured, the marquess resolved to call in Brook Street as early as it would be proper to do so. He had spent the last twelve hours trying out various speeches in his defense. As all of these sounded insufferably priggish, he threw out the lot and began phrasing apologies. But here too he was at a standstill. He could think of no combination of words that would convey his sympathy for the hurt Frances had suffered, his assurance that the opinions of Vanessa were completely without foundation or the concurrence of the *ton*, and a total disavowal of any interest in that manipulative woman, while still managing to retain Frances' respect. At last he tossed out all his carefully constructed phrases and resolved to be guided by the situation— an unheard-of attitude for a man known the length and breadth of the British Empire for his judicious and diplomatic conduct.

It was with some trepidation, a feeling he had not experienced since his days at Eton, that Julian knocked at Brook Street. Higgins greeted him with his usual dignity, while trying desperately to make his well-modulated "Good day, Lord Mainwaring" carry to the morning room. The butler need not have worried. Lady Frances, prey to her own unsatisfactory thoughts, had been pacing back and forth in front of the window and had witnessed the arrival of Mainwaring's curricle. With a desperate effort she stopped her perambulations and assumed a calm and dignified demeanor that was in total contrast to her feelings.

She presented a charming picture with her newly cropped curls catching the light that streamed in behind her. However, the marquess was too intent upon his mission to take in such a minor detail. In fact, in contrast to Lady Frances, he seemed singularly ill at ease. "Lady Frances," he began abruptly, "I wish to apologize for the epi . . . ah, encounter in the park." He cursed himself for this bald way of putting it. Her gaze remained calm and steady, giving him no clue to her thoughts and no help in organizing his own. He began again. "I am aware that my companion . . . I mean, that you may have suffered some discomfort from the . . . ah . . . for which I apologize." This was hardly better, and he bit his lip uncomfortably.

Fortunately, Frances' pride and social graces came to the rescue. "Think nothing of it, my lord. If I were someone who craved public acclaim, I might have been upset, but as you know, someone with my preferences cares perhaps too little for such things. Therefore, I was not the least concerned. It is kind of you to apologize, but I assure you I do not regard it in the least." Lady Frances congratulated herself on her delivery. It was all she could have hoped for—rational, detached, gracious. She only wished he would leave before her carefully constructed facade crumbled into a million pieces.

Mainwaring was left with nothing to do but murmur, "You are too kind," before bowing over her hand and departing. Once outside, however, the last shreds of his dignity disappeared. "Damn and blast! What a cowhanded fool you are, Mainwaring!" he cursed. No, he thought bitterly, it wasn't that I was so lacking in address, as that she was so completely mistress of hers. Why did she have to be so gracious and understanding? No, why did she have to be so damned cool, so completely unaffected? That last, he realized, was what tormented him.

Though he sympathized intensely with the hurt he was certain he had seen in her eyes yesterday, he had secretly been glad of it because it showed him that she cared for his friendship. Today she acted as though this disastrous encounter had changed nothing between them because there had been nothing there to be changed. Infinitely more uncomfortable though it would have been, he found himself wishing that she had raged at him for spending time with someone as useless as Vanessa Welford, for allowing his mistress to be seen with him in public, for not coming to her, Frances', defense. At least then he would have known where he stood. Now, as he was beginning to be aware of just how much their friendship meant to him, she gave him ample proof of how little it meant to her. With this gloomy conclusion he was forced to be satisfied for quite some time, because the moment he arrived at Grosvenor Square, Kilson put into his hand a letter from one of his captains requesting that he come down to Plymouth to inspect a new merchantman under construction there.

Frances' hard-won composure deserted her the instant the sound of the carriage wheels died away. She sank limply into a chair and bowed her head in her hands. Wellington, sensing his mistress's distress, swallowed his scruples—he scorned lapdogs with passionate intensity—and climbed into her lap, sighing sympathetically. Frances knew she had done the only thing she could have. Under the circumstances, she had carried off the interview magnificently. Why, then, did she feel so utterly wretched? Gone was the easy camaraderie, the trust between friends. But what could she have done to change all that? Nothing. The tears slipped through her fingers onto Wellington's rough coat. He sat looking curiously up at her. This was a behavior he had never witnessed before, and he was not at all sure what he should do about it. Finally he placed a paw gravely on her hand. She gathered him closely in her arms. Much as he scorned lapdogs, he felt this was not the time to stand on principle, and contented himself with licking the tears on her cheeks. She soon came to herself. "And why should *I* be miserable? *I* have not behaved badly. *I* have not put a friend in an awkward situation. Come, Wellington. We need some fresh air.'' Relieved to see that he had recalled her to her senses, Wellington barked his approval and frisked on ahead of her as she went to fetch a bonnet and pelisse.

25

While Frances was taking a brisk salutary turn around the park, the other party in the contretemps was bowling along at a spanking pace toward Plymouth in a rapidly decaying frame of mind. At any other time he would have welcomed the opportunity to inspect the ship, the chance to use his brain and swap stories of foreign ports with the captain and crew. During any other Season he would have been delighted to have an excuse to leave the stuffy ballrooms, smirking young ladies, and rapacious mamas, but now he damned it as an inconvenience of the highest order. He was determined to reestablish his friendship with Frances. Recognizing her as a woman of decision and character, he realized that it would take a great deal to regain her trust in him. A campaign of such magnitude required his constant presence in London, at the balls, operas, and plays Frances was likely to attend. It was this campaign and the strategy called for, rather than the upcoming business, that occupied his mind as he tooled along, mentally rehearsing one scene after another. If anyone had told him that he would have spent that much time analyzing a relationship with anyone, much less a woman who was only passably pretty, and a bluestocking as well, he would have questioned his sanity. However, he was in no state to reflect on this departure from his usual attitudes.

He arrived at Plymouth late one evening and spent the next day walking the decks of his unfinished ship with the captain, discussing the fittings, requirements of the cargo, and the disposition of the crew. But all the while he was conscious of the small corner of his mind that dwelt on Frances and the state of her mind. Becoming aware of the direction of his thoughts, he would dismiss them with an impatient gesture and try to concentrate more deeply than ever on the business at hand, but he was never entirely successful.

Later that night he sat gazing into the fire as he lingered over his port, ruminating over the entire state of affairs. The longer he dwelt on it, the more he cursed himself for a fool in expending such thought and energy on the matter. Mainwaring, you're all about in the head to waste another second's consideration on any of it, he told himself sternly. Besides, you never wanted a friendship to develop in the first place. You should count yourself lucky, old man, to be so well out of it. Satisfied with this conclusion, he set down his glass with a decisive gesture and prepared to go to bed. He had not risen from his chair before he was overcome with such a sense of loss and emptiness that he remained staring moodily into the flames, his dark brows drawn together in a deep frown. How long he stayed that way he didn't know, until the guttering candles recalled his attention and he cursed softly to himself: "You know what's wrong with you, Mainwaring? You've fallen in love like any callow youth." This realization, coming as it did after their recent disastrous encounter, only intensified his somber mood. He fell to thinking of Frances and all the little ways that were peculiarly hers— Frances comforting the terrified Nelson, Frances telling the children stories, Frances laughing at Grimaldi as hard as any child, or Frances looking up at him with that special teasing look of hers. He realized that the thought of life without any of that was no longer possible.

But how shall I ever set it right with her? he wondered. Ordinarily Julian Mainwaring was never at a loss for an answer. In point of fact, it was known in business and diplomatic circles that the stickier the situation, the more he enjoyed it. Nor did he ever doubt his ability to win a point in the end. Now, when so much was at stake, he found his usual confidence had vanished, leaving him with only a desperate desire to do the right thing. I mustn't fail. I can't fail! he told himself. And with that, he resolved to return to town at the earliest possible moment.

Frances, in the meantime, was allowing herself no such thoughts. On the contrary, she had thrown herself so vigorously into the social whirl that she was astounded at herself. In this endeavor she was aided and abetted by the Comte de Vaudron, who seemed to be everywhere at once.

He squired her to the opera, drove her to the park, and escorted her to a variety of routs and balls. And always he seemed to produce the most amusing companions. Following his lead, she found herself enjoying conversations that only a few months ago she would have been too shy to enter. Much to her surprise, they were not as trivial as she had imagined. Also, to her surprise, she discovered that people seemed to think she had something to say, even to find her amusing. If the shadow cast on her life by her disappointment in Mainwaring kept her from being happy, she was at least occupied and amused. And always at a distance there was the *comte* noticing and encouraging the change in her. With smug satisfaction he saw her respond to admiration and begin to sparkle and grow more witty.

He was congratulating himself as he stood one evening at the Mountjoys' ball watching Frances whirling around the floor with the totally captivated son and heir of the house. "You have done very well, my friend." It was so much his own thought that it took some minutes before he realized that the dowager Marchioness of Camberly had come quietly up behind him.

"Ah, from you, Marianne, that is high praise indeed."

She nodded at him, smiling slyly. "My grandson will have something to think about when he returns from Plymouth. He will have a run for his money." She nodded sagely. "Not a bad thing for either of them, I should think."

The marquess did in fact return the very next day, but in spite of an hour spent circling the park and religious attendance at a very dull ball indeed and an equally uninspiring opera, he did not lay eyes on Frances. After one particularly frustrating day spent sauntering with studied casualness along Bond Street and persuing more tomes at Hatchard's than he cared to remember, he repaired to Brooks's. His unpropitious mood was destined to be further impaired by the conversation he overheard as he entered the gaming room. "I quite agree with you, Wytham. She is all that is charming," drawled a well-known man-about-town. "But she's quite above my touch. Don't know her that well."

"Meaning that she knows you ain't too full in the cockloft," interposed his friend.

"I don't argue with you, Wythy. I'm the first one to admit that I ain't all that bobbish. Now, Alvanley here is just her sort. You ask him. He seems to be quite taken with her. Leastways, he spent the longest time at the Marlowes' rout discussing some dashed picture on his snuffbox."

"Sounds suspiciously like a regular bluestocking to me." Wytham dismissed the subject of their conversation with an airy wave of his hand.

"That's just it, she ain't at all," chimed in another young buck. "She's as easy to talk to as your own best friend. Don't put on all of those die-away airs. Don't expect you to bow and scrape and do the pretty all the time. I like her. I can tell you, it's a great relief to dance with a female who can laugh and who don't expect much. Besides, she's quite a taking thing too. Oh, she ain't exactly an incomparable, because she don't look like a dashed china doll, but for my money she's a lot prettier than all those peaches-and-cream misses everyone admires." A brief pause ensued as he conjured up an image of his favorite. "Tell you what. She's got the most beautiful eyes. They look right into you. Let you know what she's thinking too," he concluded enthusiastically.

"Good God," Wytham's sardonic voice broke in. "She must be a diamond if Langford likes her. Can't remember when he ever liked a female that wasn't a horse. Can it be he's going to become leg-shackled at last?"

"No." Langford sighed. "She's as friendly to me as she is to everyone else, but I don't stand a chance, with Alvanley and all those others who surround her all the time. And Wolvercote is so taken with her, he's ready to do battle with anyone who even looks at her. Tell you what, he's making a dashed cake of himself with his poetic airs and constant haunting of her house. Wonder she doesn't get demmed sick of it. But she's too kind to upset anyone, even someone who's as big a gudgeon as Wolvercote.''

Mainwaring turned to the Corinthian who had entered with him. "Who is this, Boxford? A female that isn't silly or a diamond but is all the rage? Only tell me the name of such a paragon."

Lord Boxford looked at him with surprise. "Where have you been, old boy? You need catching up with the *ton. She* is Lady Frances Cresswell, Charles Cresswell's daughter. Apparently she had a Season several years ago, but when her father died she went back to Hampshire to manage the estate and hasn't come to town since. Now she's going about with the Comte de Vaudron, who stands as some sort of godfather to her. She isn't exactly a diamond, but she's got great elegance and style, and what's more, she's pleasant to be with. Doesn't put on any of the airs and graces that our usual incomparables seem to feel they must adopt."

Lord Mainwaring had the oddest sensation in the pit of his stomach, as though someone had broken through his guard and tipped him a leveler. Lady Frances, an incomparable? *His* Lady Frances? But she wasn't the sort to appeal to bucks like these. It took a man of intelligence and perception—someone such as himself, for example—to appreciate her very special qualities.

This turn of events killed all his interest in Brooks's and he returned to Grosvenor Square to throw himself into a pile of correspondence that had accumulated during his absence. After two hours of intense concentration on some very delicate diplomatic issues, he was in no better state. His thoughts and feelings were still in a turmoil. There was nothing to do but possess himself of as much patience as he could muster until the Duchess of Devonshire's ball that evening. It was the event of the Season, and Frances was sure to be there.

In the meantime, his staff crept about quietly making their own observations and reaching their own conclusions. "He's in a bad way," Kilson commented to himself. "Never seen him as blue-deviled before, especially over any woman. Wonder if he knows it?'' Ordinarily Mainwaring's henchman had the highest respect for his master's intelligence, but lately it had seemed to him that Lord Mainwaring had been unaware of the simplest situation. Any fool could see that the mere mention of Lady Frances Cresswell caught his immediate and total attention. And one didn't have to spend much time in that lady's presence to know that she was the one for him. Why, he never talked to other women the way he talked to her, or cared to hear their thoughts on any subject. Why, the other day he had even asked whether or not she had used the latest seed drill. And, what's more, what she had thought about it. However, it was more than that. There was a certain warmth in his eyes whenever he looked at her or mentioned her that Kilson had never seen before. He only hoped that Lady Frances was of the same mind. Of course, he didn't know her very well, but he rather thought she was. But something must have happened to upset this nicely progressing state of affairs. Discreet inquiries among the coachmen and footmen had revealed nothing, and Kilson, at a loss to know what had occurred, was at an even greater loss as to how to remedy it. Like his master, he finally decided that all he could do was to await developments with as much patience as possible.

26

The Duchess of Devonshire's ball was predicted to be the most important event of the Season. No member of the *ton* worthy of that appellation would have even considered missing it. No more did Lady Frances, though she was certain it would prove to be a sad crush. Much to her astonishment, she had rather enjoyed her social transformation. At first she had been inclined to doubt the Comte de Vaudron's opinion that the more elegantly she was attired and the more fashionable she was, the more confident she would feel. In fact, he had been astoundingly accurate. Her locks, shorn of their heavier tresses, felt light and frivolous, encouraging her to toss her head, laugh, and smile in a manner totally foreign to her previous, more dignified self. She knew her toilette to be the height of elegance, and this, to her total amazement, actually did give her the absolute composure she had lacked before in the face of social scrutiny. Before, a stare, no matter how ill-bred, left her quaking in her boots, wondering if her dress were horribly dowdy, her toilette in disrepair, or her conversation lacking. Now she could attribute such stares to envy rather than to censure, and this envy, though she was loathe to admit it, gave a certain spice to social affairs. It was, of course, a lowering thought for one bred to disregard the superficialities and appreciate the finer points of people's characters, but that made it no less true. It was thus that she looked forward to the ball. Despite Lady Frances' protests, Madame Regnery had insisted on creating a ball gown for her out of the material carefully brought from Lyons. Because of the uniqueness of the silk, which shimmered between green and a rich gold, the dress was of the simplest design, cut low over the bosom and softly gathered above the waist. Its only ornamentations were several heavy rouleaux of the same material at the hem, which served to make it mold to the elegant lines of her figure, and a Medici collar of rich blond lace at the neck. It was true that silk was now less favored than muslin, but this was of a type that had never before graced the ballrooms of London—or Paris, for that matter. A magnificent parure of her mother's emeralds and a matching brooch in the corsage completed the ensemble, complimented the color of her eyes, and emphasized the creamy richness of her skin. Her hair, brushed into a riot of golden curls, shone with the same highlights as her gown.

"Oh, Frances, don't you look just like a princess!" Kitty exclaimed when she saw her. "No, much grander than that . . . a queen, I think," she amended.

Kitty was not alone in her opinion. Bertie, who came to escort her, was equally appreciative. "I say, Fanny, that's a bang-up rig. I am certainly lucky to be with you. You'll take the shine out of all of 'em. Did you get it from Fanchon?"

"What a complete hand you are, Bertie. You always know just the right thing to say, don't you?" Frances was gratified.

"Now Fan, you know that's a plumper. I ain't one of those poetic fellows who knows just how to put things."

"You can't flummery me," she interrupted sternly. "Whether or not you or anyone else acknowledges it, the most important words are those that come directly from a kind heart, which you have in abundant degree."

"I say, Fan," he stammered, pleased in spite of his evident embarrassment. "Now it's time for you to cut a dash with a larger audience. Are you ready for it?" he inquired as he escorted her to the carriage.

It was gratifying to Frances, slowly making her way up the

magnificent staircase, to see so many familiar faces. How different from her first Season, when everyone was not only strange to her, but critical as well. Now, though many of the familiar faces were no closer friends, they represented no threat to her equanimity. And much as she disliked admitting it to herself, she enjoyed causing a stir, however minor, when she entered. Heretofore Frances had looked upon vanity with distaste, but she allowed herself to indulge in it just briefly when Lords Alvanley and Boxford, closely followed by the Viscount Wytham, hastened over to secure dances and form a laughing coterie around her.

It was thus that Mainwaring first saw her in the glow from the chandelier directly overhead, laughing gaily at a sally of Alvanley's. Mainwaring's ordinarily bored expression deserted him and he stared at the warm, vital creature who caught the light with every graceful gesture.

Long hours spent staring into the fire had brought Julian to the conclusion that Lady Frances Cresswell was someone he cared enough about to consider spending the rest of his life with. She would make a fine wife. She was intelligent in a greater variety of areas than most men of his acquaintance. She faced life with courageousness and purpose. She had a quick wit that teased and delighted him, and the heavy responsibilities she had borne so competently and quietly endeared her to him. But tonight, for the first time, he saw her as a beautiful woman. It quite took his breath away. Never had her smile seemed so bewitching or—his jaw tightened at the thought—intimate. The slim perfection of her body and grace of movement were emphasized by the material of her gown, which clung to her and shimmered enticingly at the least motion. The brilliant parure called attention to the beautifully molded neck and shoulders, not to mention a décolletage that might even have been called daring. In the midst of all the pale fluttering gauzes she stood out like a gilded vital young goddess with a warm and vivid beauty that would have taken any man's breath away.

In a daze, Lord Mainwaring guided partners around the floor, nodding and commenting mechanically at the appropriate moments, but his eyes never left Frances as she whirled by with one partner after another. Just as he felt he could stand it no longer, that he simply must talk with her at whatever cost, he saw her disappear through a French window onto the terrace. Not far behind her followed the besotted young man Wolvercote, a great deal the worse for the effects of the punch. Barely staying to restore his partner to her party, Mainwaring strode off after the pair, his blue eyes smoldering dangerously in a face dark and threatening as a thundercloud.

If he had not been beside himself with rage and jealously, he might have appreciated the picture that met his furious gaze. Slim and ethereal, her dress shimmering in the moonlight, Frances leaned on the parapet surveying the garden below. Wolvercote, who, whatever his faults, was a picturesque and graceful youth, had just flung himself to his knees and caught her hand to his mouth in a passion of youthful ardor. But Mainwaring was in no mood for aesthetics, nor did he register the look of intense annoyance that crossed Frances' face as she tried to recapture her hand. All he saw was the woman he wanted, being ardently kissed by another man. By this time Wolvercote, intoxicated with his own boldness and the romantic atmosphere, had risen, grabbed Frances inexpertly in his arms, and was trying unsuccessfully to kiss her.

"Most affecting." Mainwaring's harsh voice shattered the idyllic scene.

"Lord Mainwaring!" Frances exclaimed, striving for a normal voice and wishing fervently that the earth would open up and swallow her. "I had not thought to see you here." There! She had achieved at least a semblance of conversational tone, though the thudding of her heart threatened to suffocate her.

"Obviously not," he responded grimly.

The contempt in his face goaded her as she realized the infelicity of her last remark. "I had *thought*," she continued with emphasis, "I had *thought* you were out of town on business and had not expected to see you for some time."

"And so made yourself the talk of the town in my absence."

Thoroughly roused, she flashed back. "*You* are certainly not my chaperone, my lord. And if I were looking for models of propriety, I certainly shouldn't look to you."

"Oh, wouldn't you? Let me tell you, my girl, I was on the town and conversant with all its rules and restrictions long before you were out of the schoolroom. And disappearing to an isolated terrace with besotted young men has never been acceptable behavior." Here he turned to the miserable Wolvercote, who had been standing, his mouth open, observing this astounding scene. "Get out of here, you puppy. And don't you go compromising Lady Frances again."

Wolvercote fled with relief, but Lady Frances, thoroughly enraged, drew herself to her full height and turned to Julian. Eyes flashing, she responded in a low passionate voice that she could barely keep from trembling with anger. "What right have you to interfere in my affairs or comment on my conduct?"

Mainwaring, as angry as she, lashed out, "The right of any sensible person who sees someone behaving like an idiot."

"And what concern is it of yours, my lord, whether or not I choose to behave like an idiot?" In fact, Frances did feel like a complete idiot. She had been as intensely aware of Lord Mainwaring all evening as he had been of her, and, upset at her own interests and attraction to someone so obviously a cad, she had sought the solace of the terrace, never dreaming that her escape would be noticed or that she would be followed. She had been as revolted as Mainwaring by young Wolvercote, but her censor's next words forced her to adopt a totally opposite position.

"I never thought to see you with such a foolish young jackanapes."

Lady Frances thoroughly agreed, but would have died before admitting such a thing. "Wolvercote happens to be a serious young man who shares many of my tastes. We admire many of the same things, and *he*, at least, respects and admires me." She was thoroughly disgusted at the petulance of this last remark, which, in spite of its childishness, seemed to be the last straw for Mainwaring.

"If it's admiration you want . . ." he hissed, grasping her by the shoulders and pulling her roughly to him. His arms tightened painfully around her as his lips came down on hers fiercely, possessively, angrily demanding.

Caught off guard, Frances felt herself overwhelmed by the hardness of his body against hers, the insistence of his lips as they moved on hers, exploring, forcing her to respond. For a moment she gave herself up to the warm tide that was flooding her, spreading languorously up from her trembling knees to the pit of her stomach and her breast. For an instant she wanted to free her arms, pull him to her, and return the kiss as passionately as he. But at the back of her mind a cold little voice admonished. "He is doing this out of anger and disgust. He despises you. Get away. Run!" Marshalling her fading resistance, she pulled away, her eyes dark with passion, and in a voice throbbing with emotion demanded, "And I suppose *this* is proper conduct? You seem to forget I am not Lady Welford, sir." Then, in a swirl of green-gold, she turned on her heel and vanished into the garden.

Left alone in the darkness, Lord Mainwaring suffered a thousand conflicting emotions, chiefly anger—anger at Frances for having forced him to behave like the most callow of overheated young bucks, anger at himself for having given way so completely to his emotions. But also there was desire—desire for her as she stood facing him, her eyes alight with anger, her whole body vibrant with passion and fury. And he, who had flirted with scores of beautiful, sophisticated women in all the capitals or Europe, felt sick with longing for her, for the suppleness of her body beneath his hands, the warmth and softness of her lips against his. Surely, for a moment, she had responded, her lips clinging to his with equal fevor before she ran off into the night?

You're a cad and an utter fool, he derided himself bitterly. And now you have ruined whatever chance you ever had of getting her back. In his despair, he realized now exactly how much he did want her back, not just as a friend, but because he needed her, desired her, wanted her more than anything he had ever wanted before. With his painful discovery, he too strode off to find his carriage and the dubious solace of a bottle of brandy in his own empty library.

Lady Frances, hardly knowing where she was headed, except away from Lord Mainwaring, stumbled through the garden in the vague direction of her carriage. Just when she was beginning to despair of finding a way out and wondering how she could possibly face returning to the ballroom and the curious eyes of the assembled multitude, she discovered a small door in the garden wall. Mercifully, it opened quietly and she found herself on the cobblestones of the stableyard. Somehow she found John Coachman, was helped tenderly into the carriage, and collapsed thankfully against the squabs.

For a time she gave herself up to the motion of the vehicle, happy to enjoy the peace and darkness alone. But on alighting at Brook Street and entering her dressing room, she found that she had escaped the crush and Lord Mainwaring only to find herself prey to thoughts as unwelcome as any she had ever experienced. Her anger at being criticized so unfairly and handled so peremptorily, which had sustained her through the scene with Mainwaring, had now evaporated, and she was left with unsettling memories of the entire episode. Mainwaring had been entirely correct in his hope that she had yielded briefly to her feelings and returned his embrace. When he had first pulled her to him, she had been too angry to do anything other than resist, but as his lips pressed more insistently on hers, forcing them apart, and his arms tightened around her, molding her body against his, she became more and more aware of the warm lethargic feeling stealing over her and subduing her resistance. A quick glance stolen up at him revealed a strange intensity in his gaze that she had never seen before—almost a hunger—and for some reason she wanted desperately to deliver herself up to this hunger and to forget herself in the hardness of his body pressing on hers, the strength of his hand tilting her head to his kiss. She hadn't known whether she was glad or sorry for the small corner of her mind that had brought her to herself, to the realization of Lord Mainwaring's probable feelings for her at that moment. But, she sighed sadly as she recalled it all in vivid detail, she wished she had been able to wipe out everything, to delude herself into believing that he wanted her, Frances Cresswell, for herself and not out of anger. She wished desperately that she had been able to forget herself in one moment of passion. And that's what it was, my girl, she told herself severely. You did want him to desire you, to love you the way he loves Lady Welford. It's not respect or friendship you crave. It's love. You want him to love you because you love him that way." For a long time after reaching this totally upsetting conclusion, she sat staring at her hollow-eyed reflection in the mirror, her only thought: Now whatever am I to do?

Eventually her characteristic energy and independent spirit reasserted themselves. I must get out of here, away from him, away from London, away from everyone. And she feverishly began planning and packing for her immediate return to Cresswell. It was not her customary, organized preparation, but by the time dawn broke, she had a valise ready, and instructions for the servants completed. She felt slightly guilty, slipping off without saying good-bye to Aunt Harriet and the children, but she couldn't bear to stay in London a moment longer than absolutely necessary. Besides, her hasty departure was in keeping with the note she had left, implying some pressing business at Cresswell that required her immediate attention. Such haste and deception were so totally unlike her that she was not at all sure she would be able to fool Aunt Harriet or Higgins for a minute. But then, such emotions had never before entered her life. True, she had mourned her parents deeply and she had loathed and detested her first London Season, but she had never before doubted herself or the rightness of her own feelings. It was certainly lowering to reflect that a pair of dark blue eyes set in a harsh-featured face and a sardonic smile could affect her so powerfully. Inexplicable as it was, that seemed to be the case, and she was not at all happy about it.

For the remainder of the journey she allowed herself the luxury of recalling the times they had shared, the special smile that seemed to lurk in his eyes just for her when he knew she would understand some fine point. The care and gentleness with which he handed her into a carriage or entered into her particular worries over the children and Cresswell, and last, the brief moment when he had seemed to want her as much as she now admitted to wanting him. But upon arriving at Cresswell, she resolutely put all thoughts of Lord Julian Mainwaring out of her mind to immerse herself in a flurry of activity.

By day she kept up a backbreaking regimen of riding over the estate checking crops, fences, tenants' cottages, and listening to complaints, problems, or just neighborly chatter. In the evening she pored over accounts or studied the authors and texts she wished to share with Freddie and Cassie, until she was exhausted. Despite her best efforts, the occasional memory of some shared moment with Mainwaring or speculation as to his whereabouts or the state of his emotions would intrude. At that, she would shake her head briskly, call to Wellington, who, much to his delight and pride, had been the one being allowed to accompany her in her flight, and head off for a vigorous walk, whatever the weather or the hour.

By degrees, she soon recovered her equanimity, but it was a peace without much joy or expectation. Odd to think that the very same life, the same daily round of activities that had seemed so full before she went to London, could now seem so flat, so empty. But she knew from experience that time would restore much, if not all, of her former sense of herself.

In the meanwhile, those she had left behind were reacting in their own particular ways to her escape. As she had suspected, neither Higgins nor Aunt Harriet believed for a single moment her pretext of pressing business at Cresswell. Both knew her to be far too good a manager and far too judicious in her choice of stewards to be caught unawares by some crisis. Contrary to her expectations, they both, without knowing precisely the true circumstances, immediately divined the cause of her departure. "Drat all men," muttered Aunt Harriet, swiping viciously at a faded blossom. "Why must they be forever imposing themselves on women? They make 'em love 'em and then make 'em miserable. There's not a one of them worthy of a good woman, especially one like Frances. With all the ladybirds in London dying for him, why did that Mainwaring have to go and upset my precious girl? Why, I'll give that arrogant, interfering so-and-so a piece of my mind if I get half the chance."

Higgins was taking out his frustrations on his particular pride and joy—the family silver—and mumbling to himself. "Something certainly has overset Miss Frances. It isn't any emergency that has called her away." Buff, buff. "And she is running away. That's certain. I've never known her to run away from anyone or anything before, so it must be his lordship that has upset her so. She has never known anyone like him before. Top-of-the-trees, a real out-and-outer, he is." Buff, buff. "Or was," he amended darkly. "If he's done anything to cut up Miss Frances' peace, we shall certainly see what will have to be done.'' And setting down a sauceboat with an ominous thump, he marched off to set investigations in motion, beginning with Lady Frances' Daisy.

''Ooh, I don't know, sir. I didn't see her ladyship till this morning, but she didn't sleep a wink, that I'm sure. Her bed wasn't touched and she did a powerful amount of packing.''

In the breakfast room, Frances' departure was being discussed with some dismay. ''But, Aunt Harriet,'' wailed Cassie, ''she couldn't have gone! She promised to take Ned and me on another trip to the Tower and then to Gunters.' ''

Freddie's consternation was just as real, though premised on more complicated circumstances. With Frances went his only link to Lord Mainwaring, and he had dearly hoped that his lordship would remember his promise to take him, Nigel, and Ned to see a cricket match at the recently established Lord's.

''Well, Cassie, she has more important things to attend to than taking a pair of schoolchildren on outings and for ices,'' her aunt responded tartly, covering up her own concern over the situation by appearing more brusque than usual. All of these various household members had their suspicions—Frances being one of the most organized, least impulsive of mistresses, sisters, or nieces, as the case was. They were all alike, however, in that each one struggled with his or her doubts in silence, not daring or deigning to confide in anyone else.

Freddie alone of the assorted interested parties engaged in unraveling the MYSTERY. He had A PLAN. It had seemed to him that just as he had begun to recognize that Lord Mainwaring, though a real out-and-outer, was not at all toplofty where truly inspired young schoolboys were concerned, his lordship had become a noticeably less-frequent visitor in Brook Street. After nearly an hour spent scowling over a most boring passage that Fanny had assigned for translation, he began to see a PATTERN to the situation. It all dated back to that odd encounter in the park. It was after that that he had noticed his sister's unusual social gaiety. Really, she had almost completely ignored him and Cassie while she ran around buying clothes or going to parties. It must have been something to do with that episode that he didn't fully understand. For after that, Fanny, ordinarily so willing to discuss Lord Mainwaring's manifold accomplishments with him, had been positively put out every time he brought up the subject for conversation. Her usual response, "Really, Freddie, Lord Mainwaring is far too busy to be interested in any of us," made him think that perhaps she was mad at his lordship. In that case, he, Freddie, who was out of favor with Lady Frances more than anyone else and knew exactly how unpleasant that could be, felt it his duty to apprise his lordship of the situation and perhaps suggest some remedies.

It was with this laudable goal in mind that he set out, not exactly stealthily, but with a good deal less commotion than ordinarily accompanied his comings and goings, for his lordship's mansion in Grosvenor Square.

27

A s Lord Mainwaring's constant and sometimes only
companion in his travels, from huts in the West Indies to
palaces in Persia, from boats on the Nile to elephants in India,
Kilson had encountered and protected his lordship from many
strange people and many even odder requests, buy he had never
been more taken aback than when he opened the door to young
Master Frederick. Events have taken a most interesting turn,
he remarked to himself. Behind his impassive face, speculation
ran wild. Not even the flicker of an eyelid betrayed that anxious-
looking lads of eleven were not Lord Mainwaring's most
frequent visitors.

"Master Frederick Cresswell to see you, sir," he announced
impressively, ushering Freddie into the library.

Lord Mainwaring was no less astounded than his butler, but
detecting the unease that would flit momentarily across Freddie's
face despite his valiant efforts to hide it, he said in a tone that
implied these visits were a regular occurrence, "Hallo, Freddie.
What brings you to this part of town?"

With an effort, Freddie, who had been gazing in awe at an
imposing ancestor astride a horse over the mantelpiece, pulled
his thoughts together and said in as offhand a manner as he could

muster, "Well, sir, as we haven't seen you this age, I just thought I would pay you a call to see how you are doing."

Mainwaring was amused. "That is most kind of you. I am doing very well, thank you."

"I am glad of that, sir," his young guest responded politely while he sought desperately for some conversational gambit to introduce the subject occupying his mind. No such phrase came to him, so, in characteristic fashion, he blurted, "Well, you see, sir, you used to come to see us all the time, and now you don't. And, well, the last time we saw you it seemed as though Fanny was not best pleased with you." The quizzical lift of his host's eyebrow did nothing to encourage him, but he plunged bravely on. "Well, sir, you see, sir," he began unhappily, "it seemed to me as though you and she were as thick as thieves. I mean . . ." He blushed guiltily at his cant phrase. "You seemed to be such good friends. And then you weren't, and . . ." He looked fleetingly, pleadingly, at Lord Mainwaring's impassive countenance. "I thought you might like to be friends again, sir."

"Ah," said his lordship.

"So I thought if I explained to you what a right 'un Fan is and how she never holds a grudge or keeps harping on it after she's let you have it, I thought you might feel brave enough to go tell her you're sorry she got mad and you'd like to be friends with her again." He looked up appealingly, adding ingenuously, "And then you wouldn't feel at all odd about coming to call or taking Ned and me to a cricket match at Lord's, or whatever."

With a supreme effort Lord Mainwaring was able to keep his lips from twitching at this clincher to Freddie's argument, but for a moment his eyes twinkled with barely suppressed amusement. This was quickly replaced by the strained hollow look that had been worrying Kilson all week. He smiled and laid his hand on Freddie's shoulder, saying, "I appreciate your coming, old man, but it is more serious than that. It's not that I have made your sister angry. It's that I have given her a disgust of me and my life that could hardly be remedied with an apology. She's not mad at me. She simply does not like me." In this simply put speech to a boy who could not possibly understand all the bitter thoughts with which he had been torturing himself, Mainwaring revealed more of his feelings than he had ever let slip to another human being.

Freddie stood silent for a moment, his brow wrinkled in a fierce effort at concentration. "Well," he said in a burst of perspicacity that took even him by surprise, "I think she must not dislike you, because if she did dislike you, she wouldn't have been the least upset if you had done something very bad. And she *is* upset. I could just tell by the way she looked. When she's blue-deviled she likes to walk in the country. And she went to Cresswell because she's in the dismals, not because there's anything amiss there," he concluded triumphantly. "The staff there can take care of anything that comes up. She herself said that the day we left. So you see, sir . . ."

A slightly conscious look stole across Lord Mainwaring's features. "You may not be too far wrong, lad. We may just have to put your theory to the test."

"Oh, please do, sir," his youthful mentor begged. "I know I am not wrong. You could say you have come to visit Cassie and me. Promise to try, sir."

Mainwaring seemed to consider the invitation, though anyone privileged to observe how quickly the gloom had lifted from his brow would have known this hesitation was purely for effect. "Very well, Frederick. I shall put it to the touch. But you must run along now before you are missed."

"Splendid, sir! You won't forget about the cricket, will you, sir? We shall be going down to Cresswell ourselves at the end of the week, so we don't have much time." And with this parting shot he was gone, leaving Lord Mainwaring to stare pensively into the ashes of last night's fire.

"By God, the scamp just might be right. Kilson!"

Kilson, who had been standing suspiciously close to the library door, took some time before answering his lordship's bellow. "Yes, my lord?"

"Pack my bags. I think it's high time we found out how things are progressing at Camberly."

"Very good, my lord." Once outside the door again, Kilson's wooden countenance relaxed into a smile of heartfelt relief. "Bless you, Master Frederick," he breathed to himself.

Young Master Frederick was not at all above congratulating himself. "Cassie! Cassie, I say, where are you?" he bellowed up the stairs the minute Higgins had shut the door behind him.

"I'm up here, Freddie, with Ned. Whatever do you want?" his twin responded with some annoyance. She and Ned had just completed the laborious construction of an elaborate card castle, whose instant doom was imminent the moment her rambunctious brother appeared. Sure enough, he had only to enter the doorway of the drawing room for the entire structure to collapse. "Really, Freddie! You're worse than Wellington!" Cassie began disgustedly, but broke off at the sight of her brother's face. He was obviously bursting with information and quite obviously put out at finding her with company. Cassie was at a loss. On one hand, she was dying to discover what had put Freddie in such a state. On the other, she was very fond of Ned, and though wishing him to leave, knew that the last thing someone as quiet and shy as Ned needed was to be made to feel like a third party. "Ned is such a good castle builder, you can't think, Freddie," she began, seizing the first thing that came to mind. "He knows ever so much history, and so many stories that he's been telling me as we have been building this." Ned blushed uncomfortably. He appreciated Cassie's efforts to draw him into the group, but he would so much have preferred to be called a clever cricketer or a bruising rider.

"Does he now?" Freddie looked curious.

"Yes, he does, and what's more, he told me all about going to see the Horse Armory at the Tower with Nigel. Did you know they have effigies of all the kings of England, from George II back to William the Conqueror, mounted on horses and wearing their armor?"

"No." Freddie's interest was stirred. "Did you see all kinds of weapons too?" Fortunately, Ned had an excellent and exact memory. This, coupled with his true interest in the subject and a talent for narration, soon had Freddie listening with rapt attention, his momentous visit completely forgotten.

"Perhaps we can go together again sometime before we all go back to the country," Cassie suggested. Ned looked gratefully at her.

"That would be famous," her brother agreed enthusiastically.

"But who would take us?" They all agreed that this was indeed a puzzler, and all three of them realized, not for the first time, how seriously they missed Frances. Ned soon made his exit, promising to hint to Kitty so that she might hint to Lady Streatham that a second excursion to the Tower might be in order.

"Now, what has happened to put you in such a state?" demanded Cassie the minute he had gone. "I feared that if you had to wait another minute you might burst your buttons."

"Now, Cass," her twin began heatedly. Then, adopting a tone more suitable to the important nature of his mission, he continued coolly, "It's nothing. I've just been calling at Mainwaring House and thought you might be interested in how Lord Mainwaring is getting on."

Cassie was suitably impressed. "Freddie, you didn't! Weren't you dreadfully afraid? After all, he hasn't come to call in weeks."

"Well, I thought that might have to do with Fanny's being so mad at him in the park. I thought he mightn't understand that she doesn't stay mad long and she's always willing to cry friends, so I thought I'd tell him that."

Cassie was awed into silence by this worldly pronouncement. She soon recovered and added thoughtfully, "You're right, of course, but I'm not sure Fan would like us meddling in her affairs."

"I'm not meddling!" he retorted indignantly. "But I don't see why we should lose such a bang-up friend just because of a silly little brangle. You know how grown-ups are. They think the least little thing is terribly serious and important."

"You might be right," she began dubiously. "But what did he say he would do?"

Freddie tried to recall his lordship's exact words. He didn't remember Lord Mainwaring actually promising anything, but from somewhere he had come by the impression that Lord Mainwaring, feeling a great weight lifted from his mind, was on the point of immediate departure for Hampshire.

In fact, Lord Mainwaring's departure was forestalled in a slightly frustrating manner by the most amiable of friends, Bertie Montgomery. Bertie had an innately sympathetic nature, a quick, observant eye, and a finely tuned sense of social situations. Perhaps sooner than anyone else, the dowager Marchioness of Camberly and Lady Streatham included, he had foreseen Frances' and Julian's friendship developing and continuing into something more. He sensed, even before they did, the understanding that had grown up between them. Without being party to their last two disastrous encounters, he had a fair sense of what might have occurred. He had visited Frances not long after the episode in the park and had instantly noted the change in her and put it down to his friend's account. From her subsequent transformation he was able to surmise that somehow another woman, presumably Vanessa Welford, had been involved. Mainwaring, of course, had been out of town, so Bertie had had to wait some time to see how the situation was affecting him. Because he was fond of both Frances and Mainwaring and continued in his original conviction that they would suit each other very well, it was with some satisfaction that he observed the restless behavior Mainwaring had exhibited upon his return to the metropolis. The man who ordinarily scorned the social for more weighty affairs now haunted the opera, the theater, routs, balls, and even Almack's. To the casual observer, Mainwaring remained as aloof as ever, cutting the presumptuous and the insipid with his usual quelling hauteur, but there was a look in his eyes that spoke volumes to Bertie of his friend's unhappiness.

For a while it had seemed as though Frances, under the tutelage of the Comte de Vaudron, not only had recovered but also was discovering and truly enjoying the delights of society. Bertie was delighted. He had long thought she was dreadfully unappreciated and was glad to see her coming into her own. Perhaps even more gratifying was that she seemed to be enjoying herself immensely as well—a rare but well-deserved state of affairs. Still, a small part of him was sad that she seemed to have outgrown her friendship with Julian so quickly. Frances was so convincing in her role as a young lady enjoying taking the *ton* by storm, indeed she had almost convinced herself, that Bertie was unaware how much she too missed Mainwaring's companionship.

Then came the night of the Duchess of Devonshire's ball.

Bertie had been part of the general circle around Frances and had happened to glance up at the precise moment Mainwaring had entered the room. He saw the look that Mainwaring had been unable to hide completely, read the admiration, the jealousy, and the longing in it. He also observed, by the way she studiously avoided looking in Mainwaring's direction, that Frances was as intensely aware of his movements in the throng as Mainwaring was of hers. Having thus established that neither one of them was as indifferent as he or she hoped to appear, Bertie set himself to watch them closely. Thus it was that out of the corner of his eye he saw Frances go out on the terrace, trailed by young Wolvercote and shortly followed by Julian. When the only one of the principals to reappear was Wolvercote, he developed fairly accurate suspicions as to the nature of the scene and its outcome. The suspicions were confirmed the next day by Higgins, who informed him, "Lady Frances has gone to the country, sir. Urgent business at Cresswell required her presence, you understand." Though a confirmed lover of London, Bertie was well enough aware of country life and Frances' excellent managerial abilities not to be fooled a moment by this flimsy excuse to escape a difficult situation. Furthermore, he knew that it would not fool the sharper members of the *ton* either. Partly out of a true desire to offer her sympathy and companionship, and partly out of a desire to offer the type of support that would mislead the rest of the world and ensure her continued good standing in society, he gathered together a house party of the most witty and socially brilliant of his friends and, to his mother's complete astonishment, retired posthaste to his own nearby estate.

It was just as he was about to embark on this journey that he encountered Mainwaring. Both were caught in the crush of traffic on Park Lane. Mainwaring, on a handsome but nervous bay, was on his way to work off some of its skittishness and his own impatience as well. He was astounded and slightly alarmed to see his friend ensconced in a traveling coach. Knowing that Bertie never willingly left the bustle of the city, he inquired his destination with genuine concern. His amazement grew when he learned that Bertie was actually returning to his ancestral acres. "Is Lady Montgomery ill, then?"

"Oh, no. Quite the contrary, chipper as ever. I just felt in need of rustication and have invited Alvanley and some others to bear me company."

Lord Mainwaring might not have been as socially aware as his friend, but he was no fool. He was well aware that Bertie's friendship with Frances arose from the proximity of their estates. He had always thought of Bertie as a perennial bachelor, never the type to become serious over a woman, but as he quickly reviewed the past months, he realized uncomfortably that, aside from himself, Frances' most constant companion had been Bertie. The more he thought about it and of the warm way in which Bertie always spoke of Frances, the more jealous and suspicious he became. His face darkened as he said shortly, "Enjoy yourself." This ill temper was not lost on Bertie. It had not been part of his plan in the least to make Mainwaring jealous, but if he were, so much the better. Jealousy sometimes drove intelligent men to take steps they might otherwise avoid.

Bertie's visit to Hampshire was at least partially successful. He had managed, via his customary grapevine, to keep the *ton* informed of the picnics, the excursions, and the fêtes in which Frances always played an important role. Certainly Frances enjoyed all the company and the activity, but Bertie, catching her in unguarded moments, saw such sadness in her eyes that he longed to comfort her, to offer her anything—himself even— that would dispel it even the tiniest bit. And Bertie was someone who had a pure and unadulterated horror of the married state. Still, he advised himself, if one had to marry, Fanny would be the one to choose. She was so easy to get along with. But fortunately, before he moved too far in this vein, he realized that however comfortable it would be for him to live with Fanny, it would not be the least bit comfortable to live with the other Cresswells. Nor, when he thought about it, would Fanny be happy with him. She needed someone as intelligent and articulate as she was—someone like Lord Julian Mainwaring. In fact, he became so much more convinced of this than ever that he soon found himself returning to town in the hopes that he could effect some sort of reconciliation.

On the slimmest of pretexts, a totally false interest in the affairs at Camberly, he presented himself at Mainwaring House.

"Place is looking a bit run-down, you know," he reported to a surprised Mainwaring. "Wouldn't dream of telling you how to run your affairs, old fellow, but I know you've got so many of them you can't be everywhere and, well, I know Frances never trusted that rascally agent of yours."

"Oh, you saw Lady Frances, did you?"

"Oh, certainly. Called on her almost every day." Mainwaring's brows lowered threateningly. "She was perfectly charming. Always an addition to any party, and there were a good many of them. But she seemed a bit pulled."

"Oh?" Mainwaring would allow himself to reveal no more than that of his intense curiosity.

"Yes. She seems quieter than usual, almost worried. Something's upsetting her. 'Course, knowing her, she'll take care of it, but I don't like to see her tackling so many things on her own." The seed successfully planted, he rose to go. "Just thought I'd drop by and let you know how things are at Camberly. Might not be a bad thing for you to go down with Ned and Kitty when they return, and cast an eye around." And having given his friend the perfect excuse to pursue his happiness on his own, he departed, well-satisfied with his morning's work.

Bertie was more successful than he could have hoped. In fact, he was almost too successful. Mainwaring at first was infuriated by the thought of Frances flirting and enjoying herself with such a gay crowd while he suffered in London, tortured by an uncomfortable conscience. This brought back thoughts of the confrontation that had driven her from London in the first place. Bertie had mentioned her fatigue. Was she still upset over his unpardonable behavior? Or was it really some problem at Cresswell Manor that was wearing her down? Bertie's concern, damn him, had seemed almost proprietary. Mainwaring wanted someone to share and ease Frances' burdens, but Bertie Montgomery was not the person he had cast in the role of her supporter. Bertie was too much the gay dog to take on such burdens. Still, and there a shattering doubt crept in, Bertie cared a great deal for Frances, was an old friend, and possessed the kindest heart in London. Perhaps, despite his horror of anything remotely intellectual, he was the very person for her. Bertie, in any event, never upset her, never made her angry or acted reprehensibly toward her. How could he, Mainwaring, outstanding for his calm diplomacy, have forced his attentions upon her out of pure jealousy and anger? Again he cursed himself for having treated her so roughly at the Duchess of Devonshire's ball. She would never forgive him. At least, he consoled himself with a bitter smile, his further alienation of her brought with it the memory of her in his arms, a memory so intense that he ached with the longing to feel the softness of her, to bury his hands in her delicately scented hair and kiss her until she was forced to respond, to admit that he had been correct in interpreting that brief instant of yielding as passion for him. But no, Lady Frances had too much pride and independence. She would never allow herself to become a victim of passion. Even in her greatest moment of anger she had always been in command of her thoughts, her words. What had she said? "You seem to forget I am not Lady Welford." A passionately involved woman would not have been able to respond with such presence of mind. A woman less completely in control of herself would have raged at him or wept. Not Frances. Always mistress of herself and her surroundings, she had left rather precipitately, but in full possession of her faculties. Perhaps she did love Bertie. He was another one who never allowed his passions, if he possessed any, to obscure his delicate social sense. Yes, perhaps Bertie was the man for her. He, Mainwaring, should stay away from Cresswell and allow them a chance to pursue their friendship in peace. No! his mind and body protested. She is too vital, too spirited, too adventurous for him. She would be wasted on Bertie, bored within a month. They won't do together. He can't have her! Worn out with thinking, he poured himself a glass of brandy, and another, and another, savoring the burning in his throat as he slouched in his chair, head in hand.

He decided at last to set out for Camberly. But first he resolved to do something for Frances—and Freddie as well—that would please her, no matter what the outcome of future encounters. He fulfilled his much-longed-for promise and took Freddie, Nigel, and Ned to a cricket match at the grounds recently set aside by Mr. Thomas Lord. The boys were ecstatic. Even Ned, who ordinarily was more interested in bookish pursuits, his only outdoor activities centering around horses, was enthralled. The marquess himself had a surprisingly enjoyable afternoon. Though he'd since transferred his athletic interests and prowess to the boxing salon and equestrian pursuits, he had not forgotten his own days of glory on the cricket pitch. It was refreshing to return to those scenes, to discuss it all with such eager spectators, to talk with people too young to dissemble, to pretend interest that they didn't feel or feign boredom. Infected by their enthusiasm and undisguised admiration, he found himself unbending and enjoying himself in a way he hadn't since he had returned from his travels in the colonies.

He was not alone. Freddie, seeing that Lord Mainwaring was the true sport he had expected him to be, was more determined than ever to reestablish easy terms between the Cresswells and Mainwaring. This resolution extended even to the inclusion of Ned in his conversation. Ordinarily he would have written him off as a rather dull stick as he had in the past, but Cassie had seemed to see something in him. Now, as he got to know him, he realized that this dullness stemmed from a natural reserve and being raised in a feminine household. Ned wasn't necessarily unadventurous. He had just never had anyone to encourage him. Freddie resolved to visit Camberly more often in order to offer him the boon of male companionship. Of course, the chance to bring himself and his family to Lord Mainwaring's attention did nothing to weaken this admirable resolve.

28

The subject of these various machinations continued in her routine, totally oblivious of the stratagems of those interested in her welfare. In spite of admitting to herself that she was in a fair way to being in love with, or certainly attracted to, Lord Mainwaring, Lady Frances had never entertained the least thought of marrying him. She had never even seriously considered marrying anyone, and she would have been astounded and probably highly annoyed to learn that no fewer than all of her nearest and dearest, with the possible exception of Aunt Harriet—and the Comte de Vaudron was working on that redoubtable lady—not only pictured her married to Lord Mainwaring but also were actively promoting the match.

She was glad to welcome Cassie, Freddie, Aunt Harriet, and the staff home. In truth, after the first few days when she had relived past events, reinterpreted various scenes, and wrestled in general to put her thoughts and emotions in order, she had begun to find her solitude more upsetting than restful. Bertie's house party had certainly provided diversion. It was delightful to discuss antiquities with Lord Alvanley and match wits with Bertie's more brilliant friends. She had even enjoyed the blatant admiration of some of the younger members of his group, who trailed her everywhere, hanging on every word. And she had been warmed and comforted by the support and sympathy she read in Bertie's bearing toward her. But instead of dispelling unwelcome thoughts, these people, so closely connected with the life she had led in London, brought back the memories even more vividly. She longed for the simple trust and companionship of her family. Thus when one beautiful June afternoon the dusty carriage finally appeared, she greeted them all with unusual warmth.

"Fanny, Wellington, Nelson! We're here!" Cassie yelled, leaning perilously from the coach and waving vigorously as it rounded the bend in the drive. The twins were bursting with energy, eager to get back to the freedom and delights of the country.

"Has Jim arrived yet with the ponies?" Freddie wanted to know. "And has Ned come home yet?"

Frances was somewhat surprised by this last query, as Freddie had been less than interested in his neighbor before.

"I don't believe so, but I don't know when they plan to return."

"Oh, soon, I expect. He told me the other day it would most likely be sometime this week."

Frances' curiosity increased. "Oh, did you see Ned and Kitty while I was away?"

"Oh, yes. Lord Mainwaring took Nigel, Ned, and me to see a cricket match at Lord's. And, Fan, it was the most bang-up thing ever." Her brother had begun blithely, but observing the slightly rigid look that came over his sister's face, he broke off abruptly. "Wellington, Wellington! Come on, you silly mongrel," he called. "Let's go to the stables and see what's up."

"He's not a mongrel," Cassie protested indignantly, but then, recognizing the meaningful look cast in her direction, realized that Freddie had purposely chosen a taunt that never failed to rouse her, with the sole object of getting her attention. She trotted off obediently with him and Wellington to the stables.

Once out of earshot, her twin hissed, "She's still angry at him, so be sure you don't let on that he's coming down here."

She nodded, looking at once mischievous and approving. "What a strategist you are, Freddie."

"Nothing to it," he responded loftily, but spoiled his superiority the next minute by adding confidently, "Grown-ups aren't at all difficult to manage, you know. They aren't any better at covering up their feelings than children are. They just seem to want different things. Though why they want them, I can't understand." He frowned disapprovingly at this afterthought. In fact this had been puzzling him a great deal. Except for Fannie and Cassie, who were both great guns, awake on every suit, and pluck to the backbone, he had no use at all for females. They were weak, silly things who never knew when to be quiet and had no interest in the finer things of life—dogs, guns, horses, boxing. In fact, he had decided in a meditative moment that he liked his sisters precisely because they didn't act like other members of their sex. Given this misogynistic outlook, it was only natural that he should look upon love and lovers with the highest scorn. Most boys of eleven would have been totally oblivious of the existence of this phenomenon, but Freddie was a medievalist at heart. He delighted in tales of knights and dragons and bemoaned the cruelty of a fate that had caused him to be born in a civilized age when even duels were illegal. He read voraciously, anything and everything, even tackling Froissart and Malory in his enthusiasm. Though he skipped over the parts concerning fair ladies and concentrated only on the incredible feats required to rescue them, he was aware that their approval was a motivating factor in knightly conduct. Much as he loved and admired Lancelot and Arthur, he deplored their apparent foolishness over Guinevere. And now, another, more fleshly hero seemed to share their only weakness. Not only had Freddie been disgusted that such a nonpareil as Lord Mainwaring should want to spend time with someone as clinging and languishing as the lady who had been hanging on his arm that day in the park, but he had even found it difficult to believe that his lordship could prefer driving Frances around the park to joining him and Nigel on a return trip to the Tower.

At first he had thought Mainwaring escorted Frances so that

she would not feel left out when he returned to the more manly companionship of Freddie, Nigel, and Ned. But it had soon been borne in on him that Mainwaring enjoyed his sister's company, in fact actually preferred it to his. It was not to be supposed that Freddie could overlook this flaw in his hero, but in view of his other outstanding qualities, he readily forgave it. And, after all, Lord Mainwaring was not acting foolishly over just any female. Just before the unfortunate encounter in the park, Freddie had begun to recognize the advantages of this otherwise disturbing state of affairs. Lord Mainwaring was increasingly to be seen at Brook Street and could always be relied on to lend a sympathetic ear to the problems of perfecting one's cricket techniques or to offer advice on the management of recalcitrant ponies. And then that overdressed lady with the mean eyes had somehow ruined everything. Freddie didn't quite understand it, but he knew that his elder sister was very angry. He also knew that though she was seldom upset, once she was, she didn't give in easily. He also knew that a man who had successfully dealt with pirates in the West Indies and angry natives in Africa would not be the least bit worried by a furious woman, even if she were Lady Frances Cresswell. He was far more likely to ignore her and sooner or later forget all about her and her family. And Freddie certainly did not want that to happen. He felt that the best course to reestablish relations was to take a leaf out of Malory's book and hope for some situation that would offer Mainwaring adventure and challenge, while at the same time rendering a service to Lady Frances. In this boring day and age, such dramatic situations were not readily available, but Freddie felt certain that time and some ingenuity on his part could produce one. In the meantime, it would be better if the two principals in the drama were kept apart and not allowed to annoy each other further.

At his wits' end as far as the creation of such a situation went, he decided to enlist the aid of his twin. Cassie listened breathlessly while he outlined his plans. Sympathetic as she was, she was no more forthcoming with ideas than he had been. "If only all the dragons hadn't been killed or died off," she sighed.

Wistfully, Freddie thought so too, but there was no use in wasting time and energy lamenting the glorious past. "Come

off it, Cassie. Think!'' he ordered. And the two of them sat
in the hayloft with furrowed brows until Wellington summoned
them to tea. Ferreting out the twins in all their many hideaways
was one of Wellington's prime duties. Aided by his sharp eyes
and no less acute nose, he was justifiably proud of his skill,
for Cassie and Freddie were past masters at hiding in out-of-
the-way nooks and crannies.

Meanwhile, the object of all these plans was worrying over
the state of affairs himself. Well aware that it behooved him
to tread carefully where Lady Frances Cresswell was concerned,
Lord Mainwaring did not take Bertie's suggestion and escort
Kitty and Ned into Hampshire. Lady Frances was too damnably
self-assured as it was when trapped in the most unexpected and
uncomfortable confrontations. He certainly did not want her to
be forewarned of his presence at Camberly. He made certain
of arrangements for his wards' journey and bade them a warmer
farewell than anticipated. Really, he had almost grown fond of
Kitty's enthusiasms and Ned's youthfully serious air.

He then retired to business of his own—reports to be made
to Lord Charlton, problems with a greedy maharajah who was
making trouble with his agents in the East, and recalcitrant
tenants closer at hand on his smallest estate in Buckinghamshire.
He dealt with all of these in his usual incisive manner, but at
times his mind would wander back to Lady Frances and conjecture on a variety of possible receptions at Cresswell. His
shipping agent found him unwontedly cautious and several times
his solicitor was forced to recall his errant thoughts. Both
instances were so uncharacteristic of his lordship that these
worthy men were slightly dismayed.

"Hit's as though 'is 'eart wasn't in it,'' the agent complained
to an overripe widow of indeterminate age who shared his
predilection for the Mermaid tavern in Cheapside.

"I can't think what must have been worrying him. Everything
has been settled most advantageously,'' Mr. Wilkins confided
to his worthy mate as they sat over their dinner in Russell
Square. Both of these ladies, springing from backgrounds as
dissimilar as one could have imagined, had no difficulty in
interpreting this behavior. "It's a woman, sure as I'm
breathin','' sighed Nell gustily.

So it was that the Cresswells and their neighbors enjoyed a week of activity unconstrained by the presence of Lord Mainwaring. In fact, only Lady Frances would have been uncomfortable in his company. A Season in London had taught Kitty that formidable though he might be, her guardian was well-versed in the ways of society. In the main, Lord Mainwaring, concerned with more important problems than the latest style of tying a cravat or the tailor best capable of fitting a coat to perfection, spent too much time in diplomatic and financial circles to be acknowledged as a leader of the *ton*. However, his excellent taste in all the arts, coupled with tremendous wealth, pleasing personal appearance, and undoubted prowess in athletic pursuits of all types made him sought after by hostesses eager to lend cachet to their various functions, damsels aspiring to distinction or a great catch, sporting bloods in search of an amateur who posed a serious threat to the nation's champions, and hoary members of the Foreign Office in search of a well-considered opinion. In short, better than being one of its leading lights, Lord Mainwaring commanded the respect of the fashionable world, which was no mean feat. And in doing so, he had won the grudging admiration of his ward, uncomfortable as she occasionally still was in his awe-inspiring presence.

Ned, who could have cared less about society, or even whether or not his guardian noticed him at all, had first been impressed by his lordship's library. Not only was it well-stocked, it appeared to be well-used. Its shelves were never dusty and the volumes stood irregularly enough on them that even the most casual observer must recognize that they were frequently consulted. Ned was thrilled to have access to such a place. And, being a sensitive lad, he could see the trouble the marquess, obviously a busy man, went to to make certain his young charges enjoyed themselves. Though quiet, Ned was well aware of all that went on around him, and he grew to admire his uncle as he had never admired anyone else. He envied his calmness and assurance, the analytical approach he took to complications, and the way he interested himself personally in any problem, no matter how trivial.

Of course, Freddie and Cassie would have welcomed such a knowing 'un as the marquess. They had never stood in the least awe of him and were more ready than the others to recognize the qualities that made him an intriguing companion for even the most imaginative of eleven-year-olds. They were vociferous and frequent in lamenting his absence, and were carrying on in their usual manner one day to their sister. "Lord Mainwaring would let us go to see the Gypsy fair. I know he would," protested Cassie.

"You know he wouldn't allow Squire Tilden to convince him that it was dangerous. He would know what an old woman the squire is," her brother scoffed.

"That may very well be," Frances retorted. "But Lord Mainwaring is a man, fully able to scare respect into a band of Gypsies. No matter how well I am able to look after Cresswell, not to mention you two hellions, I don't scare Gypsies. And besides, he isn't here," she concluded triumphantly.

Here she received unexpected help from Kitty, who had ridden over to visit at the earliest opportunity. "You know, Freddie, everyone says that all those wonderful feats—sword-swallowing, fire-eating, conjuring, and the like—are the basest trickery. They don't really do it at all, but rely on their own quickness and the *stupidity* of their audience." She looked meaningfully at the twins, then concluded with a master stroke: "I am told they are hideously cruel to their animals. They beat their poor ponies unmercifully and they're too nip-farthing to feed their dogs properly. That's why they steal dogs wherever they go, because theirs are always starving to death." Kitty's cheeks pinkened and her large velvety eyes glistened with tears. In her earnestness, she remained oblivious of Frances' quizzical smile.

Lady Frances by no means believed these hair-raising stories, but if they kept the redoubtable twins from a situation bound to land both of them in some sort of trouble, so much the better. "Come," she said briskly, taking pity on their very genuine disappointment. "We must plan a great picnic instead to welcome home Kitty and Ned."

The twins were mollified with this idea, and when Frances discovered that the elder brother of the youngest housemaid added knowledge of a few magic tricks to a far-reaching reputation as an accomplished juggler, they were almost completely reconciled to the loss of the Gypsy fair.

The day chosen for the outing dawned clear and warm but not hot. In short, it was a perfect day for an expedition to Shooter's Hill, a spot beloved by picnickers for its commanding view of the surrounding countryside. Frances and Kitty had planned to travel sedately in the barouche, but the day was so fine and both of them had missed their long country rides so much while they were in the city that they chose to join the children on their ponies. Aunt Harriet had been offered a place in the carriage but had responded acidly that moments of such peace and quiet as this were too precious to waste, and besides, she must see to her precious plants after their upsetting journey. So the only traveler in the carriage was the well-stocked picnic hamper.

Ned, mounted on a recently bought chestnut his uncle had helped him select at Tattersall's, was the envy of the twins. And Freddie, seeing how well he sat a mount that was quite obviously full of spirit, was impressed. He wanted to know Xerxes' history, parentage, and fine points in minutest detail, and once again was surprised to find himself enjoying Ned's company so much. More inclined to conceal his accomplishments than call attention to them, Ned at first resisted Freddie's urging to "Show us what he can do, Ned." But when Cassie begged, "Oh, Ned, please do put him through his paces," he showed himself and his animal as proudly as though he were in the ring at Astley's. The twins then could no longer contain themselves, and itching for some violent exercise, galloped on ahead at breakneck speed, doubling back every once in a while to admonish the others, "Do hurry, we'll never get there at this snail's pace, and we're so hungry. Do come and look at Farmer Stubbs's new bull, Fan. Isn't he the most monstrous mean-looking beast you have ever seen?"

Ned fell back to listen to his sister and Frances discussing the progress of Frances' book. "In truth, I neglected it sadly while I was in London, and of course the first few days I was back at Cresswell I had my hands full, but I now am coming along better." Ned shyly asked what period of history she had chosen to present to the public first. "I've decided to try the most difficult first, the Greeks, and then, if I can make a go of that, I shall be so encouraged that I shall try the easier things—the Crusades, the Wars of the Roses, the Tudors. But, Ned, how have you come on with your own Greek studies? I know you had set the most ambitious plan to fill your days in London."

The boy flushed with pleasure. He had always regarded the twins' sister with awe. That she could be so learned, but so warm, adventurous, and gay, seemed a miracle to him. For years he had secretly envied Cassie and Freddie their close relationship with someone who could teach them so much. Dearly as he loved Kitty for her sweet and affectionate ways, he recognized that her mind was not as keen or inquiring as his. And here Frances was talking to him as a fellow scholar. He was in heaven.

Kitty rode on, amused by his admiration and happy in his pleasure at being treated as an equal. She was the only one of the party who seemed to feel anything but relieved to be back at home. Such an attitude was understandable in one who had exchanged exquisite ball gowns for a riding dress, a constant throng of admirers at a variety of dazzling social occasions for a family outing, and letters and bouquets for the complaints of the housekeeper and her elderly cousin. But the air felt so fine, the country looked so fresh, that she was content to ride along enjoying the fineness of the day and the peace and quiet of the countryside. She would have been astounded to learn how often Lady Frances' thoughts strayed back to the gaiety of the past Season and that her "Do tell me about the rest of your stay, Kitty," was as much to indulge the listener as the regaler.

Kitty was only too happy to oblige with dance-by-dance descriptions of the last of the Season's balls, as well as repeating word by word the conversations and detailing flounce by flounce the gowns at the final routs and fêtes. Young Lord Willoughby's name was featured rather frequently and always alluded to in such an offhand manner that Lady Frances was able to gratify her narrator by remarking on the apparent interest of that young peer. "Oh, yes, I daresay we did see a good deal of each other. He seems to enjoy the same things I do," replied Kitty with her adorable blush much deeper than usual. "He is all that is gentlemanly and attentive, not like so many of them, who only care whether one is impressed with the set of their coats, the intricacies of their cravats, or their athletic prowess. The tone of his mind is extremely nice. I think you would like him, Fan. At least, I hope you would. I do. I don't think I could like anyone else half so well," she concluded in a rush, with such a glowing look that her friend refrained from the obvious observations on the extreme youth and inexperience of both parties.

And, she thought to herself, just because I would not be happy with someone as naive and innocently optimistic as Willoughby doesn't necessarily mean that Kitty wouldn't be. Experience of the world does not ensure freedom from bitter disillusionment any more than naiveté assures it. After all, there was never a more naive and sentimental pair of lovers than Kitty's parents, nor a happier one. No need to be hard on them or her because they weren't to my taste. This last thought brought forcefully to mind the deep blue eyes and tanned face of one who was infinitely wise in the ways of the world, an image which, despite its instantaneous banishment, caused a warm fluttery sensation in the pit of her stomach and a certain breathlessness that had begun to affect her recently.

Kitty could not divine any of this complicated thought process, but she could recognize and correctly identify Frances' own blush and distracted air, and was instantly intrigued. For a while it had seemed to her that her guardian and Lady Frances had shared some special understanding, and she had hoped, not very optimistically, that something would come of it. She did not set such store by the relationship as Lady Streatham and her great-grandmother did, but then, she was not as well-acquainted with her uncle as they were. At any rate, she had been far more impressed with the *ton*ish group paying court to her friend just before her abrupt departure from London. Perhaps one of Bertie's friends? She began her investigation adroitly, she thought. "But you were quite gay down here yourself. Didn't Bertie Montgomery host a large party of friends directly after the Season ended?"

"Yes, he did," was the totally unsatisfying reply. There was no betraying consciousness, and the air of abstraction still remained. Kitty was at a loss to explain, but renewed her efforts. "Who was here?"

"Oh, Lord Alvanley, Lord Petersham, the usual, you know." Frances was patently uninterested in this select group.

The thundering of hooves ended any further questioning. "Do come on! However can you be so slow?" demanded Cassie.

"Women!" Freddie muttered, looking at Ned with all the world-weariness of an eleven-year-old who had just come home from a London Season. "Can you believe they would rather talk than ride or eat? Come along, Fan, we're so ravenous we've got pains in the breadbasket."

"In your what?"

"Well, that's what Jim calls it. Ain't it a great expression?"

"It is, I admit. And it's all very well for Jim, but it isn't for you."

"But, Fan, you're always telling us to write descriptively and enrich our vocabulary."

"Freddie Cresswell! You know very well that I refer to refined richness and not some stableboy cant," she retorted crossly.

Her brother grinned engagingly. "Come on, Ned. Cook made some delicious game pies and we must get to them before Cassie does or there won't be a crumb left." Having provoked both his sisters to his satisfaction, Freddie dashed on ahead to oversee the laying-out of the picnic.

The rest of the afternoon passed in the deliciously lazy way a perfect summer afternoon should. The children, under the critical eye of John Coachman, put their mounts through their paces, and Freddie even essayed the feat that had brought him to grief earlier. After many unsuccessful attempts he was able to stand on Prince's back long enough to ride in a circle at the end of the rein. "Fan, Fan! Look at me, I say," he was able to shout just before beginning to lose his precarious balance, but he was able to keep dignity intact by turning a slip into a jump off his mount's back and finish with a flourishing bow.

There was nothing for it then but for the others to try. Frances resumed her reading of *Guy Mannering*, just received from

Hatchard's in the morning post. Kitty was once again, after the Season's absence, busy with her sketchbook. Frances found the companionable silence and the hum of the bees very restful after the emotional turmoil of London and her own recent feverish activity at Cresswell. Slowly she drifted off and, for the first time in several months, fell into a deep sleep unbroken by any dreams or thoughts.

She was awakened by the rattle of tea things being set about and the arrival of William, complete with top hat and pet rabbit. The children spent a blissful hour stuffing themselves with jam tarts and exclaiming in delight as he made various articles disappear and reappear in the twinkling of an eye—and in the strangest places. He totally mystified the sharp-eyed Cassie with card tricks she thought she knew completely, and dismayed them all by making a dear little rabbit vanish altogether. He won all their admiration when, keeping five fresh eggs in the air, he reached deep into his empty hat and produced the rabbit, contentedly munching some dandelion greens. All in all it was a splendid afternoon and the Gypsies were totally forgotten.

29

While the Cresswells and their neighbors were thus enjoying the summer, the marquess was tidying up a few last details in town before descending on this unsuspecting crew. At last, two weeks after Kitty and Ned's departure for Hampshire, he was tooling toward Camberly, savoring the freshness of the country air and the chance to spring his grays after the crowds, noise, and claustrophobic atmosphere of the city. He did enjoy the wealth of interesting companions and the variety of entertainments to be found in London, but feeling sated with sophisticated pursuits, he welcomed the exhilaration of the drive, the test of his physical rather than his mental skills. For a while he gave himself thoroughly to the managing of his horses and the challenge of driving to an inch, but it wasn't long before unwelcome thoughts began to intrude. How was he going to convince Lady Frances to see him? And even if he were able to, what would he say? "I love you"? She would laugh in his face. No, that was not true. She would never allow herself to be unkind or vulgar. She would merely look at him in patent disbelief. How would he ever show that he cared about her? Well, then, should he tell her that she was the only woman he had ever wanted to marry? Despite the truth of this he knew her disbelief would turn to sheer incredulity. He would show her, make her see that he loved her, but how? In his frustration he took a corner much too fast and nearly locked wheels with a lumbering farm cart. Cursing himself, his stupidity, and his mismanagement of the entire situation, he gritted his teeth and drove the rest of the way, concentrating rigidly on nothing but the road ahead.

Before he was halfway to Camberly, Lord Mainwaring, for all his years and experience, was in no better shape than any young man in love. I was resisting matchmaking mamas and determined young women and carrying on liaisons with dozens of delightful ladies while she was still in the schoolroom, and now I am no better than someone in his salad days—or perhaps I'm already in my dotage, he thought bitterly. Humiliating as it all was, he reflected ruefully, it must mean he was in love. He had never in his life put himself out for a woman, and now he was allowing one to inflict agonies of self doubt—a hard lesson for a man who had been accustomed to holding his own alone in any situation, anywhere, for so long.

These serious reflections occupied him so that it seemed no time at all before he was in the yard at the White Hart, claiming the attention of several eager ostlers and the genial Crimmins. "Well, my lord, it's been some time since we've seen you here." Beaming, he ushered Mainwaring into a private parlor. "How are they all at Camberly? I fancy Miss Kitty did fairly make them stand up and take notice in London. We heard she's just come back. A lovely lass. And will you be staying on at Camberly or just passing through?"

"Thank you, Crimmins." The marquess gratefully accepted a mug of his host's best home brew. "Actually, I was hoping you could put me up. I'm sure they're all at sixes and sevens at Camberly, having just gotten back. I don't know how long my business here will take, and I don't want to put them out."

"You're more than welcome here, my lord." Crimmins completely accepted this barefaced lie. If he suspected that his wife's excellent cooking and his genial hospitality were luring Lord Mainwaring from Cousin Honoria's parsimonious housekeeping and smoking chimneys, he was welcome to. Mainwaring was not prepared to admit to anyone, even to himself, the real reason for his choice of accommodation. His presence in the neighborhood was much less likely to be brought to Frances' attention if he were at the White Hart than if he were at Camberly.

He had not reckoned on the sharp eyes of Master Frederick and Miss Cassandra Cresswell. The twins had just escaped from their lessons and had ridden straight to the village to see William's latest crop of baby rabbits. Since his performance at the picnic and subsequent offer to teach them the simplest of his tricks, that young man had become quite the favorite of the schoolroom set. William was at work mending fences in Squire Tilden's lower fields, but he had instructed his mother to show the rabbits to the children. He had not told her to regale them with freshly baked currant buns, but this offer was eagerly accepted and Cassie and Freddie came away more than satisfied, despite having missed their friend. They promised to visit Mrs. Tubbs next week when they came to check on the progress of the dear little bunnies.

As they rounded the bend in front of the inn, Cassie said, "Look, Freddie, there's Lord Mainwaring's curricle. Isn't it beautiful?"

"It couldn't be. He's doing business in London. You must be mistaken." The brotherly scorn in his voice implied that no mere girl could be capable of distinguishing one equipage from another, no matter how magnificent it was.

His twin was not so easily dismissed. "You are an odious boy, Freddie Cresswell. I can recognize Lord Mainwaring's grays just as well as you can, and well you know it! You might as well own up, Freddie. You know I'm right."

By now they had come abreast of the vehicle and there was no question as to whom they belonged. "Well, you may be right," her brother conceded unwillingly. Then he resumed with his superior air, "But don't tell Fan, whatever you do. I don't want you upsetting her."

Which, Cassie thought indignantly, was outside of enough and just like her toplofty brother. He never could stand to be bested at the least little thing. After all, *she* had not fallen off her pony and given her sister a week of worry in London.

But when they reached Cresswell in time for tea, both Frances and Nelson looked so agitated—an extremely uncharacteristic frame of mind for both of them—that they completely forgot this interesting turn of events. "I can't think where Wellington has got to," worried Frances. "Cook says he didn't show up for breakfast, and he hasn't bothered me for a walk the entire day. You know he always appears at teatime to tussle with Nelson and upset things as much as possible. Besides, Nelson has been meowing and trying to get my attention since I got up. And you know he's become so fat and lazy he wouldn't stir a paw if his life depended on it unless Wellington were playing with him."

"Mrrow," her companion agreed dolefully.

"Perhaps he found some stoats," volunteered Freddie. "Farmer Stubbs told me he thinks there's a family of them living in Hanger Wood. He's been meaning to go after them, but he's just too busy."

"Perhaps you are right," His sister agreed with little conviction. "He usually is here dropping them in my lap the minute he's caught one, though."

"Maybe they're very clever stoats and he's having difficulty catching them," ventured Cassie skeptically.

No one wanted to be the one to suggest what they all feared and suspected most. It was Cook, bursting in wrathfully to inform them that the chicken she had planned to dress for dinner had been stolen, who articulated their worst fears. "It's them rascally Gypsies, buffer nappers all of 'em, miss. They'll take anything that isn't tied down and locked up."

Frances interrupted soothingly. "It may have just gone off to find a nice private nesting place, or maybe a fox got it."

Cook was not to be mollified. "Humph. I don't believe no such thing, and it's my belief that they've stolen that pesky cur as well."

"You've no right to call Wellington that when you sneak as many scraps to him as anyone," protested Cassie. "But, Fanny, what would they steal Wellington for? They wouldn't . . . they wouldn't . . ." Cassie couldn't go on.

"Lord, no, you silly clunch," her brother exclaimed. "They've kidnapped him to turn him into a performing dog. They know that terriers like Wellington are very good at that sort of thing. And anyone looking at him can tell he's highly intelligent. That stupid nit has probably forgotten all about us and is having himself a fine time learning all sorts of tricks. You know how he likes to show off. He certainly enjoyed it when I tried to teach him some of the things I saw the dogs doing at Astley's.''

Hearing the name of his friend, Nelson howled and got up to scratch at the library door.

"Not tonight, Nelson. But if he's not back tomorrow, we'll go find him,'' Frances promised. "Now, what do you say? I think a little of Caesar's *Gallic Wars* to take our minds off this.''

The twins groaned more out of habit than anything else, for they realized as well as Frances that since nothing could be done for Wellington that night and they were more likely to fret impatiently if they were unoccupied, they might as well direct their energies somehow. "But,'' Freddie pointed out, "there are lots more pleasant ways to drown our sorrows or forget them.''

"Yes,'' his sister agreed. "And none of them is nearly as productive.'' All resistance squelched, the lesson began.

Freddie was wrong about one thing. Wellington was not enjoying himself in the least. In fact, he could not remember a time in his short life when he had been more miserable, he thought to himself as he sat morosely under one of the Gypsy caravans. He'd been happily following the fresh scent of stoat when he'd been roughly snatched up and thrust into a foul-smelling bag. He must have been tied to a saddle, because there was a distinct smell of horse and he was jolted quite dreadfully. It must have been an underfed pony. Wellington had ridden occasionally with Frances and he'd been behind the marquess's team of grays and he knew full well that no horse of any breeding would have as rough a gait as the one to which he had just been subjected.

They had bounced along for some time and then the air was suddenly alive with commotion. Women and children were shouting, dogs barking, ponies whinnying, and babies crying. The bouncing stopped. Wellington was jerked from his bag and pawed by a thousand curious hands, pulled and mulled like some object instead of a purebred West Highland Terrier of

impeccable lineage, he thought huffily. Then, as if this man-
handling by the common herd weren't enough, he was subjected
to the final indignity—a dirty rope was tied around his neck and
he was rudely pulled under a caravan, to be ignominiously tied
there alone with his thoughts under the baleful eyes of the ill-
assorted mongrels of the camp. One by one the fires were put
out. The appetizing smell of stew died out, and as the cold
evening fog descended, he sat alone, miserable, hungry, and
sorry for every time he hadn't come when Frances called, hadn't
sat down when one of the twins told him to, had nipped Nelson
a little too hard when they were wrestling. With a gusty sigh
he buried his nose in his paws and tried to sleep.

"Mrrow."

One ear lifted cautiously. Just a dream, he told himself,
shaking his head.

"Mrrow."

This time, both ears shot up. "Arrph," he responded
cautiously. A soft, furry body snuggled up next to him and
purred loudly in his ear. Unable to persuade Frances to look
for Wellington that evening, Nelson, his partner in crime and
adventure, had set off to do so himself. Following the elusive
trail and relying on a good deal of feline instinct, coupled with
the conversation he had overheard at tea and a natural distrust
of Gypsies, he had found him at last. All Wellington's loneliness
and misery vanished, but it would never do to show Nelson how
overjoyed he was to see him. Not only did someone now know
where he was, but he had a friend and ally of his own. He had
stuck out his square little jaw and showed himself completely
unimpressed by those ravenous Gyspy dogs, even though all
the while his insides were quaking. Together he and Nelson
worried the rope, but it resisted all their determined efforts.
They were at last forced to abandon the project, and Nelson
slunk off in the dark, promising to round up reinforcements.

He arrived back at Cresswell only a few hours before dawn—
just enough time to take a catnap at the end of Frances' bed
before waking her. This he promptly did, just as the faintest
streaks of morning light appeared in the east. He was loath to
let her complete her entire morning bathing ritual, and

complained loudly when she sat down in the breakfast parlor for some muffins and chocolate.

"Nelson, I *am* coming, but I shan't be able to help anyone on an empty stomach," his mistress admonished. "And what's more, you won't be able to either. Come, have some breakfast." She poured some cream in a bowl and laid on a saucer the kipper that Cook insisted no breakfast table be without. Despite the dreadful state of his nerves, Nelson succumbed to the delicious aroma of the kipper. Once that was finished, he needed the cream to wash it down. Much of his anxiety vanished once his stomach was full, and he was able to wait with a reasonable amount of patience for Frances to finish her repast. This she did with dispatch, fearing the descent of the twins and the inevitable delay while she told them her plans and dissuaded them from coming with her. As it was, she left the briefest of notes informing them that she and Nelson had left to search for Wellington, but not giving the slightest indication of their direction. In this way she hoped, without much confidence in the effectiveness of her stratagem, to prevent them from following her.

It was still quite early when she and Nelson set out, Nelson running a few feet ahead of her, tail waving proudly. It was a beautiful hour of the day, bathed in the golden glow of early-morning light. The grass, wet with dew, and the air, unsullied with the dust of the day, were fresh with the just-washed newness of a summer morning. In spite of her anxiety over Wellington and the emotional strain of the past few weeks, Frances felt glad to be there and alive with the sheer delight of ripening fields, singing birds, and trees in full leaf.

She was just a bit glad no one else knew of Wellington's disappearance, because it did seem a trifle absurd to be so upset over a mere dog. How Wellington would scorn her for such a heretical thought. And he would have been right to do so. To her, he wasn't a mere dog. He'd been a constant companion as she walked or rode the estate. He had sat up nights with her while she pored over the accounts or agricultural journals. When she had longed to rest her head on the shoulder of a parent or friend, he had snuggled up to her, beaming loyalty and encouragement out of his bright black eyes, and licked her face.

Absorbed in her thoughts, she tramped several miles, always keeping her eye on Nelson's tail but otherwise not paying a great deal of attention to her surroundings. All of a sudden Nelson stopped so abruptly that she almost tumbled over him. She looked about. Several hundred feet away was the Gypsy camp. In the early-morning light with the smoke rising from breakfast fires, it looked like some ghostly caravan from an Oriental tale. Frances stood taking in the scene a moment before collecting her thoughts to plan the next step. She had barely begun to do this when there was a rustle behind, a sharp pain at the back of her head, a flash of light, and then darkness.

30

"Freddie, Freddie," shouted Cassie as she raced up the stairs two at a time. She was usually an earlier riser than her slugabed brother, who remained warm and cozy under the bedclothes until the last possible moment. Today her matinal energy had been rewarded, as she was the first to discover Frances' note and was able to impart the news with an important air to the rest of the household that her sister had gone to look for Wellington.

Cassie had already apprised her Aunt Harriet of the news as that lady frowned over a botanical journal in the breakfast parlor while she absently crumbled a muffin into her morning chocolate. "Gracious, even Frances can't have been so pigheaded and independent as to have gone off to tackle those Gypsies alone," she remarked before returning to the latest theories for propagating orchids in England's inclement atmosphere. But an inquiry among the staff revealed that Frances appeared to have done exactly that.

Armed with this illuminating discovery, Cassie tore off to rouse her somnolent twin. For a moment he gaped owlishly at her from under a rumpled thatch of blond hair. "All alone, was she? That was dashed selfish of her to go off on a splendid adventure just like that when she knew we were dying to see . . . ahem, when she knew we would be worried to death about her. Perhaps we should go help her,'' he suggested. Galvanized by the prospect of such excitement, he leapt up and pulled on his clothes.

He was forestalled by the venerable Higgins, who, knowing his young master's mind better than anyone else, appeared just in time to put a stop to any such plans. ''Now, Master Freddie, you know as well as I do that Lady Frances doesn't want any interference from you.'' He silenced the indignant objections that burst forth with an admonitory gesture. ''No! You know that anyone who is capable of standing up to that villainous Mr. Snythe is not to be put off by a few vagabond Gypsies. No, Master Frederick, and Miss Cassandra too, don't try to gammon me. You know it's as good as my position is worth to keep you here even if it means tying you two up and locking you in the schoolroom. If Miss Frances had wanted company, she would have asked for it. Now, that's an end to the matter.'' Determination was written large in every line of his countenance. The twins sighed and contented themselves with topping each other's speculations as to Frances' probable course of action once she reached the Gypsy camp.

The day dragged on. Noontime came and went. Cook reluctantly served luncheon, but there was still no Lady Frances. By this time the twins were beginning to worry. It was so unlike their elder sister to be gone so long on an errand that should not have taken outside of an hour or two. ''Perhaps she stopped in the village,'' Cassie suggested. ''I heard her say that Mrs. Stubbs's youngest had the mumps.'' The only response she got from her brother was a look of pure scorn.

By teatime they were seriously alarmed, but they allowed Higgins to serve it as usual, just in case Frances should arrive tired and thirsty, looking forward to it. But both of them felt they couldn't eat a bite. Just as Higgins was setting down the bread and butter, there was a scratch at the door and in bounded Wellington and Nelson, both rather the worse for wear, but ecstatic to be home again.

''Wellington, you scamp,'' cried Cassie, hugging the bedraggled body close and surreptitiously feeding him a thickly buttered scone. "Whatever have they done to you? Freddie, look. The rope has rubbed his neck raw, and look at this cut over his eye. You look dreadful, Wellington, you really do."

The little dog was disappointed to hear her say so. He'd evaded no fewer than two Gypsy mongrels, nasty snapping beasts with gaping jaws and sharp teeth. He thought the cut gave him quite a rakish appearance. It lent a definite air of distinction. Nelson's game eye was also slightly puffy. He'd been dealt a swipe by one of the dogs in the fray. His already tattered ears looked to be even more so, but he seemed to be quite cheerful, and ever so proud of having discharged his old debt in rescuing his friend. It had been his perseverance and sharp teeth that had finally severed the rope and freed his companion.

The animals allowed themselves to be welcomed and fussed over for a little while, but it soon became plain that theirs was unfinished business. Wolfing down a final scone, Wellington headed for the door and barked peremptorily. "Freddie, he knows where Frances is. He's going to show us," whispered Cassie excitedly.

"Of course he does. Just a minute, Wellington. I must get a gun."

"Freddie Cresswell! When did you ever learn to handle a gun?" his sister demanded suspiciously.

"Well, I don't say I've ever killed anything, but I can hit a target most of the time," came the defensive reply.

"Stuff! Those Gypsies can throw their knives farther and faster than you can hit anything with that. I tell you what. I think we want a grown-up."

Her brother protested. "Cass, they'll just rant and rave about how children don't know what's to do and that their place is in the schoolroom, and then we'll never get to Frances before the Gypsies. Besides, we'll miss all the excitement because they'd never let us join them in looking for her."

"We don't want just any adult. We want . . ." Cassie thought for a moment. "We want Lord Mainwaring!" she exclaimed triumphantly. Much as it cost him to admit, Freddie grudgingly agreed that Mainwaring was the perfect solution, and the two, having scrawled a brief note intended to reassure Aunt Harriet and the staff, headed off toward Camberly with Wellington and Nelson in tow.

The marquess had just stepped into the library to go over some household accounts when the butler Chamberlain announced, "Master Frederick Cresswell, Miss Cassandra Cresswell to see you, sir." He hid his surprise quite creditably as he ushered them to chairs and asked the butler to bring some tea. "What? You've had yours, have you? Never mind, then, Chamberlain. Oh, yes, hello, Wellington . . . hello, Nelson. Of course I'm delighted to see you all, but if I'm correct, this looks like a deputation with a mission. How did you know I was here?"

Freddie explained their having seen his curricle a few days before and then began hesitantly, "It's about Fan, sir."

The marquess raised one mobile eyebrow, a gesture that seemed more indicative of surprise than interest.

"Well, it's like this, sir. We think the Gypsies have kidnapped her."

Both brows went up. There was no doubt as to the expression now. It was one of patient disbelief.

"I know it sounds like nonsense, sir, but Wellington disappeared and, having heard that Gypsies were in the area, Fan thought, we all thought, they might have stolen him. So she went to look for him. And they must have—stolen him, I mean—and done something to Fan, because here he is and Fan hasn't shown up for luncheon or tea and her note said she left very early this morning to look for him. So you see, I think Wellington escaped but she's a prisoner somewhere because just look at the rope around Wellington's neck. Both he and Nelson appear to have been in a scuffle, and now they keep trying to get us to follow them."

"Arf!" Wellington confirmed the veracity of Freddie's suspicions.

During the discussion, Lord Mainwaring had gone from being slightly incredulous at such a wild tale to thoughtful, and now he looked distinctly forbidding. "I think, wildly improbable as this seems, you may be right. Now, and don't argue with me, I shall take Wellington and Nelson with me. You and Cassie must return to Cresswell on the off chance that Frances returns.

No! I know you feel you should come with me, and in any other instance I would be glad to have two such plucky companions, but I think it's best if I go alone. It's much easier for a single person to surprise the enemy and rescue someone than it is for a crowd."

The twins, object though they would, were forced to bow to superior knowledge and experience and admit the sense of this plan. After wishing the marquess luck, they allowed themselves to be persuaded to return to Cresswell. The unadventurousness of this course of action was palliated somewhat by their being driven in his lordship's curricle behind his famous grays.

In the meantime, Mainwaring, Wellington, and Nelson repaired to the stable, where his lordship's powerful hunter was quickly saddled. He would have preferred to take a carriage, as Lady Frances might be in no shape to ride, but after nearly a day's delay there was no time to be wasted. It had taken a bit of doing to convince Wellington and Nelson that the twins were putting the responsibility for the search for Frances into the marquess's capable hands, but at last they understood and were soon bounding along a few feet in front of him and Brutus, feeling extremely important.

The early evening was as lovely as the morning had been when Lady Frances set out. Soft light was slanting across ripening fields, bathing them in gold, and a light breeze was stirring the leaves. The marquess, his eyes fixed on the small figures leading him, barely noticed his surroundings. The grim set of his jaw and worried line of his dark brows revealed the unpleasant turn of his thoughts. If only she had gone to the squire or one of the local farmers instead of charging off completely on her own. How foolish and how very like her, in the interests of efficiency and speed, to take the entire problem immediately on herself without stopping to consult anyone. Though he cursed her for having put herself in such danger, Julian admired the spirit that had prompted it. His face softened as he thought of the self-reliance and the willingness to tackle and solve whatever unpleasantness came her way. And once again he, who could do so much to help her, had been unable to spare her. At least this time he could still do something. But what state was she in? Had the Gypsies, fearing the law, decamped already and taken her with them? How had they kept her from escaping? A lady as resourceful as Lady Frances would be difficult to detain without resorting to some sort of violence or drugs or both. He could not bear the thought of any of it.

After what seemed miles and hours of agonizing over Frances' possible state, he and Brutus nearly stumbled over Wellington and Nelson, who had stopped to reconnoiter before advancing cautiously on a tumbledown shack that at one time must have held laborer's tools. The four approached carefully, but there was no sound or sight of any guard. There was no sound of Frances either. Most likely, the marquess thought bitterly, the Gypsies, panicked by what they had done, had gone off as quickly and inconspicuously as possible, leaving her to her fate. From Wellington's eager look it appeared as though she were still in there. Mainwaring dismounted, tied Brutus to a tree, ordered Wellington and Nelson to remain out of the way, and advanced warily on the hut.

There was a rusty lock hooked through an equally rusty hasp on the door, but these were easily broken with one well-placed kick. The door burst open and the marquess stood aside, fists raised. His powerful shoulders and businesslike stance proclaimed him more than a match for any Gypsy guard. None appeared, so he stepped in. As his eyes became accustomed to the gloom, he saw Frances in the far corner. Her hands and feet were bound, and a dirty handkerchief gagged her, but at the sound of an intruder she struggled into as combative a position as possible, her eyes blazing defiance.

"My poor girl," he exclaimed. With one stride Mainwaring crossed the hut and knelt beside her to untie the gag that was painfully tight around her head.

She gasped for air and then in her coolest drawing-room voice inquired, "Whatever are you doing here, my lord?"

"I *thought* I was rescuing you," he replied, busy with the cords at her hands and feet.

It took all her willpower not to collapse when they were loosened, but she was damned if she were going to reveal the slightest weakness to her rescuer. In the past few minutes Frances' emotions had run the full gamut, from fear, to relief, to something else that she refused to recognize.

When she had first come to her senses after her capture, Frances had been too weak to do anything. Her head throbbed so much it had been impossible even to think. Gradually, though, she had felt better and had done her best to try to undo the ropes at her hands and feet. All her twisting and wriggling of her extremities had only succeeded in chafing the skin badly and not loosening them the slightest bit. At the outset she had been certain that the Gypsies would eventually recognize her and release her, but as no one came, she concluded they must be writing a ransom note of some sort. She had not been too afraid, only uncomfortable and thirsty. The day dragged on. She had kept track of the sun's passage through a hole in the roof, thinking hopefully of the note she had left back at Cresswell. Surely someone there would rouse the neighborhood and come to the camp in search of her. Still no one came. When far away came the sound of horses stamping, dogs barking, and harnesses jingling, she concluded in despair that the Gypsies were leaving to put as much distance between them and Cresswell as possible before her disappearance was noticed. Try as she would to think of some way to escape or to make her presence known, she could come up with nothing. She could only hope that somehow Freddie or Cassie would remember where the Gypsies had been camping and organize a search party. Certainly they would. Frances had settled down to wait with as much fortitude as she could muster, but her spirits, aggravated by hunger and thirst, would sink, and despite her best efforts, despair would creep up on her. It was when she began to feel her courage at its lowest ebb that the door had burst open and a tall, powerful figure strode in.

Frances had done her best to put on a face of defiance for the intruder, but she was quaking inside. Her biggest fear was that the Gypsies had come to take her off with them in order to thwart any search parties. When she recognized the square jaw and fierce blue eyes of Lord Mainwaring, she had nearly burst into tears of relief. Just in time she had recalled their last meeting and was able to summon up, with her last bit of energy, enough anger to restore her calm. In fact, she was quite proud of her coolness as she asked him how he had come to find her.

"Freddie and Cassie had seen my curricle at the White Hart

in the village before. When they discovered you were missing, they came to Camberly first to find me as it is closer to Cresswell than the White Hart.'' Though he couldn't help admiring the indomitable spirit that gave Frances such calm composure after the ordeal, Mainwaring wished rather ruefully that for once she were less spirited. Looking at the white face and dark circles under eyes large with fatigue, he wanted more than anything to take her in his arms and kiss away the strain of the last hours. But one could hardly comfort a perfectly composed lady who was asking in the most rational way about the events leading to her release. For a moment he had felt sure he'd seen her face light up when she had recognized him. For an instant he had been sure the gladness he had seen in her eyes had been for himself and not just any rescuer. But now, agonizingly, he wasn't sure, and a corroding sense of disappointment and sadness washed over him. Could it be that he really was nothing more to her than just another London Corinthian to be danced with and then dismissed with scorn for his frivolous tendencies?

Fortunately for both parties, at this juncture Wellington, who despite Lord Mainwaring's firm command to STAY could contain his impatience no longer, burst excitedly into the hut, heading straight for Frances and covering her face with reassuring licks. It was too much. The strain, followed by the relief at being rescued, and now the joy at finding Wellington unharmed, completely overset Frances and she burst into tears. Mainwaring pulled her gently to her feet and gathered her in his arms, murmuring into her hair, ''Oh, my poor love. Hush, now. It's all over. My poor dear.''

Frances had had no idea that a solid chest and strong arms could be so comforting. For some minutes she stayed there giving herself up to the soothing effect of his strength and the feel of his hands as he gently smoothed her hair. At first she had been totally incapable of stopping the tears that poured down her cheeks, but gradually, under Mainwaring's comforting influence, she became calmer.

Julian felt the tension slowly drain out of her, but he continued to hold her thus, his cheek resting against her hair, relishing the feeling of her in his arms at last. But then, looking down at the tousled head on his chest, he asked softly, ''Why did you run away?'' She remained silent, head bent. ''Frances?'' He forced her to look up at him, tilting her chin with long fingers.

She at last looked up to see him regarding her with a more serious expression in his eyes than she had ever seen before. Unable to sustain the intensity of his gaze, she dropped hers. ''I . . .There was something at Cresswell that had to be dealt with right away.'' A slight blush crept into her pale cheeks.

''Frances, I have been managing businesses and estates since you were in the schoolroom. Nothing, no problem, is that urgent. It couldn't have been.'' There was a pause. ''Surely it wasn't the Duchess of Devonshire's ball? Frances, please tell me. Did I put myself beyond reproach? I must know what upset you so much that you left without a word to anyone.'' Much as she wished to make some reply, Frances was simply incapable of saying anything. ''Frances,'' he pressed desperately, ''please, I must know. I must know because I love you.''

That jolted her out of her bemused state. Her eyes flew to his in astonishment. ''You what?''

''I love you. I have . . . oh, for quite a while now, you know.''

''But you couldn't possibly!''

It was his turn to be astounded. ''And why ever not?''

''Well, because . . . because I'm not the sort of person you fall in love with.''

''And what brings you to that conclusion?'' he demanded with some asperity.

''Well, I'm just not the type.'' The skeptical look on his face deepened. She tried again. ''Well, I'm not that amusing, sophisticated sort of woman who would interest you.'' Frances still didn't appear to be making herself clear. ''What I *mean* is that I'm not at all sensual and alluring like . . . like Lady Welford.''

The skeptical look was replaced by one of pure amusement. ''My dear girl! How do you know that you're not sensual or alluring? You have a great appreciation and enjoyment for beauty of any and every kind. You see it all around you, and you enjoy it. That is far more sensual than dousing yourself with perfume and draping yourself on pink satin pillows all day long.''

Frances was intrigued. "Is that what she does? I must say, it doesn't sound nearly as interesting and exciting as I thought it would be."

His arms tightened around her. "And furthermore," he continued, ignoring her last remark, "I find you quite alluring. If you hadn't been so damned alluring, there never would have been that scene at the Duchess of Devonshire's ball. You were absolutely breathtaking, and I couldn't even get near you! I can't remember ever having felt jealous before that night. But when I saw you sparkling and laughing in one man's arms or another's, but never in mine, I was furious with jealousy. Then, when you disappeared on the terrace, that was more than I could take." His voice grew husky. "You looked so beautiful there that I hardly noticed that puppy on his knees. I just knew I wanted you more than anything in the world. I had to have you! I apologize for making you so furious, but I am *not* sorry for what I did."

Stealing a quick glance up at him, Frances was taken aback at the intensity in the depths of his eyes. "I wasn't exactly furious. I was more confused, upset. I—"

She wasn't allowed to continue. He pulled her to him fiercely. His lips came down on hers and began to kiss her with a passion that left her weaker and more shaken than all the rest of the day's events combined. For an instant Frances remained there, transfixed by a feeling she had never felt before. Then his hold slackened, his hands slid caressingly up her arms to her neck, his lips became warm, tender, insistent, and her arms crept around his neck and she molded her body to his, responding to the warmth that enveloped her as he kissed her eyes, the line of her jaw down to her throat, her shoulders. Somehow, it seemed she had never felt as alive, as aware of all her senses as she did at this moment, feeling the strength of his back and shoulders underneath her hands, the warmth of his lips against hers.

He lifted his head at last, breathing hard. "We'd best get married at the earliest possible moment. I don't want to wait any longer for you than absolutely necessary."

"Married?"

He cocked his head. "It *is* customary, you know." He saw

the doubt in her face and remarked with some exasperation, "My dear girl, a proper young woman does not kiss someone the way you just did unless she is planning to marry him."

"But I never thought . . . The children . . . I couldn't . . ." Her voice trailed off as she realized just how much she would enjoy life with someone who thought the same way she did, who was interested in the same things she was, who respected her judgment and would let her go her own way. Her eyes filled. "It sounds lovely, but I can't leave Freddie, Cassie, Wellington, and Nelson to Aunt Harriet."

"I would never ask you to do that, my dear one. I like the twins. In fact, if it weren't for Freddie I wouldn't be here now." She was puzzled. "Well, why do you think I happened to arrive in Hampshire at such an opportune moment?"

"I don't know. I suppose you came to check up on Camberly."

"Lord, Frances, don't be a cloth-head. I have an agent who can do that. I came at Freddie's special request. No need to look so astonished. That's a very perceptive young man. When I was in flat despair over you, he came to me at Mainwaring House and hinted to me that you might be more amenable to an apology than I had hoped."

"Freddie?" Frances looked incredulous.

"Yes, Freddie. He surmised, and quite correctly too, that we had had a falling-out. He reasoned that you would never waste your time being angry at someone you didn't like; therefore, anybody who truly made you angry must be someone you truly cared about. He urged me to come down here. I must say I wasn't all that convinced of the accuracy of his theory, but I was so desperate that I was willing to try anything. So, here I am. Here we are."

"But Aunt Harriet . . ."

"Aunt Harriet can stay exactly where she is. We can live at Camberly. It's large enough for all of us and more. We shall foist Kitty off on the first young man she becomes intractable over. Cousin Honoria can have the seaside cottage she's been pining for for her and that dutiful niece from Bath. And Aunt Harriet can turn all of Cresswell into a conservatory if she wishes. You won't be missed in the slightest. Any more foolish objections?'' Overwhelmed, she shook her head. ''Good! Then we had better get along to let the others know you are safe before they murder each other out of impatience. But first . . .'' He looked at her soberly. ''My girl, I don't want to push you into anything you don't want. It's a difficult thing to contemplate sharing your life with someone. I don't want you to do something just because I want it so much. I can understand your wishing to remain the same as always . . .'' He paused uncertainly.

She shook her head and smiled mistily up at him. That was all the encouragement he needed. He kissed her again—a long, hungry, demanding kiss that left them both breathless—before picking her up and carrying her out into the fading light to the waiting horse and her faithful companions.